HORRIBLE

SARAH MCCORMACK

This is a work of fiction. Unless otherwise indicated, all names, characters, businesses, places, events, and incidents in this book are either the product of the author's imagination or used in a fictitious manner. Any resemblance to actual persons, living or dead, or actual events, is purely coincidental.

No part of this book may be reproduced, or stored in a retrieval system, or transmitted in any form or by any means, electronic, mechanical, photocopying, recording, or otherwise, without the express written permission of the publisher.

Copyright 2021 Sarah McCormack
All Rights Reserved

Poem written and provided by: Rachel Barnard.

HORRIBLE

A good thing
Shirks from the dark,
Points a shaky finger
And screams,
"DIABOLICAL!"

Ha

My love, do not desire
that
Fetid wretch, that
poorly designed
existence.

You can crouch with
me a while,
Beholding all and
fearing none.

That lacking good
thing is frightened of
what feeds us.

To the man who makes my heart go bump

Chapter 1

"It's the houses," Mark would tell people later, "they are my muse."

The spookier the better. The more chilling, the more enticing.

"The creak of a floorboard, the rattling of a branch against a windowpane, the little bumps in the night - those are the things that make horror what it is," he will say. "Turning the ordinary into the macabre, making innocuous things terrifying, and playing heads-or-tails with ambiguity is the name of the game, and where better to find them but in the false sense of security of your own home?"

"But aren't you scared to stay in all of those scary houses?"

"Yes," he would answer. "Wouldn't you be?"

He can imagine it now, a hungry-eyed reporter sitting in the velvet armchair on the other side of his desk, cross-legged with a notepad in her lap, jotting down snippets of his words to sieve through and hopefully strike gold. If she didn't, perhaps she would embellish his words- re-order them to make them fit. He knows how these things go; he has been in the industry for over two decades.

Now, if only he could write something.

He stared down at the blinking cursor of his new Toshiba Dyna book in front of him. It was taunting him. Goading him into spending hours typing out of desperation to only return to find a mess of words, nonsensical and indefensible in their worth, and only good for backspacing. No. He would not succumb, he would wait it out.

Tap, tap, tap…

The tapping of his nail against the edge of his keyboard stopped as he lifted his hands over the letters, an image coming to the forefront of his mind. At last, a scene revealing itself to him. But just as it had appeared, it disintegrated. With a yawn, Mark ran his hand the length of his face and leaned over, scratching the hair under his chin, and went back to staring at the screen.

A loud crash from downstairs offered him a reprieve but when silence followed, he faced his computer once more and in a wave of inspiration his fingers touched the hard plastic keyboard and were off.

The words began to flow freely, leading his antagonist up the winding stairs, towards the door at the end of the hall - his footsteps silent on the red carpet – as his unsuspecting victims lay sleeping, their arms wrapped around one another in an embrace as the moon hid behind the thick clouds; there was something about to happen that it didn't want to see. What didn't it want to see? The image dispersed, the running reel of film at the end of its spool. Mark left his fingers poised over the keys, but the words eluded him.

His eyes drifted down to his stomach. Slouched over his desk, his belly hung over his belt buckle like the slob he felt he had let himself become. When had that happened? When had those extra pounds snuck onto his midsection? *Probably when you stopped exercising,* he answered himself. It didn't matter. He went back to work, making a conscious effort to sit straighter, even typing a whole line out, but he could not avoid the distraction of his stomach touching his belt, trying to creep over the barrier.

He stood, running his hands down his front, over the rise of his t-shirt as his palms moved past his middle where the extra weight sat, keeping him warm. His mind wandered, recounting his meals. And whiskey. There had been more of both lately, he supposed, but not *that* much. That couldn't be it. Maybe age? Age and a sedentary job – that must be it. Years ago he could have (and would have) eaten rings around himself, drank until he couldn't stand, and gone out for a run as soon as the sun rose. Not now.

From the half-zipped case by the wardrobe at the end of the bed, Mark pulled out a pale blue sweater and pulled it on, burying the belly, and vowing to get back to regular exercise.

How much cardio do middle aged, slightly overweight, whiskey drinking men need these days? Five years ago he completed a marathon. Last year he could have run a 5k with only one break. Now? He grabbed a handful of his stomach and sighed. Life was a killer sometimes.

He sat at his desk, his eyes scanning the words on the page while his thoughts were fixed on how tight his jumper felt around his shoulders.

BANG!

"It is the house," Mark would tell them later. "The house and my kids," he would say when he told his agent why he hadn't sent over his draft.

Mark pushed back from his desk, letting the wheels of his chair travel along the warped wooden floor as far as his bed before he stood up and went to the door, the candle on the desktop flickering wildly, and left his laptop lid open, the cursor blinking madly, calling him back.

"I didn't take it!" The voices were already travelling towards him. By the time Mark reached the centre of the long, red-carpeted hallway, the argument had moved into the large foyer and his two children stood at the end of the winding staircase. Light from the square of painted glass in the front door streamed a beautiful rainbow of colours on the hardwood floor and set a perfectly picturesque setting to an otherwise ugly scene.

"Dad, can you please tell Daniel to stop eating my food!" Amelia Owens called out when she spotted her father. Her hands were working through her auburn hair, pulling cereal out of the dark strands. Daniel, his oldest, was standing against the banisters with the smug grin of an eighteen-year-old boy, holding a bowl over-flowing with oats. His hand slipped into the pocket of his shorts and, when his sister's gaze was fixed on Mark, he flicked a piece of cereal at his sister.

"Dad!" Amelia exclaimed, her brows coming together in annoyance.

"Mu-be it was yur boyfriend who ate it!" Daniel said between chews, his short blonde hair pushed back from his forehead and gelled to the side as if he were going to dinner rather than on the jog he did every morning. No doubt it was to impress their new neighbour. *Like father, like son,* Mark mused.

"Daniel, stop it," Mark said, pointing a warning finger at his son. "You have a boyfriend?" Mark asked Amelia, setting his hand on the banisters. Immediately his daughter's cheeks were ablaze, and she lowered her eyes to the floor before shaking her head.

"No. Of course I don't," she muttered so he could barely hear her from the top of the stairs.

"Daniel, leave your sister alone. I need to get back to work," Mark said with a sigh and turned his back on his two children just as Daniel threw the rest of his cached cereal at his sister. Amelia cried out just as Mark turned back around. "Where's Cora?"

Cora Owens, dark hair like her father, bright eyes like her mother. Four and a half years old. She wasn't old enough to walk alone to the shop back home, but she was allowed to make herself breakfast, as long as it was cereal or toast, or cereal on toast. She liked dogs well enough but loved cats more than any dog she knew, and her favourite colour is orange. She thinks orange gets a bad name for itself, that not many people see how nice it is. Oranges, for instance, are delicious and are orange. Kiwis on the other hand are sour and bitter and she doesn't like them at all - and they are two colours, green and brown. Cora doesn't always hate green and brown, but she does always hate kiwis. For instance, she likes the dirt which is usually brown unless there's some grass or moss in it and then there's some green too. The dirt sometimes gets her clothes dirty, but that doesn't bother her all that much; it's fun and they always end up clean and in her drawer a couple of days later.

"Cora!"

Cora looked up from her pile of dirt and gathered sticks for her fort, and at the side of her dad's new house. She didn't see anyone so she went back to her dirt. Her dad had at least a hundred houses at this point. Every summer, once Daniel and Amelia were finished school, he would whisk them away to one of his new 'old-time' houses and they would pretend like it was their normal one until hundreds of days went by and there was no more summer. Cora didn't mind though, not like Amelia and Daniel did. But, she wondered, maybe she would mind when she started school. Maybe then she would understand why they always hated it.

"What are you doing out here?" Amelia asked. She was kneeling next to Cora now, still in her pyjamas, with their new cat sidling up next to her. Cora shrugged.

"Just playing," Cora replied, running her hand along the cat's back.

"Come back inside, I'll make you some breakfast." Without waiting for Cora to say if she even wanted breakfast - or to finish playing - Amelia, who really likes kiwis, pulled her by the hand to her feet and brought her inside through the huge door with the massive handle that Cora could barely reach without stretching up on to her tiptoes.

Cora didn't really like their new house when they first got here. It was old and dark and sometimes smelled funny. The stairs were never-ending, and Cora hated having to go up so many whenever she wanted to go to her room to play. She loved it when Daniel let her come back down them on her bum with a pillow though. The house was weird, Cora thought. It had a room downstairs, like downstairs of the downstairs. That room, at first, had scared Cora. But now she didn't mind it so much, especially because Daniel sometimes played with her down there. Right then, though, he was in the kitchen and when he saw Cora, he stood up from the wobbly table where she eats her cereal or toast.

"Cora!" Daniel cheered and lifted her into the air. She started to giggle and laugh when he threw her into the air again and again.

"Will you be careful, Daniel. You nearly hit her off the ceiling!" Amelia said in her angry Amelia voice that she uses when Daniel is around. Cora loves Daniel and she loves Amelia, but they don't always like each other.

"Would ya relax?" Daniel set Cora into the chair with her booster seat and tickled her sides. Cora wriggled in her seat, almost spilling the cereal that Amelia put on the table for her.

"Stop. It." Amelia pushed Daniel on his shoulder. Cora watched as Daniel took a single Cheerio from her bowl and threw it at Amelia. It hit her on the cheek. Daniel shot Cora an expression that made his eyes wide and his mouth turn into the shape of the cereal. She couldn't stop laughing. Daniel always made her laugh! Amelia suddenly had the look she sometimes got just before she started shouting: when her cheeks would go red and her nostrils puffed out hot air like a bull, except Amelia didn't have a ring in her nose. The picture of one in her nose made Cora laugh again.

"Ah, there she is."

Cora swung her legs beneath her when her dad, who liked all of them, planted a kiss on her cheek. "I have to go out to try and get some work done."

Cora knows her dad writes stories, and she knows she isn't allowed to read them until she is much, much older. Maybe not until she is a teenager! It didn't matter right now, she could barely read as it was. "I need you both to look after your sister," he said, leaning with his two hands on the back of Cora's chair so she had to look up to see his hairy chin above her.

"Sounds like your job." Daniel was halfway out the door with an apple in his hand, chewing on a chunk and pointing at Amelia.

"Hey-"

"What? I've t'go for a run to keep my stamina up!"

Amelia let out a huff, one that moved her shoulders, and squeezed her hands by her sides, staring at their dad.

"He'll do it next time. Besides, it'll be fun! You can read the first new chapter!" Cora liked it when Amelia spent time with her, especially when she wasn't in a bad mood which seemed less often since they came to this new house at the start of the summer. But she didn't mind because she had her new cat who was probably more fun.

All Daniel could hear was the sound of his feet pounding into the mucky ground along the forest trail. All he could see was the blur of green and brown from the trees around him as he sprinted past them; all he could feel was the air in his lungs and the innate urge to continue.

When they had first moved in for the summer, packing up all of his shit for yet another shitty summer spent in another shitty house so his father could write another shitty novel, the trail he ran on was nothing but overgrown grass and weeds. Since then, Daniel had managed to run a trail a few kilometres long each day so that now there was a clear pathway going from the backdoor of their rented shithole, up to the crest of the hill and back down to go in a giant, runnable loop that was long enough for him to forget that all of his friends were back home, enjoying their last summer before college while he spent his in the arsehole of nowhere doing absolutely nothing. Well, not nothing.

He was on his second run of the loop when he bent over, his hands planted on his knees, taking deep breaths of the too-fresh air. His throat was on fire, his quads were burning. He stood and shook them out, one at a time.

"You'd want to be careful; you're going to give yourself a cramp." Daniel raised his head, his breathing heavy in his ears, and looked towards the sound. Through the trees came his something.

"And what time do ya call this?" Daniel asked, standing up straight as Ellen joined his trail, her house just about visible through the dense trees of the forest from here. He checked his wristwatch and raised a teasing brow at her.

"Some of us like to sleep," she retorted, extending a bottle of water out to him. He took it and gulped half of it, watching as Ellen stretched her arms across her chest and then bent to touch her toes. His eyes travelled the length of her legs. He swallowed.

"It suits you," Daniel said, tilting his head to watch her closer still. She paused, met his cheeky grin, and rolled her eyes.

"Let's go. I'll give you a head-start," she said once she finished stretching. Daniel handed her back her water bottle and started into a jog, slapping her on the butt as he passed her.

If it were Halloween, it could be considered festive, fun… cheesy, even. But it was the middle of June and the house stood formidable and daring, huge and haunted with its peeling paint and single glazed windows; the dark slates above each one looking as though they were angry, slanted brows tormenting Amelia, even in her sleep. Its wooden frame was weather-worn and looked as though it might topple with a stiff Irish wind. The trees, standing sentinel in a half-circle around the house and lining the long driveway, had sheltered it for as long as it had been standing, she supposed.

It could have been a pretty house at one point, with a fresh lick of paint and some baskets hanging from the porch, full of flowers surrounded by bees, but now it looked derelict and damned, as if over time something grave had moved into the empty walls.

Since coming here, her dreams had been plagued by creeping shadows with shining eyes, watching her from afar, never showing their faces. And the noises... the house creaked at night, as though someone was tapping a metal rod along the old pipes, and there were scratches on the walls, as though someone was trapped behind them, begging to be freed.

"It is the atmosphere of the house," her father told her once. "It's fantastic," he said. Amelia couldn't agree any less. And Daniel... she kicked her foot further into the soil at the thought of announcing her concerns to him. No, this, it seemed, she would be facing alone.

"Why are you still standing?" Cora asked. Amelia watched her younger sister, her clothes filthy, her face and hands covered in dirt, and let out a disgruntled sigh.

"Because the ground is wet and cold," she said, wrapping her arms around herself, her hands buried in her sleeves for warmth. "Come on, let's go inside." Without protest, Cora got to her feet, wiping her hands onto the legs of her flowery leggings, and skipped ahead of Amelia, towards the stairs leading up the wrap-around porch, their black stray cat keeping up with her. Amelia followed, a chill spiking down her spine as she climbed the creaking steps; splintered and thin, they threatened to give way any day.

The house, Amelia had decided, was too big for the four of them. And unfamiliar – never had Amelia seen an Irish home with a wooden exterior or that wide veranda. It was out of place and sent uncanny tingles down her spine. With tall ceilings, bad insulation, and that musty smell from moth-eaten curtains and past damp issues, the house was cold and uninviting. This sentiment was enhanced by the dark corners that stayed unlit no matter the number of lamps or candles used. That and the creepy carved mouldings of hooded figures in the hallway, living room, and on the landing that watched you wherever you went and often made Amelia scurry past them as if they might try to reach out and grab her as she went by. If there were more of them then perhaps the house would not be so dull, that maybe life could be injected into it through the habitants. But, as it stood, the house seemed to reject them as much as Amelia did it.

And quiet. Too quiet, as though it swallowed sound.

Set back from the road and with no noise coming from partying neighbours or screaming children, the house was eerily quiet. So uncomfortably so that Amelia felt the stillness in the house stifling – suffocating - at times. She longed for the busy street back home, the barking dogs that set off pets two streets over so a symphony of howls angered sleeping neighbours. Or the learner driver in their first car that tested their speakers by blaring their music outside the window, the base like a drum vibrating her room.

Under a flickering sconce, her father had left the first draft of his new novel on the old console table by the living room for her to read. She picked it up and flicked through the pages, catching snippets of the sentences, before crossing the large foyer and pushing open the door which led to the basement. The stairs were shrouded in darkness, the only light coming from the lamps at the bottom. Cora had already made her way down the stairs, her little musings traveling up in sweet tones. Amelia tucked the manuscript under her arm and flicked the switch on the wall. The bulb made a small attempt at lighting the stairs before giving up with a crackle. With a sigh, Amelia set her hand onto the rickety banisters and started down. Mucky footprints left a trail to where Cora sat on her honkers, playing with the dolls in her hands.

"Cora! Look at the state of the floor after you!"

Cora glanced at the muddy prints and up at Amelia.

"Oops." She dropped her doll to the floor and pulled her shoes off. Amelia shook her head, considered if it would be easier to clean the dirt when it was dried up- a part of her knowing that it would never be cleaned - and sat in the armchair, pulling the throw on the back over herself and tucking her legs under her.

Chapter 2

"**Where did you find that?**" Amelia asked. Setting her father's manuscript down, she covered her shoulders with the blanket and stood, going to kneel next to Cora. The cat, previously curled up in a ball at Amelia's feet, meowed in protest.

An empty box lay on the floor, the lid turned face-up. There was a picture of two sets of hands placed delicately on a tear-drop-shaped wooden planchette over a board inscribed with the alphabet arching over the word 'Goodbye', with 'Yes' in one corner above it, and 'No' in the other. The game's name was faded so that the 'j' of Ouija was all but gone, with the other letters not much clearer, only echoes of their former vibrance.

"Under here." Cora's voice was muffled from beneath the faded yellow couch with her feet the only visible part of her. "Help!" she called, wiggling her feet, and kicking Amelia in the shin. Amelia tugged on her leg and pulled her backward. With a heap of dust puffing out in a cloud, Cora appeared holding the board from the box. She blew the loose, dark strands from her face and wiped at the dust on the game board, smiling. "Wanna play?" Amelia reached for the board and examined it. Of course, she knew what this was. The letters of the alphabet were peeled in places and faded in other parts so that most of them were indiscernible and the filigree at the edges looked like faded snakes coiling around the 'Yes' and 'No'. The only clear inscription was the 'Goodbye' at the bottom of the wooden board.

"No, I don't," Amelia answered, setting the board atop the upturned lid, and stood to go back to her armchair. "And maybe don't touch that, it looks old and smells musty."

From upstairs there was a clatter and a bang as though the front door had been pulled open and slammed shut. Amelia hesitated, looking at the dark, shadowy stairs, and listened.

"What's it called?" Cora wondered, running her fingers along the dusty surface of the Ouija board. Amelia held on to the banisters, one foot already on the bottom step. "O-o-o." Cora tried sounding out the letters behind her.

"It's *Ouija*," Amelia said, turning away from the stairs at last and looking at Cora as she traced her fingers along the faded letters. "I told you not to touch that." The door at the top of the basement stairs opened with a loud creak. Heavy steps thundered down the staircase and Daniel appeared at the bottom, his shorts and white t-shirt stained green and brown. Next to Cora's little ones, Daniel's huge feet left massive muddy patches on the floor. Amelia regarded her brother's wobbly steps and glassy eyes and shook her head before she plonked herself back down onto the armchair and picked her father's manuscript back up. Over the top of the page, she watched as Daniel went to his knees next to Cora and fell back onto his backside.

"Where did you manage to find this?" he cheered, his last words were slurred. The smell of vodka came off him in plumes. Amelia checked her wristwatch: 2 pm.

"It was under the couch- wanna play?" Cora asked. Her eyes were two round bulbs in her little face.

"Sure, I'll play- but we'll have to wait until it's dark." Daniel rubbed furiously at the sticky dust that clung to the board before wiping his hands on the rug. Eventually, he gave up and set the board on the top of his knees before he twisted his wrist to check the watch there. He squinted down at the numbers, closing one eye in the end before letting his head fall back against the old couch.

"Why do we have to wait until then?" Cora whined. Amelia waited, expecting to hear Daniel's snores any second now as he slipped into a drunken coma, but to her surprise, he lifted his head back up and ruffled Cora's hair. She giggled along while Amelia's frustration grew and she began to seethe from the armchair.

"Well, you know what this is, don't ya?" he asked. Amelia lowered her feet to the floor, readying herself to interject.

"Daniel-" Amelia warned.

"What?" His head turned towards her.

"Don't tell her."

"Why not?"

"Tell me what?" Cora chimed in. "I want to know. That's not fair, I want to know- you never tell me anything-"

"Alright, alright, shush." Daniel squeezed his eyes shut and set one hand on the side of his head, the other in a *shushing* motion towards Cora.

"She won't be able to sleep, Daniel," Amelia scolded. Ignoring her, Daniel lifted the board and turned to Cora. He pointed to the faded ink on the game.

"Just because this shit scares you it doesn't mean Cora is a baby, does it, C?"

Amelia could feel her pulse in her ears. She wrapped her arms across her chest, her jaw clenched, and prepared in her mind what she would tell their father later when Cora wasn't able to sleep alone.

"You swore!" Cora giggled but silenced herself when Daniel waved her words away.

"Yeah, yeah. Now, listen up, this could save you one day." He reached over and lifted Cora by the arms to sit on his lap, threatening to topple sideways before managing to straighten again.

"This here is a threshold to-"

"What's a threshold?" Cora asked.

"How old are you again?"

"Four and a half," she told him, angrily.

"I was testing you," he teased, meeting her sceptical gaze with one of his own. "This is a *doorway* to the spirit world. It lets you talk to all those ghosts that tickle your toes at night," Daniel said, pretending to grab her feet. "If you're lucky, you can talk to a nice one." Amelia listened in, knowing that if he said any more Cora would be spending the night in her bed.

"Really? Can they tell you things?"

"Oh, yeah, they tell you all kinds of stuff- like... if it's going to rain tomorrow or...if Amelia is going to ever cheer up-" Daniel flinched when the pillow hit his head. Amelia glared at him, scoffing loudly, and forced herself to go back to reading, but she was unable to focus on the words.

"Can you talk to people you know?" Amelia knew where this was going. She set the paper down and went to sit with them, a bubble of anxiety forming in her stomach. She *knew* this would happen.

"Sometimes- only if they want to talk to you," Daniel told her, oblivious to his sister's trail of thought.

"Do you think we could talk to Mam?" Cora asked. Amelia let her head fall, her eyes focusing on the old game on Daniel's lap and waited to see how 'drunken-Daniel' would back out of this hole without upsetting Cora.

"To Mam? Well..." Daniel paused, staring down at the peeling letters on the board. He stayed like that for another moment, and when it seemed like he wasn't going to say anything Amelia cleared her throat.

"Well, the thing about this, Cora, is that you can only really talk to people who are in between... the ones waiting to go to Heaven or Hell. Mam, well, she's definitely in Heaven," Amelia said, smiling at her. Cora considered this for a moment before her little nose crinkled up.

"So, you can talk to bad people, too?" she asked. Again, Daniel hesitated to answer.

"Eh, yeah, you can." His jaw had tightened, his gaze drifting away, his thoughts seemingly elsewhere until Cora tugged on his arm and brought his focus back to her.

"Would they haunt me?" Cora asked, her face a mask of horror. Daniel shrugged.

"Oh yeah! They hide your things, whisper horrible things to you at night, scratch your arms until you bleed-"

"Daniel! You're terrifying her!" Daniel frowned at Amelia, ready to argue, but turned when Cora dug her face against his chest, screaming. With a shrug of his shoulders, he rubbed her back. "I told you not to tell her!" Amelia scolded and stood, pulling Cora to her feet.

"Oh, relax. She's fine. She'll probably forget in an hour."

"She's not a goldfish, Daniel. Why don't you go and sleep off that drink." Amelia hugged Cora to her. "And shower - you stink of vodka and B.O," she told him, heatedly.

"When did you become such a nag?" Daniel asked, staggering to his feet. The Ouija board toppled to the ground in a clatter and with a fright, the cat scurried past Amelia and Cora and ran up the stairs, disappearing into the darkness and away from the commotion.

"I'm telling Dad."

Daniel raised his brows. "Fine. Tell him. And I'll tell him about your little boyfriend that you've been sneaking in and out of the house," he replied, burping. They stared at one another, daring the other to break their eye contact. Amelia's cheeks were on fire. She broke away first. Infuriated, she ushered Cora to the steps and nudged her up.

"The dark! What if they're in the dark?" Cora cried. Over her shoulder, Amelia shot Daniel a look of disdain.

"Truce?" Daniel asked, holding out his pinkie finger mockingly. In return, Amelia stuck a different finger up and led the way to the top of the stairs.

Chapter 3

Cora usually slept well, even in the new houses. Once she had her bright yellow blanket from home, her favourite stuffed elephant teddy that she had gotten when she was only a baby, and her nightlight that made her ceiling inside look like the sky outside without it being scary, she never even had a bad dream. But that was before she knew about that scary game from under the couch from the downstairs' downstairs.

She was in her bed, holding onto her blanket so tightly that the tips of her fingers were starting to hurt, staring at those stars on the ceiling. They looked funny on this ceiling, like they didn't really fit between the lines of wood, their legs wonky on the wooden sticks that ran across the space.

"I promise I'll be good," she whispered to the ghosts that might be listening, hoping that they would stop making those scratching noises on her walls.

There it was again.

Cora squealed and ducked beneath her blanket. Her skin was cold with fright.

The ghosts. They were coming for her.

What sounded like a muffled growl and heavy monster breaths had her in tears.

BANG

Cora cried out, desperate for safety, and bolted for her bedroom door. Terrified, she let out another yelp when a shadow shifted on the wall. She reached for the door handle and pulled on it. Light from the dim landing entered the room, shedding its yellow beam across the messy bedsheets and forgotten plush elephant teddy. Cora's steps made little to no noise even as she raced to the other end of the hallway where a sliver of light under the last door offered some promise of protection. Her sweaty fingers grasped at the brass handle, and she opened the door, tears streaming down her cheeks as she gasped for breath.

"Cora! What's happened?" Mark turned at the sound of the door opening to find his youngest daughter in floods of tears, her cheeks pink, her breaths coming out in hiccups as she rushed towards him. "What is it?" He pulled her to him and lifted her onto his knee, hesitating only a second to glance at his open laptop, before tucking her head under his chin.

"There's a weird noise coming from the walls! I- I- I think it's the gh-ghost!" Cora cried out.

"Ghosts? What do you mean? Slow down, Honey. Take a breath." Cora sniffled and gasped, catching her breath, before her hiccupping set in. Mark wiped at her wet cheeks. "Shh, now, it's okay, you're alright." He rubbed at her hair and gave her a tight hug. "Now, tell me what's happened."

"There's a ghost in my room. I can hear him scratching on the walls," she confided, wiping her face with the sleeves of her pink pyjamas. Mark took a deep breath.

"This is an incredibly old house, Cora. Old houses sometimes make noises, it's just something that happens- there's nothing to be afraid of," he said in his most soothing tone as he was bombarded with memories of his other daughter, sitting as Cora was sat, crying about the ghosts in her room. Amelia, Mark remembered, had a particular fear of shadows at Cora's age.

"But I heard it! It's real. And I *saw* it too- the shadow!" Mark lifted his daughter and sat her on the edge of his bed. Swinging his chair around, he sat facing her, his hands clasped in front of him.

"How about we go check it out together?" Immediately Cora was shaking her head vigorously, "And if there is something there, your big old dad will have some words with it and make it leave you alone. How does that sound?" She considered this for a long time, no longer crying.

"What if he doesn't leave?" she whispered tentatively. Mark raised a brow and lifted his arms, flexing his biceps in funny ways so that Cora couldn't stop herself from giggling. His shirt barely lifted as he twisted his arm towards himself and he was reminded of his softening figure.

"Do you really think a ghost would go up against your dad? Come on, be serious!" He reached over and tickled her sides until she was laughing and falling back on the bed, trying to escape. "Let's go check this out, see what ghost thinks they can stay in this house without paying rent!" Mark stood and extended his hand out to Cora.

Cora hopped down from the bed and took hold of her father's hand and went with him, bravely, back to her room. Reluctant to face the ghost again, she stood back and let her father go into the room first. Mark pushed open the door and entered, leaving Cora to watch after him as she peeked from around the doorframe. He pulled back the curtains, letting the pitch-dark sky from outside fill his vision; it knocked on the glass as though it were a guest looking to be let in. In it, he could see his reflection. He looked old, the deep etching of wrinkles on his forehead, the crow's feet stamping his face like a branding from middle-age as time accepted him into their club, *Come on in.* But what if you don't want your membership? He pulled the curtains over and went to the wardrobe, stepping back so Cora could see the hanging clothes within, the emptied, pink suitcase stacked beneath it.

"See?" Cora was shaking her head again and pointing a single, uncertain finger towards her bed. Mark gave her a small grin and got onto his hands and knees, his joints cracking as if to agree with his wrinkling face with a mocking cackle. Other than dust bunnies and a few odd socks, the space was monster-less. With one more cursory glance around the room, Mark picked up her elephant toy and set his hands on his hips.

"I think it's safe, but just to make sure, I better give a warning," he said with a wink. "If there is a ghost in this room, I demand you leave, right now! You are ruining Cora's sleep and she doesn't want you here! If I have to come back, there'll be *big* trouble for you!" he said, and beckoned Cora in with a wave of his hand. She took a cautious step in before there was a flicker of a shadow on the wall. She let out a squeak and ran to her father, grabbing the elephant from his hands. Mark twisted to inspect.

"It's still here, I saw the shadow again!"

"Hmm." Mark stepped away from Cora and waved his hand around. His shadow moved across the wall, among the twirling stars. Behind him, Cora's night light glowed in its socket. "Maybe you can sleep in with your sister for the night? Does that sound like an idea?" he asked her. "Give this guy some time to pack his things and find somewhere else to go- maybe he'll stay with Daniel." Cora nodded her head enthusiastically, squeezing her elephant close to her chest. "Okay, let's go knock on Amelia's door." As Cora went back into the hallway, Mark reached down and unplugged the night light, setting it atop the tall wardrobe. Closing the door over behind him, he felt tiredness wash over him- he needed sleep, but he needed to write more.

Cora was at Amelia's door, knocking on it. Mark went to her and set his hand upon her shoulder, adding his own tapping to it. When there was no answer, he tried the handle. The lock jiggled in the door, stopping him from entering. With an open palm, he slapped on the wood loudly.

"Amelia, open the door." There was some movement from inside her bedroom, as though she was fumbling. Mark knelt next to Cora, turning his head when a peculiar sound from the other end of the landing hallway alerted him. His gaze shifted to the top of the stairwell, expecting something to happen - to see the black cat which had made itself at home, appear. Then, another creak and a distant sound of voices.

Amelia's door unlocked and opened a crack. "Dad, is everything alright?" Amelia's sleepy voice pulled his attention away from the stairway. He pushed the door to get a wide view of the room.

"Why is your door locked?"

Amelia hesitated. Behind her, her lamp was on, a book opened on her bedside table. She had a pair of shorts and a tank top on.

"I was just about to change."

"Okay," Mark set his hand back on Cora's shoulder. "Well, don't have it locked late at night. It's a fire hazard," he told her. *Especially in this house,* he added internally.

"Sorry. I won't. Is there something wrong?"

"No. Cora is going to spend a night or two with you in your room, okay?" Amelia let out an irritated sigh but nodded as she reached behind her door, tugging an oversized jumper from the hook and pulling it on.

"Sure," she muttered, checking over her shoulder at her bed.

"Cora, honey, I want you to know that there is no ghost in your room-"

"But I *saw* one!" Cora moaned.

"Well, if you did, then I'm sure it was only Mam coming to say 'hi'. Probably making sure you were tucked in, is all," he told her in reassurance. Beside him, Amelia shifted uncomfortably in place while Cora smiled.

"Do you think so?"

"I know so," Mark said, kissing her forehead and standing. "Now, knowing that it could have been your mother, well, she is one ghost that *could* kick my butt!" He gently ushered Cora into Amelia's bedroom and watched as she jumped onto her sister's double bed, paying no attention to the book that she knocked over in the process, and dove under the covers, snuggling into the blankets and already closing her eyes.

"Dad, Daniel was the one-" Amelia began but stopped when Mark raised his hand.

"We can talk about it tomorrow. I need to get work finished." He checked his watch: 1.34 am. "Goodnight, sweetheart." Amelia shook her head, rolling her eyes, and closed over her door.

Mark was alone in the hallway, free to go back to his work, but something was bothering him. He had heard something from the other end of the hallway and with his curiosity spiked he walked the carpeted floors, barefooted, to the top of the stairs. Peering down the winding steps, the foyer was in total darkness with not even the moonlight coming through the glass of the door. His night vision was still coming to focus so he couldn't be sure, but...

A trick of his mind, he was sure of it.

A shift in the darkness.

He took a single step down the stairs, trying hard to see in the dark when-

There it was again-

That same noise-

But this time he was certain it was coming from behind him.

Mark let out a heavy sigh and ran his hand the length of his face when he stopped outside the first door on the left-hand side of the hallway. With an aggressive knock, he waited with his hands upon his hips, growing more irritated as the seconds passed. There was immediate shuffling from the other side, hushed voices, and even a couple of swear words before the door was cracked open a couple of inches and Daniel's face appeared, the rest of him turned away from the door in a state of undress.

"Oh, you're up late. You still working?"

"Cut it out, Daniel." He pushed open the door by several more inches before turning away and shielding his face with the side of his hand from the neighbour girl who was covering herself with Daniel's bedsheets. "For fuck's sake, Daniel!" he cursed in hushed tones. His eyes flickered to his daughter's bedroom door, which was still shut, and he lowered his voice.

"Hello, Mr Owens," the girl called politely.

"Sorry, I didn't think anyone was awake-"

"You have your sister terrified. She thinks there are ghosts in the house because of you two," he scolded his son. "Bring Ellen home. Now." Daniel was reaching for his trousers, stepping into them, and pulling them up, before he stepped out into the hallway and closed the door over on Ellen.

"Yeah, no problem. Can I've the keys for the car?" he asked, following as Mark started walking back towards his room. He stopped and sniffed the air around his son.

"Where'd you get the drink?"

Daniel hesitated, his eyes darting away before he shrugged, pulling his t-shirt over his head. "You're not driving after you've been drinking. You may walk there," Mark said.

"What! But it's like two miles away! And we drank that hours ago!" Mark turned and gave Daniel a warning stare.

"It'll help with your stamina, son - build up your character, isn't that what you say?" Mark said, repeating Daniel's own words back to him as he stepped into his room. His laptop screen was dark as it waited on standby, like a mistress, for his return. He doubted very much if he would be getting any more work done tonight. "Tell Ellen I said goodnight." He closed the door over and went to his bed. Sitting on the edge, where Cora had been earlier that night, he looked at the picture frame on his desk; a beautiful blonde woman smiled back at him, her eyes a soft grey. He couldn't help but let out a soft chuckle.

"Ghosts, huh."

He rolled back onto the mattress and closed his eyes, thinking of his wife and wishing that she were there in the bed, waiting for him.

Chapter 4

The road was treacherous in the dark with holes in the tar that could break an ankle if you were to slip into one. The moon offered cold light where it broke through the gathering clouds, but other than that and the flickering torch Daniel had brought along, they were walking blindly down the road to Ellen's house. Beside him, Ellen hooked her arm into his and shivered.

"Your dad was pretty calm," she said. Daniel shrugged and tapped the torch against his palm. The batteries within jiggled loudly as they bounced up and down, up and down, until the flickering light stilled and a beam lit their path with a yellow glow that bounced off of the reflective eyes of the foxes in the forest as they waited for them to pass. "My dad would have blown a fuse."

"I'm surprised he noticed, to be honest," Daniel replied. Ellen jolted away from him, her foot sliding into one of the many potholes along the way. She pulled at his arm to get her balance back. Daniel took a step sideways, pulling her with him, and dropped the torch. It rolled along the ground, stopping when it touched the grass at the edge of the bank. Its light returned to its urgent flickering.

"Are you alright?" Daniel asked, holding onto Ellen's shoulders to steady her. She hissed when she set her foot down flat, pressing her weight on it.

"I think it's twisted." She gasped and clung to Daniel for support. Shifting his arm under hers, he helped her take the weight off her hurt foot. Together they retrieved the blinking torch, and with one loud thump against the ground, the light steadied to a solid stream.

"We aren't too far from yours; do you think you can make it?"

"Yeah, I think so." They moved along at a slower pace, checking the road in front of them closely for any more holes. Concentrating, they didn't speak for a moment, their heavy breathing joining the night-time noises of the nocturnal creatures. Daniel focused on the road ahead but couldn't ignore the heat from Ellen's hand on his arm, the way she squeezed it each time she felt uneven ground under her feet. Beyond the bend in the road there was the twinkle of lights as Ellen's house came in to view, her porch lamps attracting them like moths. Together they hopped towards the house as if it were sports day and they had been tied together in a three-legged race

"Thanks for walking me back," Ellen said breathily when they reached the house. She limped to the freshly painted porch and leaned against it, sliding herself under the wooden railing so that her feet dangled freely. Daniel watched the front door, expecting another interruption, but none came. He pushed one of Ellen's legs aside and stood before her. She smiled up at him. Leaning in, he kissed her softly as her hands caressed his arms.

Mosquitoes and moths filled the air around them, darting back and forth between the lamps on the wall. Daniel slapped the back of his neck, feeling the small pinch of a bite.

"I hate it here," he grunted, checking his palm and seeing the tiny, squished bug there.

"It's not so bad," Ellen said, tugging him by the shirt closer to her. She kissed his cheek. "I was thinking that maybe we could hang out over here the next time?" she suggested.

"If it's because of my dad... that won't happen again. It's just because Cora woke up- he's never heard us before," Daniel told her, a grin complemented his raised brow as he thought back on their summer nights spent in his room, shoving pillows behind the headboard, the duvet on the floor.

"No, it's not that. I mean, that is going to haunt me for like forever, but it's not because of that," she said, dropping her eyes down to her hands. "It's... silly, but..."

"What is it?" He waited while she was quietly chewing her lower lip. Using his hand, he pushed all her hair behind her ear. Finally, she rolled her eyes and sighed.

"It's that house. It creeps me out," she said, meeting his gaze with furrowed brows. Daniel tried his best to keep a straight face, but she pushed him away when he failed. "Don't laugh at me!" she demanded, her head lolling backward.

"I'm not," he assured her, unable to stop himself from doing so. She stared at him stonily and pulled her two legs through the wooden rails. Putting her weight on her good foot, she went to stand. Daniel reached through the beams and held her in place.

"I'm sorry, I won't laugh," he promised. She paused before easing herself back down so that Daniel could return to his standing position between her legs. "Tell me why."

She wet her lips and took a breath. "Fine," she exhaled through her nose and watched as a bat dove to collect dinner, disappearing into the trees, camouflaged by night.

"You know what happened to the previous owners, right?" she asked. Daniel frowned, shaking his head. "Really? It's like *the* haunted house of the town- it may be the most haunted house in the country."

Daniel shrugged his shoulders nonchalantly; this didn't surprise him, considering his father's track record of bringing them around the country to write his horror novels. They have stayed in quite a few *haunted houses* in his time.

"Wow, okay. So, like twenty-five or twenty-six... maybe like thirty years ago a man and a woman moved here from the States and built the house, doing it all up before moving in with their new-born baby. They loved the house, but strange things started happening in it."

"Like what?" Daniel asked, trying his best to sound intrigued, but knowing he was never good at faking anything.

"You know, like strange sounds from the walls and they would hear people whispering to them when there was no one in the room with them, things like that."

"And they told people this?" Daniel asked, fighting to keep the scepticism out of his voice. If he started to hear voices in the walls, the last thing he would do would be to tell his new neighbours about it.

"*You* asked me to tell you this," she reminded him, her Mayo accent accentuated with her temper.

"I know, keep going," he prompted. Ellen shifted closer to Daniel and ran her hands up and down his arms.

"So, this went on for ages, apparently, and then Mr Evans- the husband, started to say some really weird things around town, like how he wished the voices would stop and that he could never get a minute's peace with all the screaming from the walls. People used to see him walking up and down this road," at this, she beckoned to the road they had just travelled along, and gulped, "at all hours of the night with an axe- some said that it used to be bloody, but I'm not sure if I believe that." Daniel raised his brows in mock surprise.

"Really?"

"Yeah, but it wasn't until months later- maybe like a year or so, even- that people got really worried. It was when they stopped seeing Mrs Evans and the baby around town. She just suddenly stopped going to the shops with him and whenever anyone would ask after her, Mr Evans just said that she was at home with the baby, but like... she was *never* out!"

"So, what happened to her?" Daniel asked, setting his hands on either side of Ellen's legs, and leaning closer. He watched her lips as they moved, still shiny, her cheeks a light pink, a remnant of their romantic tussle.

"He killed her," Ellen whispered, her exposed skin rising like gooseflesh when she said the words. He held her steady gaze. The night was still, even the crickets had quietened to hear the story. "They found her chopped up into tiny pieces and scattered around all the rooms of the house. He left her head on her pillow - and he slept next to it - every. Single. Night. Can you *imagine* that? Sleeping next to your wife's bloody head? And it must have been for weeks - she wasn't found until a neighbour from the other side of the lake came by to visit her, to check how she was doing. But they found her hand on the bottom step of the steps outside, like a welcome mat." If there was any truth to the story, even Daniel had to admit that it was pretty grim.

"Did they get him in the end?" Daniel asked, his voice suddenly matching Ellen's in pitch.

She nodded. "Oh, they got him. After the neighbour rang it in, the Gardai arrived and found that Mr Evans had slit his own throat in the basement with an old razor blade. He was found naked, covered in his own shit... well, I don't know how true that bit is either, but it fits his character, right?" Daniel's mind reeled through every moment he had spent in that basement, not knowing that there could have been a shit-covered murderer lying dead in that same room at one point in time. He thought of earlier that day when he, Cora, and Amelia had all been down there at once, and a flashing image of the dead man in the armchair Amelia had been in shot across his imagination. But, he supposed, this story was most likely bullshit...

Then another thought emerged.

"What happened to the baby? Did he kill that too?" Daniel asked. Ellen's eyes darted to the right as she recalled the details of the scary story.

"That's the crazy bit," she told him.

"*Oh*, I was wondering when it would get out of hand," Daniel said. She pushed her blonde hair back from her face, her blues eyes twinkling, and scooted even closer to him, so she was on the edge of the porch. He felt her legs wrap around him, her hot breath graze his mouth.

"So, one of the first things the guards did was a search for the baby, right, afraid of what he had done to her after doing all of that. But," she paused. Daniel leaned in, as though gravity was pushing him towards her. "They didn't find her. And they never did."

Daniel hesitated as he processed what was being said. "What do you mean they never found her? Where did she go?"

Ellen shrugged and visibly shivered. "They looked for her for weeks; dug the whole garden up, thinking he might've buried her alive. For a while, they believed he had drowned her in the lake, but they couldn't find any proof of that either. There are some weird things suggested, like that he sacrificed his baby to some demon or Satan, or whatever- other people think he ate her."

"Jaysus, people are nuts!" Daniel physically recoiled from the thought of those things.

"Yeah, they are," Ellen agreed. "There is *one* rumour that most people seem to lean towards," she said.

"What?" She regarded him as though wondering if she should tell him, and he waited. "Well?"

"Some people think that he might have hidden his daughter somewhere in the house, somewhere she couldn't have been found- that house is huge, and you never know- maybe when he did the house up they put a secret hiding place for things, like passports and shit in case the house got robbed or whatever." Daniel shook his head, doubtfully. Of all the theories, people were believing the least likely.

"The bloke probably chopped the kid up with his wife and buried it in the forest. You'd never be able to find it out there," Daniel surmised, pointing to the dark woods that surrounded the house. "If that ever even happened," he added.

"Oh, it happened. You can look it up in the old newspapers. Or even ask some of the old men in pubs, they'll tell you," Ellen assured him.

Yes, because they are reliable, he thought to himself.

"Okay, so if that all happened before you were even born, then why does it scare you now?" Daniel asked.

"Didn't you hear the start of the story? The Evans' said that they could hear things in it- whispers when they were alone and strange noises from the walls... I mean, what else could cause someone to do that to their family? The house is *obviously* possessed by… something!" This was where Daniel's humouring ended.

"Or else, that guy was batshit crazy and those voices were all in his head," Daniel suggested. Ellen shook her head, using a hand to point to her chest.

"Me and my friends used to sneak around that house when it was empty and we would hear the strangest of things coming from it. There's *definitely* something gross happening there. Even Cora heard it tonight."

Daniel couldn't hold it back any longer. He laughed loudly, much to Ellen's dismay.

"Cora heard *us*!" he reminded her. At Ellen's glare, Daniel raised his hands in surrender. "I'm sorry, I just don't believe in ghost stories. I've spent enough summers in *haunted* houses to know better," he said, bending his fingers into bunny-ears, as Ellen shimmied out from under the railings and stood next to him, leaning her weight off her twisted ankle.

"We'll see what you say when the ghost of Mr. Evans starts talking to you!" she warned him, her mouth tilting into a smile.

"His sweet nothings will keep me warm at night when you aren't around," he teased, leaning over to kiss her on the neck, jaw, cheek, and then lips.

"Get out of here," she shook her head, laughing. "I'll see you tomorrow."

"See you." He watched her limp up the steps with a sort of adoration and couldn't help smiling. The door opened and the light from the warm lamps inside streamed out onto the porch, the heat of the house a welcoming reprieve from the bitter night air. In a fleeting thought, Daniel compared that homely scene of walking into Ellen's house to the shadowy, empty one that awaited him. Just as it circled his mind, he shoved it away.

"Hey, Ellen?"

"Yeah?" She turned to look at him.

"Can you do me a favour and not tell my sisters about all of that? They already shit themselves in the house."

"Of course." She gave him one last gentle smile before turning. The door closed with a click and in the quiet night Daniel heard the lock turn in the door and wondered who it was that she was locking out.

Chapter 5

Daniel chose to walk back through the forest, along the worn trail that he and Ellen ran each morning. That was how he had met her; one morning, while out on a run at the beginning of summer, he had gone so far that he came to her house. She had been in her garden, wearing a pair of pink shorts. He had stopped to stretch before he stood at the treeline, waiting to introduce himself. From then on, they had been running together a few times a week and doing *other* things the rest of the time. She was the only thing keeping him sane.

The pathway wasn't much darker than the road and he was confident that there were no potholes along the way to twist his ankle on. The torch still flickered but was yet to fail altogether, and if it did, Daniel knew the trail well enough to make his way home; he could even run it if he wanted to.

The night was growing colder, his breath was starting to puff out in white clouds. Around him, the forest animals kept their distance with the odd fox or hedgehog crossing his path, paying no attention to him as they moved along in search of food. This way was probably safer, Daniel had thought to himself when he crossed Ellen's garden to find the beginning of the trail, yet he was on edge, felt himself twitch at the rustling of leaves or the unexpected cracking of a twig.

He hoped he wouldn't come across an angry badger, remembering his primary school teacher's warning, and momentarily considered wrapping a twig against his shins in case he did bump into one.

His breathing was deep and shaky. It was his hangover. His head was pounding, he needed sleep. Of course he was antsy, his head foggy. If Mark had just given him the car keys, he would be in bed snoring by now.

A howling dog in the distance made Daniel stop and listen to the sounds around him again. The hoot of an owl, the small scurries of little creatures through the foliage, and... the snapping of a branch.

Daniel swung round, the shine of his torch bouncing off the trees and leaves and shrubs.

Movement-

Daniel stopped spinning, concentrating the light into the trees on his left. He squinted into the darkness, searching. He thought...

Did he see...

No. He hadn't seen anything; he was walking through a forest full of animals, there was going to be some things moving, some branches breaking. This hangover was making him see things. Knowing this, he moved on, walking slightly faster now as around him trees morphed into leering shapes, their limbs outstretched and reaching for him until he cast the light on them to reveal their true identity.

He should probably get used to this forest trail in the dark anyway. If Ellen wanted to spend less time at his he would be doing this journey a lot more. It was ridiculous, he thought. How old were they? Twelve or nearly twenty? And still believing in ghost stories? Daniel often wondered had he been desensitised to these things, what with having a father who got off on horror, but then he thought of Amelia, who seemed to be getting worse, getting more terrified every year. But, he supposed, Amelia was a few years younger - practically a child.

Daniel, however, knew that houses are made from brick and mortar, cement and stone. They aren't haunted. The real horror in life is people. They are the ones that do the real damage, not some smoky projection of a being. The real thing is much, much worse. *That* is what Daniel has learned over the last few summers while living in these haunted houses. They all claim to be haunted, a mecca of paranormal deviance, however, they all started with people in them, people who did terrible things, murder sprees, child molestation, kidnapping, torture. And the guilty participants all said the same thing- the house told them to do it, the voices- they made them kill their family.

No, it was the lunatic that decided to take a shotgun to his wife's head that pulled the damn trigger.

This house was no different.

Even if what Ellen said to be true was the house's *haunting*, his opinion still stood- Mr Evans had a noggin full of crazy. It's awful, but it ain't supernatural.

What did border on supernatural was Mark's obsession with this shit, and the fact that he dragged them along with him. All Daniel wanted was to spend one summer at home where he could be with his friends. Just one more summer- that's all he had to get through. One more and he would be out. College was calling his name. He would be going to school far away from home, get a job, share a shitty apartment with his friends, and pop round to see the family on Christmas, if even. What would he study while at college? That was to be decided.

But…

He hated that 'but' that niggled at him. It said, *'But what about Amelia and Cora?'*, 'but what will they do when Mark is out for twelve hours *working*?', *'but what if the house is broken into and only the girls are home?'*.

He shouldn't have to think about that.

But, he did.

The end of the trail was coming up. The ground started up into a steep incline, his breath catching as he took long strides towards the top, thinking how at the crest of the hill, you could see into some of the rooms at the back of the house. *That*, if someone asked him, was what made the house creepy; anyone could stand at the top of that hill and look at the house. You could see straight into the three top windows. Those bedrooms belonged to Mark and Cora for the summer. You could also clearly see onto the landing. Any creep could watch them walking from the bathroom and into their bedrooms, wearing towels or in their pyjamas. But no, the talking walls are what you should be worried about.

Daniel would bet that none of the people who believed in the ghost story had walked around dodgy parts of Town in the dark. That'd show them what they need to be afraid of.

From either his hangover or his building frustration, or a combination of both, Daniel was clenching his jaw in anger by the time he reached the top of the hill. He paused, regarding the old house; it almost blended into the night, a black shape in the darkness. Surprisingly, even Mark's bedroom had lights out.

So, the beast sleeps.

Daniel grunted to the wind and started down the hill, desperate to get to bed now that he was so close. The torchlight was bouncing along the walls of the house, hitting the glass with every other step. With the motion, the batteries in the old torch shook around in the battery pack and dislodged, sending his path into complete darkness and the batteries onto the ground.

"Shit!" Daniel contemplated leaving the batteries behind until the morning but knew that if he did, they would be staying there forever, and so he knelt, running his hands along the ground, between the broken branches, and in the mud, feeling the dirt going under his nails until he felt the small manmade cylinders. Inserting them back into the torch end, he tapped the bottom off his palm until the light came back and hit Daniel directly in the eyes. Wincing away from it, he was blinded momentarily until his vision came back to focus.

The torch beam exposed the rotting exterior of the house, the weather damage it had suffered from all the years of neglect, and seemed to shine right through the windows. Daniel held the light focused on Mark's bedroom window for a few seconds longer - if it woke him up... oh well.

Okay, he had had his fun. Now he just wanted to get to bed.

But-

Wait-

The light went across the window in the centre, the one leading to the landing, and standing there, out of place, was a tall silhouette against the window.

Daniel dropped on to one knee, shielding the light against himself so that the beam was smothered against his shirt. He froze, his heart stopping momentarily as his mind comprehended what his eyes were seeing. This wasn't his hangover, was it? He lifted his eyes to the window and saw it again.

Dropping the torch and reaching for one of the thick branches that Cora and been collecting for her fort instead, Daniel raced for the front of the house, jumping up the set of steps in one leap. He pulled on the cold metal handle and sidled in, stopping the door just before the creak he had learned to avoid early in their stay, and closing it over quietly.

There was somebody upstairs.

Somebody in *his* house.

Somebody who didn't belong there.

The house was in total darkness. Daniel could barely see his own hands clutching the thick branch as he crossed the foyer. At the bottom of the stairs, he hesitated, listening to the noises of the house.

Footsteps.

He could hear them muffled on the carpeted floor above. His heart was racing. His adrenaline flowing freely. His breath coming in unsteady waves. He took the steps three at a time, missing the noisy set, and waited near the top, listening again for any signs that the intruder had gone into one of the bedrooms- into his room.

There were more footsteps. They were nearing him. Slow, unsure footing.

Daniel wasn't going to wait for him to get the drop on him. He lunged forward, swinging the branch out at the intruder. His first swing was low, connecting with a torso. There was a loud thump followed by a crashing sound as Daniel shoved his body weight into the man and forced him into the wall.

"Ahhh-" Daniel stepped back, slid his hands down his branch, and readied himself to swing again, aiming this time for his head. The branch was stopped mid-swing, the intruder catching it in his outstretched hand. Daniel let go, grabbing at the dark and feeling the fabric of a coat, and pulled them upwards, raising his other fist and punching downwards. He couldn't be sure, but he thought he heard a crack.

Then the lights came on.

"Daniel!"

"Daniel! What-" Under Daniel, cowering with his arms covering his head, was a blonde boy, whimpering and curling his legs to his chest. Daniel let go of his hold on his jacket and the boy toppled to the floor with a loud *thud*.

"Stephen! Oh my God!" Amelia went to his side, cradling his head in her arms. He groaned, holding his bloody nose.

"What the hell is going on out here?" Mark demanded.

"Yeah, what the hell, Daniel!" Amelia shouted. Behind her, Cora stood in the bedroom doorway, holding her elephant toy close to her chest, her face puffy with sleep.

"I thought he was breaking in!" Daniel tried, picking the branch back up off the floor.

"Oh, yeah, likely story- you think that just because you're older you get to do this-" Amelia was rubbing sleep from her eyes.

"What are ya talking about? I saw someone in the window, and I presumed-"

"Why would that be your first thought? What if it had been me? Or one of your sisters?"

Daniel raised his hands up in protest.

"I was just trying to leave, I swear. I wasn't breaking in-" Stephen's voice was thick as he tried to stem the blood flow from his nose. Amelia offered her jumper to him.

"Just because your girlfriend got caught in your room, it doesn't mean you need to ruin it for me!" Amelia bit, her long hair unruly as she pressed her jumper to the boy's nose.

"Wait, you had a boy in your room?" Mark asked, waving his hand when he turned to her, trying to understand the scene before him with disorientated consciousness.

"So? Daniel had girls over when he was younger than me!"

"That's different," Daniel retorted with a scoff. Amelia's face transformed from one of indignation to that of pure outrage.

"How? Because I'm a girl? It's none of your business what I do with boys-" Amelia let out a yell of protest as Daniel leaned forward and yanked Stephen up from the floor by the scruff.

"You better not have touched my sister-" He reeled back his fist but was stopped before he could land the punch when Mark stepped in the way and pulled Stephen out of harm's way. Using his two arms as a barrier, he held the two boys back from one another – or Daniel from the boy, more accurately - his sleep-filled eyes wide.

"Amelia, check on your sister, please." Mark nodded towards the bedroom door. Cora was no longer standing there and had seemingly run for cover. Amelia's jaw tightened, but she turned. "What's your name, son?" Mark asked, his brows etched together, but his tone gentle.

"It's Stephen, sir," he answered, one hand clutching his bruised torso, the other his bloodied nose. Mark sighed and eyed Daniel as he lowered his hands, a warning to his son.

"Stephen." Mark ran his hand the length of his face. "You live close to here?"

"Yes, sir. Just past Hadley's place," he said. He was Ellen's neighbour, Daniel noted.

"And you were heading home? That's one hell of a walk in the dark." Stephen nodded before his eyes widened and he rushed to assure him of his intentions.

"No, I really was, sir, I promise."

Mark patted him on the shoulder. "I believe you. I just mean it's a dangerous walk at this hour," Mark said, ignoring the fact that he had sent Daniel to do just that walk.

"I don't mind it, I'm used to-" Stephen cleared his throat, his cheeks flushing red.

"Fresh air is good for a broken nose, anyway," Daniel said, going to step around his father. Mark shot Daniel a halting stare.

"I can't let you walk all that way in the dark alone," Mark told him before beckoning to Daniel. "Take the keys to the Volvo and drive Stephen home."

"But-"

"Don't make me say it again, Daniel." Daniel took quick, deep breaths, his body almost trembling as he watched Mark casually and carefully inspect the boy's injuries. Stephen winced as Mark pressed on his nose and advised him to get medical attention the next day but promising him that it didn't look broken.

"Send me the doctor's bill, son, won't you?" Amelia appeared back in the doorway, closing it over and blocking Cora from view. Stephen's shoulders relaxed, his eyes widening.

"I'm a huge fan of yours, sir. I've read nearly all of your books."

"Well, thank you, son. If you bring them over, I'll sign them. They might be worth something one day that way," Mark told him, smiling. Daniel stood in disbelief, his ears ringing. This was a joke.

"I'd love that."

"Yeah, well, it's the least I could do. And the least you could do is stay out of Amelia's bedroom after nine. Deal?" They shook hands. Daniel's jaw dropped open ever so slightly. With a small smile and polite *goodnight* in Amelia's direction, Stephen took a step towards Daniel, waiting. Without speaking, Daniel turned and headed down the stairs.

"Dad-"

"I don't want to hear it, Amelia. I want to go to bed." Their voices were muffled by the thumping in Daniel's ears. He didn't check to see if Stephen was following before he grabbed the keys off the table by the basement and yanked the front door open, slamming it behind him.

By the time Stephen was coming out the door, Daniel was sitting in the Volvo 960 with the engine humming. He pulled the lever and flashed the full beams at him, blinding him as he walked towards the car.

Chapter 6

The journey in the car was dangerously quiet. The tension was thick as Daniel sped down the old road furiously. The light from the dash bled a cold blue glow into the interior of the car, matching the icy atmosphere. Stephen sat as still as possible and kept his breathing to a minimum. Daniel kept his sight on the road, his gaze flickering only once when they were passing Ellen's house and he spied a warm light coming from one of the top rooms of the house. He would ask her about Stephen tomorrow.

There was a loud *clunk* as the front wheel hit a pothole in the road. Stephen grabbed at his face, wincing loudly as pain seared. Daniel let out an arrogant chuckle, one that made a hard smile appear and eased the tension in his chest just a little.

"You don't have to be so smug," Stephen muttered under his breath. Daniel glanced at him.

"Unless you want two black eyes to match that nose, I'd be quiet," he warned, unable to stop his satisfaction from entering his voice. "How old are you anyway?" he asked. He looked young, with a rounded face, but he was tall and broad enough to make Daniel unsure of his age.

"I'm nearly seventeen," he replied, checking his fingers for fresh blood.

"Seventeen? What are you doing messing around with my sister? She's only fifteen!" If Daniel hadn't been driving, he would've socked him again.

"What are you talking about? Amelia is sixteen. You don't even know your own sister's age?" Daniel hesitated, thinking. Was she that old now?

Maybe she was…

"Well, either way, you shouldn't be doing it," Daniel muttered. He had known that Amelia had been sneaking a boy into the house some days, but this, this was new. "Where were you even hiding?" Daniel asked after a moment had passed.

Stephen gasped, shutting his eyes and wincing as they hit another pothole.

"In the wardrobe. I had to wait until Cora fell asleep before leaving. I nearly fell asleep myself." His accent was stronger than Ellen's, maybe because of his nearly broken nose, or maybe because he was inbred. Either way, Daniel was reminded of how ugly it sounded on some people. Daniel looked over at him, unable to hide his irritation, although the idea of him being squashed inside an old musty wardrobe did give him some enjoyment.

"It's just up here, on the left." Stephen leaned forwards, pointing to a gap in the trees. Daniel turned in, dipping the headlights when they faced against the house. He drove up behind an old Ford and reversed back to swing the nose of the car around. When he was facing away from the house, he stopped to let Stephen out.

"Listen, man, you don't need to worry- I like her. A lot." Daniel reached down and pressed a button to unlock the door of the car, punctuated with a loud click. Stephen unbuckled his belt and set his hand on the handle. "Tell Amelia I'll see her tomorrow," Stephen opened the door, letting the cool night air into the idling car. He stepped out, holding the door open to look at Daniel expectantly.

"Thanks for the lift."

"Yeah, yeah." Daniel flicked his wrist to signal him to close the door. He watched Stephen walk away from the car for a few seconds before pressing hard on the accelerator and heading home.

It was after 3 am when Daniel found the bra twisted in his sheets. The clasp was caught up in the buttons of his duvet. As tired as he was, he still smiled to himself before untangling the navy straps and laying it over the back of his chair. Stripping off, he tossed his dirty clothes into the basket beside his door and crawled under his sheets, so exhausted that he fell asleep within moments of his head touching the pillow, his hangover headache pounding in rhythm with the rattling in the walls of the house.

Amelia lay awake, freezing regardless of the extra layers she wore and the little bundle of heat that lay cuddling into her. Cora was snoring softly, a trail of drool going from her mouth down to Amelia's pillow. She had woken to the gentle tapping on her bedroom wall. She squeezed her eyes shut, trying to block out the noise by focusing on the soft sounds Cora made, with little success. She had heard Daniel coming in, slamming the front door and stomping his way up the stairs and into the bathroom, leaving the door open for the whole house to hear him in there, before he went to his room and closed the door over loudly, with little consideration for anyone else.

Some time had passed since she last heard her brother moving around, and as angry as she was at him, knowing that he was now asleep and that she was the only one awake in the house, was daunting to her, as if whatever ghouls that hid in the shadows or the carved figures in the hallway walls that feigned their inanimate states, would only come out if they knew only she would see them. Except, she wouldn't see anything because her eyes had been closed tightly since she became conscious and first heard the tapping on the walls.

It's an old house, she told herself. *Old houses make noises.*

Her breath caught when the tapping stopped, and a heavy knocking began. She held her breath as if it would make the sounds stop, but they did not stop, they only continued to move around the room, getting closer and then further away.

She was being ridiculous.

As carefully as she could, trying not to disturb the blankets, Amelia slid her hand over to hold Cora's. She felt her little hand and held on to it, afraid to move any more than that. Her heart jumped when Cora moved unexpectedly, twisting away from her and kicking her legs into Amelia's side. She hissed and pushed her sister's legs away from her so that they pointed towards the end of the bed.

She lay there, holding her side, as the knocking continued, listening until the noises seemed to stop. There was complete silence then, and when she mustered enough courage, Amelia decided to open her eyes, to prove to herself that she could.

The room was almost completely dark, with just an inkling of grey moonlight creeping in through her curtains to cast suggestive shadows. She stared at the ceiling, taking deep, steadying breaths, and wiggling her toes to gather some warmth; it was just so cold. When the knocking sounds returned, she lay there, forcing herself to keep her eyes open.

Old houses make noises, she told herself. *There is nothing to be afraid of.*

Then, as if to test herself, she scooted up ever so slightly in the bed and stared into the dark room. Her eyes traced the shapes of her desk, her chair, her mirror which reflected nothing but darkness into the room, her tall wardrobe that had stank of mould at the beginning of summer, the little silhouette of the Virgin Mary figurine - that at first had stared down at her until she faced it away - that sat atop it, and then she shifted her sight to the tall doorway on the left. With the lights off in the hallway, there was only darkness through the cracks in the frame. Between the door and her wardrobe was the darkest corner of the room. It was so dark that Amelia couldn't even make out where the two walls collided and became perpendicular to one another. She focused hard, straining to make out the edges of the room when her eyes adjusted and she gasped.

A chill spiked down her spine and her heart fell to her stomach.

She dove under the blankets, clinging to Cora, her sister's soft breathing filling her ears.

A shape.

In the darkness.

Chapter 7

The morning was damp with condensation on the thin windowpanes, and a smell that reminded Daniel of the times he spent sheltered from the rain in a friend's garden shed, huddled together while they held bottles of beer and passed a single cigarette around between them (which he always declined). Daniel tied the laces to his worn runners, playing with the hole in the toe of the shoe, and glanced out of the window. It wasn't raining, but the ground was wet. At the end of his bed there was a new pair of running shoes boxed up, the laces trailing out from under the lid like snakes. They wouldn't be ideal for running in on the first wear but he didn't fancy having soggy feet either.

He kicked his old runners off, pushing them to the side, and leaned forwards in the chair to drag the box towards him, almost over-extending the muscles in his back rather than standing up to get it. He pulled the stuffing paper out, and seeing Amelia walk past his room, still drowsy with sleep, he balled the paper up and flung it at her. It hit the back of her head, landing in her brushed hair before it fell to the ground. Amelia stopped outside his door and turned to face him with a scowl. Daniel whistled playfully and crouched to pull the runner out before he pushed his foot into the shoe.

"I hope you get a blister," Amelia grumbled in his direction before storming off. Someone had woken up in a foul mood, Daniel thought, standing and flexing his feet in the shoes. He ran on the spot until his heart rate was raised before he slowed to a walking pace. The shoes were already rubbing at the back of his heel. He went to his chest of drawers and pulled open the top drawer with a hard yank as it struggled on the railing. Bundles of t-shirts and shorts were folded inside. Between the two piles, there was an opened box of plasters. He pulled out two and slipped his feet out of the shoes to set them in place. Testing them again, the friction on his skin was somewhat lessened. It would do, he supposed.

On the porch, Daniel took a deep breath, inhaling the fresh country air. He would swap it for dusty smoking areas with falling women, and the peaceful singing of the birds for a loud nightclub where you couldn't hear a damn word, in town any day. Behind him, the door opened with a creak and he turned just as Mark stepped out, pulling his arm over his chest, and jogging on the spot. They both stopped in the act like two guilty men caught doing something illicit. Daniel bobbed his head and started scratching the back of his neck in a poor attempt to hide the fact that he had been stretching. Likewise, Mark seemed to do the same to his tri-cep, as though trying to conceal his own stretching.

"Morning."

"Morning." Daniel stood waiting; the silence was uncomfortable. Mark cleared his throat.

"Did Stephen get home alright?"

"Yeah."

"Great stuff." They mirrored one another, with their hands on their hips, both staring out into the driveway where the old Volvo 960 was parked, the stones behind it displaced after Daniel had skidded into the driveway the previous night. It was next to the much more modern XC90 that Mark had rented for himself.

"You heading out for work?"

Mark nodded without looking at him, then hesitated and shook his head, looking down at his own shorts and t-shirt. "No, actually. I was going to go for a run. It clears the head," he told him. "Trying to shift some of this too," Mark grabbed at his stomach. Daniel nodded. "You?" The question was almost rhetorical, but they both, it seemed, were keeping up the pretence.

"I was thinking of it-"

"Yeah? Which way are you going?" The question, to someone else, might have led to an invitation. From Mark, however, Daniel understood that it was an interrogation; a way for Mark to avoid the inconvenience of having to run with him. This suited Daniel fine.

"Just the trail out the back," Daniel said, his head tilting towards it. Mark's disappointment was evident.

"I see." There was a moment when neither of them said anything, ignoring the fact that only a matter of months ago they would have run together every day. But that was then.

Daniel relented. "I am actually probably going to give it a miss. I'm breaking in new runners." Daniel set his hands to his hips and tapped his foot as if to show that there wasn't even a crease in the toes of the runners. Mark's eyes drifted to his feet to watch his little dance. His expression didn't change.

"Oh, right. Well, maybe I'll head that way then." Mark headed down the porch steps, visibly relieved with his shoulders unhooking from his ears. "Oh, son, will you go to the shops today- just pick up the usual things." Mark reached into his pocket and jingled the keys at him.

"Sure," Daniel shrugged, catching the keys when they were thrown. He watched Mark jog away and let out a breath. Then, just before he disappeared around the corner of the house, he turned back and came as far as the porch decking.

"Oh and, you need to pick up something for Amelia." Mark lowered his voice so that Daniel had to walk towards him to hear.

"What is it?" Daniel set his hands on the wobbly railing. Mark seemed to be chewing his words over in his mind, his mouth tightening to a grimace.

"She needs, eh... you know- girly things." Mark's eyes squinted on the words as if he were flinching through a rectal examination.

"Tampons? She needs tampons?" Mark recoiled when Daniel said the words. Shaking his head, Daniel straightened up, wondering how this man helped produce three offspring.

"Yes."

"Yeah, grand. I'll take Cora with me." Mark nodded his goodbye and set off towards the trees. Daniel didn't wait to watch him.

"How heavy is your flow?"

Amelia paused, a Sudoku book in her hands, to stare at Daniel. In the old utility room, she was surrounded by baskets piled high with clothes; Daniel's one, brimming with sportswear, was still yet to be sorted. A hose went from the sink tap to the washing machine drawer so she could manually fill the machine with water. Amelia reached over and turned the tap off as the machine started to spin.

"What?" Amelia rolled her eyes and set her book down to begin folding colourful socks and tossing them into Cora's basket. Daniel relaxed against the doorframe, juggling two apples.

"Mark asked me 'ta go to the shop. He said you needed tampons; which ones do you want me to get?" Immediately, Amelia's face turned bright red. She scoffed and untucked her hair from behind her ear so that it hung down over her face like a shield. "So…?"

"Just get me anything," she mumbled. An apple dropped to the floor and rolled towards her. She paused, then kicked it back towards Daniel without looking up. She turned her back to him, busying herself with the laundry.

"Do you want me to get you anything else while I'm there? Any popcorn, fizzy drinks… johnnies?" Amelia spun round to face him, her nostrils flared.

"Obviously not." She glared at him. Daniel pushed off from the doorframe and picked the apple off the floor. Rubbing it against his chest, he took a bite out of it.

"Good answer," he winked at her. "I'm taking Cora with me."

What annoyed Daniel most about these kinds of towns, he realised, was not that they were boring and odd or because they had zero restaurants but had three barbers and one petrol station that they shared with the neighbouring town. It didn't have much to do with the paranoia and superstitions that were bread into them and made them avoid cracks in the path or walking beneath ladders, as though combustion was a result of not throwing salt over your left (or maybe it is your right) shoulder, either; it was because the people in it seemed to believe that it was possibly the best place in the world. They were delusional, and he found that the people who grew up in towns like this usually died eighty-five years later two doors down from their family home.

Daniel could see that after a life spent in the hustle and bustle of a city, when your children have grown and your careers have ended, that having a nest-egg here to live out the last of your days in peace, waiting for death – out of the way - could be attractive, but in a town like this, where locals grow and die without ever having left the place, any 'blow-ins' were considered a parasite, trying to burrow in and taint the town with their city roots. They were as unwelcoming as they were uninteresting. And each time they moved to one, Daniel could sense their metaphorical fly swatters raised and at the ready to squash them.

Daniel lifted Cora out of her bumper seat and shut over the door of the car. He locked the doors and slipped the keys into his pocket before handing the loose sheet of paper that Cora had scribbled gibberish on in orange crayon to match his shopping list and set her onto the ground. He held his hand out to her and waited for her to take it before they stood at the edge of the road, the cars moving slowly past them, every

second occupant rubbernecking to stare at them. (Reaching for their fly swats)
Take a picture, it'll last longer.
"Can we get ice cream? And chocolate and those, those, those white stick sweets?" Cora was oblivious to everything around her. When there was a gap between two cars, Daniel started forward, pulling Cora along.

"Sure thing, C." They walked down the wide pavement. Cora skipped along beside Daniel, swinging his arm back and forth with their interlocked hands. Flower beds dotted the street, and benches outside stores had people sitting reading the paper. Glass fronts were gleaming in the sunshine, not a sticky fingerprint in sight. The main street was clean of litter and loitering teens. One shop stuck out.

Bordered up windows and a faded notice on the door, the shop looked as though it had been closed for a long time. The plywood nailed to the shopfront had been painted on to look as though cats and dogs were sitting in windows framed by purple curtains. Daniel wondered what it had been before and stopped to read the faded notice. The words were illegible, having been washed away by time. He stepped back and shielded his eyes from the sun with his free hand and looked up. The remnants of the word 'HARDWARE' were barely discernible.

"What about a toy? Can I get a toy, too?" Cora was jumping up and down next to Daniel, tugging his arm every which way as she twirled and spun with excitement.

"Yeah, whatever," he replied absent-mindedly, Mark's bank card burning in his pocket as he took in the shopfront.

"Let's go!" Cora pulled him on, towards the shop.

A cool breeze sent shivers down Daniel's bare arms when he stepped through the doors of the shop. A bell above rang as the hum of the deep freezers sang beneath the lilting county accents of the shoppers. Several people turned and stared briefly at the *blow-ins*. He met their gaze with a raised brow before he went to grab a basket, thought second of it, and collected a shopping trolley instead before he started by the fresh produce, chucking the vegetables and fruit into the cart without checking the list that Cora waved about. She tugged on his shirt every couple of minutes, pulling his attention to anything remotely colourful, until at last, he sent her in search of her own goodies.

"Go find a toy you want," he said as her little face beamed. "I'll meet you there. Just one," he reminded her and pushed her gently down towards the other end of the shop, where he could see the stacked shelves of noisy toys. He almost called after her to tell her to test them to see which was loudest.

Daniel pushed the trolley through the food aisles at breakneck speed. He slowed in the aisle lined with toiletries, picking out shampoos and body washes for each of them, sparing no cost. He collected more plasters and a tub of Vaseline for when he would eventually get to run.

He came across the feminine hygiene section and stalled his trolley, staring up and down at the boxes and boxes stacked metres high, wondering what the difference was between them. Some were considerably more expensive than the store brand version, and Daniel wondered if that had anything to do with the quality. Compact, pearl, non-applicator- the list was endless, and then each of them had their own size, too.

He must have looked as confused as he felt because, after a minute of choosing boxes, reading the reverse side of them and then setting them back down, there was a tap on his shoulder. He spun, already pulling his trolley back.

"Sorry, am I in your way?" He glanced over his shoulder to see a pretty, brunette girl smiling at him. She shook her head and beckoned towards the mountain of products.

"You look like you need help," she said. Daniel smiled back.

"Is it that obvious?" He took the girl in; she wore pale jeans and a tight t-shirt that she had scissored a 'v' into with *Westlife* printed above a faded picture of the band, and

'*Flying Without Wings*' floating above their heads. She nodded.

"Are you picking them up for your ... girlfriend, or..." The question hung in the air for a few seconds longer, the girl staring straight into his eyes, her lips parted. They shone with her lip gloss. He knew this look. He almost spoke but stopped himself before the words '*I don't have a missus*' came out, suddenly thinking of Ellen. Daniel shook his head.

"No, they are for my sister."

"So, do you need help?"

"Yes, absolutely." Daniel watched as the girl leaned over his trolley and stretched up to the shelf, her tight shirt lifting to expose the tanned skin, a thin layer of sweat dampening her top. He wasn't a fan of the new boyband but couldn't argue that this piece of merch looked good. She pulled a box off the shelf and held it out to him.

"Well, if she didn't specify which ones to get, she probably uses these." She dropped the box into the front of the trolley, next to the toilet roll, and set her arms on the front of his trolley, only inches apart so that her chest squeezed together.

"Thanks," Daniel said. The girl stood there for a moment longer, as though waiting for something, but Daniel motioned towards the box. "Should I get more than one box for her?" At this, the girl laughed.

"No."

"Right, thanks."

"I'm Kate, by the way." She extended her hand out to him.

"Daniel." He shook it. She held onto his hand for a longer time than necessary. "Are you from here?"

"Yes. You're not, are you?" There it was again, that small town greed wanting to weed out the outsiders.

"No, we're not. We're just here for the summer until Mark finishes his book." Her face, then, changed as she realised who Daniel was. She pulled her hand back gently and set it into her back pocket.

"Oh right, well, maybe I'll see you around, Daniel." She started off in the other direction, checking over her shoulder once to watch him as he went down the aisle. Daniel didn't watch her as she went, unbothered by the reaction; it happened most places they went. As it turns out, most people don't appreciate a novelist documenting the horrors in their wholesome, family-friendly town. He imagined that half the people in the town would take a pitchfork and set it alight to chase them out if it was still as socially acceptable as when Mary Shelley was around.

He moved through the store, collecting items as he went, and made his way towards the toy aisle. When he turned the corner, he quickened his pace. Cora was standing next to a wall of toys, holding one in her hand, while a man in his late forties was knelt in front of her, talking.

"Cora, are you alright?" Daniel came to stand next to them, the front of his trolley only inches from the man's face. The man, dressed in mechanic's overalls with a dirty face, stood up. He smiled at Cora. "What's going on here?"

"I picked one!" Cora announced, holding a black cat plush toy up to show him. Daniel ignored her, however, and confronted the man.

"Is this your brother, Cora?" the man spoke politely.

"Yeah, it is. Who are you?" Daniel instinctively stepped in front of Cora. The man, sensing the mounting tension, stepped backwards and raised his hands.

"I just spotted her by herself, so wanted to check if she was with anyone. You can't be letting her run off by herself around here," the man said, not rudely, but something in Daniel reacted to it.

"Why? She didn't do any damage." The man was already shaking his head.

"That's not what I meant. I just wanted to make sure she was alright, is all." He reached forward to shake Daniel's hand. Daniel hesitated but shook it. "You're staying in that rental out by the lake, aren't yas?" Daniel nodded. "I'm looking forward to reading what your old man thinks of it." Daniel gave him a tight grin as he backed away. The man gave Cora a small wave and disappeared.

They went straight to the check-out.

Chapter 8

By the time they returned from getting the messages, Daniel's headache was a dull throbbing in his temple. It bounced around in his head with every step. With three shopping bags on one arm, another in his other hand, and Cora clinging to his back, Daniel pushed the kitchen door open with his foot to see Amelia busy folding the clothes. She held two polka dotted socks in her hands when her eyes lifted to watch as Daniel set the bags down on the counter before kneeling so that Cora could climb off, her arms leaving a red ring around his throat.

"We only do one trip in this house!" Daniel declared as Cora laughed. "I'll leave this for you, yeah? I'm going to pick Ellen up." Daniel pointed to the shopping. Before Amelia could protest, he headed for the back door and left.

―――

The afternoon slowly slipped into the evening without the sun announcing its goodbye. Daniel, Ellen, and Cora sat on the old, moth-eaten rug in the middle of the floor of the basement, pushing the wooden planchette around the Ouija board. Daniel had found Cora there, alone, playing with the board game, after he convinced a reluctant Ellen to stay for a while, promising to take her home once it got dark outside. However, without the dimming light outside being visible, they let the time go by without realising.

"Look, it's trying to say something," Daniel said. Cora's eyes were wide as she watched the piece move around the board, sliding across the alphabet and pausing on different letters. "Is there someone here with us now?" Daniel called out. The planchette pushed over to rest on the faded 'Yes'. Cora gulped, her eyes wide. Ellen watched Daniel from the corner of her eye.

"Who is it?" Cora asked, crawling closer to the board. Daniel held his fingers on the wooden piece for a moment before sighing.

"We probably shouldn't talk to them- we don't want to scare you," he said. Cora's little brows creased as she looked between the board and Daniel, her eagerness clear.

"No, no, no! I'm not scared!" she pleaded with him. Ellen was leaning on her back and raised a questioning brow when Daniel turned to her. "Pleeeeaaasssee!" Cora whined.

"Okay, if you say so." Daniel shook his shoulders in a comical shimmy and looked to the exposed beams in the ceiling, as though he was speaking to someone up there, and cleared his throat. "If you're really there, tell me what colour my jocks are!" Daniel said. Cora giggled happily when the planchette began to move over the letters.

"White," Ellen announced when it stopped moving. Daniel lifted his t-shirt up to expose the white waistband. Cora's eyes were nearly coming out of her skull.

"Ask it something else!" Cora squealed. Daniel nodded, thinking, and smiled to himself.

"Why are you here? What is it you want us to do?" Daniel said, again to the ceiling. He shot Cora a wink as she moved closer to him, ducking her head under his arm to get as close to the board as possible. She watched it move from side to side, trying to follow the letters.

"T-I-C-K-L-E," Ellen said. Cora turned to her.

"What does that spell?" she asked quietly, but Daniel's hands were still moving.

"C-O-R-A," Daniel read out this time. "That's *your* name!" Cora paled with fright, any pretence of bravery leaving her now. She clung to Daniel's arms.

"My name?" she cried out, burying her face in his chest.

"Yeah- what was the first word?" he asked Ellen. She spelled it out with a smile and roll of her eyes. "Do you know what it spells, C?" Cora leaned back. Her eyes were glassy with fear as she shook her head.

"No... I can't spell that good," she whispered, shakily.

"It spells out... *Tickle Cora!*" Daniel told her and watched while realisation hit her. She grinned and twisted, trying to escape Daniel's reach, but he held on to her, tickling her sides and under her chin as she squirmed and stretched and screamed in delight. She thrashed her legs around, kicking at the air as Daniel teased her, stopping only when she was red in the face from laughing so hard. Ellen, having retreated once Cora's flailing legs almost smacked her in the face, was putting the board away, touching it delicately, as though she was handling something rotten.

"What's wrong? I don't think dead trees can bite," Daniel said, lifting Cora and tucking her into a ball before gently setting her onto the floor. She rolled over and was pulling at his arm, trying to exact her revenge, stretching his t-shirt's neck, and making him cough as the fabric threatened to strangle him. Daniel pressed his hand on her forehead – almost covering her entire face with its mass – and pushed her back.

"I just... these things have always freaked me out," she admitted to him with a shrug. "I feel like they are bad karma, you know, like you could be messing with some bad *thing*?" She set the lid on the box and pushed it away from her with her foot, wiping her hands on her trousers. Daniel considered then if maybe he was the *only* person left that didn't believe in the paranormal.

"They aren't all bad, though." Much to Daniel's surprise, it was Cora who spoke and panted like a puppy after retreating from her brother's barricade. "You can talk to good people too... like Mam." Cora shrugged her tiny shoulders and giggled when Daniel tousled her hair. He met Ellen's sympathetic gaze and reached out to squeeze her hand. The door to the basement opened behind them, the light from the foyer lighting the stairwell. Amelia's shadow appeared on the wall. Down the stairs came the black stray cat, slinking down in smooth, graceful movements. He meowed and rubbed himself against Daniel's leg before bouncing atop the armchair, which may, or may not, have been where Mr Evans had slit his throat. The image flickered through his mind.

"Susan!" Cora jumped up to cradle the cat in her arms. She swung back and forth, hugging the meowing cat close to her chest.

"I thought that cat was male?" Ellen whispered. Daniel just nodded, rolling his eyes as he moved to sit up on the old couch and stretched his arms across the back of it. Since his return with the shopping, he and Amelia had not spoken more than a couple of words to one another.

"Cora, dinner's ready."

Daniel had his back to his sister as she stood at the top of the stairs, calling down. At the mention of food, his stomach gurgled.

"What're we having?" he asked without turning to face her. There was a moment of silence before Amelia spoke.

"Ellen, could you please tell Daniel that there's only enough food for Cora and me?" Ellen's eyes darted to Daniel and up to where Amelia stood, still at the top of the steps. Daniel sat forward, to the edge of his seat, and turned. He could only see her legs, the top half of her blocked by the banisters. If that was how she wanted to be, fine, he didn't care.

"Ellen, could you tell *Amelia* that we don't want any of her food- we will order chipper."

"Can I have pizza?" Cora shouted. Daniel twisted back to Ellen, his brows etched.

"They do deliver out here, don't they?" Before Ellen had a chance to answer, Amelia was speaking.

"Before you order, Ellen, can you tell my brother that Dad said no one is allowed to be here after half eight and that he told me I can call him if there is anyone here-"

Daniel's jaw tightened as heat travelled up his neck. He got to his feet and walked to the bottom of the stairs so that he could see his sister in her stupid oversized jumper and *his* tracksuit trousers. He was still speaking to Ellen.

"Can you tell *my sister* that her little boyfriend is going to get a punch if he *ever* comes over!" Amelia was almost halfway down the stairs now, her voice shaking.

"Ellen, do you know that this is what Daniel does everywhere we go? He finds himself a chew toy to play with and when he's finished he gets rid of her and moves on to the next shiny play-thing!" Amelia was shouting. Daniel scoffed, gripping the banisters with white knuckles.

"Ellen, could you *please* tell Amelia what Stephen said to me about *her* last night!" Amelia froze, her eyes daring him to say something, to tell her what was said.

"Daniel, stop," Ellen tried.

"No. Tell me. What did he say?" Amelia's chest was rising and falling rapidly, her eyes searching Daniel's face for fault. He stood tall, his voice steady as he spoke, and watched his sister crumble internally as he humiliated her.

"He said that there was no fear of him coming back because he got what he wanted from you." Tears were welling up in her eyes. He watched as they silently spilled over, but he wasn't done.

"No, he didn't." Her chin was trembling, giving away her tightened jaw.

"Yeah, he did. And he said that he wished he hadn't bothered because it was shit." That was it. The words were out. They were lies, but only he knew that. Amelia couldn't stop herself then. The tears fell more freely down her burning cheeks. She said nothing as she turned and ran up the stairs, slamming the door behind her.

Daniel's blood was hot. He sniffed and lifted his head to look first at Cora, who rubbed Susan's black fur quietly, and then at Ellen as she stared angrily at him. A pit in his gut told him he may have gone too far, may have stepped over the line with Amelia.

"You're such a prick," Ellen said.

Amelia just wanted to be left alone. She didn't want anyone to come after her- to see her crying. Lucky for her, no one did come after her. No one came to check to see if she was okay or to bring her up her bowl of Bolognese – a recipe she had just learned - or to tell her they were on her side, for once. That was what annoyed her so much; they were never on her side. Even when it was Daniel's fault, they didn't care that she was upset, that he had eaten her favourite snack, had punched her boyfriend - not even when he said cruel things in front of people, did they care! It was always just easier for them to leave it alone, not argue with him because he was *hard to deal with* when he was like that – but she was able to manage her emotions so that she didn't affect anyone else, didn't *disrupt* anyone's day but her own as she hid away, unlike Daniel. She was mature.

She knew she could hardly expect Cora to grasp what was happening, she was barely more than a toddler- and besides, she had always adored Daniel, always preferred him. Well, just wait until she was older and realised how horrible he actually was! But she had thought that maybe Ellen would be on her side, even just a little. But of course not, *we mustn't upset Daniel* in case he starts slamming doors.

She sat on her bed, her sleeves soaked from her tears, and cried by herself because there was no one else she could cry to. She was angry at Daniel – furious - but she was even more so at herself for letting him get to her so much. Shame washed over her as she choked back more tears, her breathing turning to hiccups as the embarrassment renewed.

She had never done that before. She wasn't a prude, it wasn't like that, but she had never felt ready to.

And now...

She flung her pillow across the room. It bounced off of the lamp on her desk and lay discarded on the floor. But why would Stephen say that to Daniel of all people? After he had practically assaulted him. Amelia sniffled back the last of her tears, resolving to the fact that all boys are the same and that she would have to settle for a life of solitude if she wanted to be happy.

A sob escaped her and she covered her mouth with a slap of her hand.

A light rattle began to sound. She leaned forward, her eyes scanning the room, searching for the cause. Her first instinct was to look to the lamp. It had stopped its flickering after the impact of the pillow and the beam was still, making no noise except for a low hum. The rattle was constant, a small, annoying sound if nothing else. Her eyes fell on the dark corner of her room; even with her two lamps on, the edges were still cast in shadow.

A chill travelled down her spine as the vision of a tall, ominous shadow crept into her memory. She had seen it last night and quickly forced herself to sleep afterwards, clinging to Cora as if she were a life vest on the safety boat of a sinking ship.

It had just been paranoia- from the Ouija board and then reading her dad's book. It was silly.

The noise was coming from the walls. The pipes, most likely. Her dad had said he was surprised it made such little noise when they first moved in, recounting a time he had spent in a haunted house several years ago. He said that the house was so loud at night that he could barely hear the keys of his laptop over the racket.

A loud bang from behind startled her. She sat up onto her knees and turned to look at the wall, her heart racing. She would be sleeping with the light on, and would have to give up reading at night, she surmised. That was probably what was making her so jumpy- the scary story. And that damn Ouija board.

It was bad news.

Was it real? She didn't know, but she wasn't about to mess around with it to find out. She had always had a morbid curiosity when it came to the occult, but she was never inquisitive enough to test it for herself, sticking strictly to stories told around torches under blankets or inside tents, or true stories in those magazine articles. Once, her dad told her a story about a friend of his who had played with one and all of his hair had turned grey within days of messing with it. She had also seen videos of people who had played with them and afterwards things in their house would go missing, doors would open and close inexplicably, and they would hear strange sounds, coming from vents. That was proof enough for her, for now.

The sounds travelled along the walls, seeming to focus mostly in the dark corner of her room. The rattle turned to more of a tapping then.

Tap...

It would happen periodically.

Tap...

Amelia tucked her blanket up to her chest, a shiver running through her. She was always cold in this house, and the crying hadn't done anything to warm her up, either. She took her book from the locker and began to read.

Tap...

Then,

Tap... Tap... Tap...

She looked up from the pages. Hadn't she read that the Devil's knocks come in three?

Tap... Tap... Tap... Tap... Tap. Tap. Tap. Tap-
Tap-Tap-Tap-Tap-Tap
TAP-TAP-TAP-

Amelia set her book down, staring at the wall in her room. The noise was growing louder and more frequent. What if a pipe was to burst? What would she do then? She didn't want to call Daniel for help- she would learn to become a plumber before she did that. She got up from her bed, her jumper falling past her hips, and stepped cautiously towards the sound.

TAP-TAP-TAP-

She stood before the wall and raised her hand to touch it.

TAPTAPTAPTAP!

She jumped back, getting frightened by the loud noise. The pipe was going to do more than burst, it sounded as though it might explode!

Knowing extraordinarily little about what she should do, Amelia moved closer to the wall, setting her palm against the cold, peeling paint, feeling the vibrations through the wood, her skin raising like gooseflesh.

TAPTAPTAP-

Then, it stopped.

The noise, the aggressive tapping coming from the walls, ceased, leaving only the sound of Amelia's quick breaths in its place. She stood there for a moment, confused. She was no handyman, but she was certain that houses were not supposed to do that. Perhaps whatever pipe was making a racket had finally come to blowing point and was now burst, spewing water, or whatever else, all over the electrics. She knew nothing of house building - could there be a fire?

Tapping the wall with her hand, she then pressed it against it. She could no longer feel the vibrations, nor could she feel any immediate dampness- at least no more than was usual in this house. Feeling as though she could not yet turn away satisfied that the house would not combust into flames from an electrical fire, she leaned in closer to press her ear to the cold wall. Her skin crawled at the sensation. It was cool, damp, and smelled strongly of the musty scent she had thought she had gotten rid of from her room. She pushed away her repulsion and focused hard on what she was hearing; she could hear no discernible sounds, no gushing water, no crackling wires-

BANG!

Amelia screamed, falling back, away from the wall and losing her footing. She fell backwards, hitting the floor hard, her wrist twisting beneath her weight, her coccyx bone taking the brunt of the fall. She hissed in pain, holding her wrist in her other hand, turning it over to assess the damage.

Her heart was hammering, her breath coming out in quick succession.

What was that?

She stared widely at the wall, in shock. It had come from the corner- where she had seen the outline of a shadow last night...

Her breathing was shaky.

Her lamp flickered just then. She was afraid to move; for fear of hurting herself somehow and more for the fear of what might happen next.

Houses make noises.

Amelia took a tentative step forward.

It is just a house.

They make sounds.

But it is just the house.

She was close enough to the wall now that her chest was almost touching it. Her fingers twitched at her side, her wrist aching. Her gulp caught in her throat. Amelia was certain that there was something wrong with the pipe now, something that was about to combust into flames and consume them.

Hesitantly, she turned her head and set her ear against the wall for the second time, straining to hear the water flow.

Sktch... sktch...sktch...

She heard a different noise coming from the corner this time. It sounded... it sounded like... *scratching-*

There was a knock on the door and Amelia's heart leapt once more. This time, however, there was a low voice accompanying the noise.

"Amelia, let me in, can we talk?" Daniel called from the hall.

"No." It was her immediate response, her instant reaction. Daniel stood there, his sigh loud enough for her to hear through the door. She could see his shadow in the gap where the saddle board should have been, waiting.

"Please?" She didn't move, nursing her twisted wrist in her other hand. When he stood there for another moment, she patted her cheeks with the sleeve of her jumper to dry her face and opened the door. Daniel was standing with her bowl of homemade Bolognese in his hands, offering it to her.

"I come in peace," he said.

"I'm not hungry," she told him. He glanced down at the cold pasta, his stomach gurgling loudly.

"We ordered pizza," he announced and turned to look at the stairs as if he was listening for something and thinking a moment before facing Amelia again. "If you want some." Amelia didn't. Or maybe she did. What she wanted most was to be left alone. She rolled her eyes to say as much and went to close over the door again but Daniel stuck his foot in the gap to stop her.

"What do you want, Daniel?" He tightened his jaw and took a deep breath. She regarded him, waiting.

"I'm sorry," he said. "I shouldn't have said those things before, I just... I was annoyed."

"You just repeated what Stephen said-"

"No, I didn't. He didn't say that to me. I was just trying to upset ya. I'm sorry." Amelia opened the door wider and watched as Daniel's eyes flickered to the thrown pillow, the lopsided lampshade. He did not comment. She chewed her lip and shook her head.

"Why? Why did you say it then?" Daniel let his head fall back, his eyes closing and his lips tightening. He shrugged his shoulders.

"I don't know. Because I knew it would be a dick thing to say? Because ya pissed me off? I'm sorry." It wasn't the most complex apology, but she knew it was the best she could hope for from him.

"I'll have some pizza too." Amelia accepted his request for forgiveness and shook his outstretched hand when he extended it towards her. "Did you, eh, hear that banging just now?" she asked and folded her arms across her chest, her wrist aching. Daniel's brows creased, his mouth turning down, and shook his head.

"No, what was it?"

"I think there's something wrong with the pipes," Amelia said. Daniel shrugged.

"He's here, you know- Stephen," Daniel told her. Amelia hadn't been expecting him. She touched her face, feeling her puffy cheeks and eyes in a panic. "Ya look fine, don't worry." Whether she did or not, it was too late to do anything about it; Stephen was at the top of the stairs, walking towards her with white sticky stitches pressed over the bridge of his nose. He was wincing with every other step, clutching at his side. He nodded at Daniel, who pressed the bowl of pasta into his hands, which he accepted without question.

"What about Dad?" Amelia asked, a fluttering of butterflies in her stomach when Stephen leaned over and kissed her politely on the cheek, much to Daniel's disdain; his brow furrowed, but he said nothing of it.

"Mark won't be back until late. He said something about working." Daniel took a step away, miming the tilting of a glass to his mouth, before stopping and facing them both. He hesitated, looking as if he might say nothing at all, before he spoke, "Keep your door open, okay?" Amelia's neck felt hot, her cheeks beginning to burn as a blush ran across her skin. She nodded. "Pizza will be here in half an hour," he told them, looking directly at Stephen as if in a warning. Stephen took her hand in his and she smiled.

"So, he's not always a dick?" Stephen whispered jokingly as Daniel walked back towards the stairs.

"Hey, Amelia?" Amelia stepped into the hallway to meet Daniel's gaze. "How old are you?" A little offended, but unsurprised, she scoffed.

"Sixteen," she said. Daniel considered this, seemingly confused, but turned without saying anything else and went back down the stairs.

Chapter 9

Daniel followed the girlish giggles into the kitchen and found Cora and Ellen laughing as they made shadow animals on the ceiling with their hands over the top of a lamp. At his arrival, Ellen turned and straightened up, raising her left brow in silent question.

"Is the pizza here?" Cora asked, running to Daniel's side.

"Not yet," Ellen answered, resting against the counter, leaning with a hand on her hip while watching Daniel cross the room to stand next to her.

"Did you order extra for your neighbour?" Daniel asked. Ellen nodded her head, a small smile tugging at the corner of her mouth.

"You mean *our* neighbour?" she teased. "He's alright-Stephen, I mean. I used to know his brother before he got shipped off to boarding school in your neck of the woods for getting caught smoking W-E-E-D," she told him, her eyes following Cora as she left the room, running up the stairs on all fours. "And it's probably nice for Amelia to have someone to hang out with."

"Can we not talk about him and my sister, please?" Daniel pleaded, thankful that Cora was now running up and down the hallway upstairs, disturbing any intimate activity.

"Did she accept your apology?" Ellen asked, not letting him off as easily as he would have liked. As soon as Amelia had retreated to her room Ellen had been straight to correct him, to scold him, but it was different from when Mark or Amelia did it.

"She accepted the offer for pizza, which is kind of the same," he said. There was a moment of silence. "I think she knows what I said was a lie." Daniel took Ellen's hand and kissed her knuckles.

"Is what *she* said true?" Daniel held Ellen's hand to his lips, hesitating. A coy smile played across her mouth.

"Why? Would you be jealous if it was?" he teased, smirking. Ellen let out a sarcastic laugh, shrugging.

"Nah, I've got a couple 'playthings' for when I get bored," she said, mockingly. Daniel felt a twitch of jealousy rise in him at this. He tried pushing it down, and when it wouldn't budge, he laughed sarcastically. Ellen caressed his chest and smirked. He couldn't tell if she was teasing him or not. He considered it and realised that if she wasn't only messing with him, he didn't want to know at that moment. He pulled Ellen to stand in front of him and tugged her close.

"Is that right?"

She giggled, twisting, and turning away when he leaned over her, kissing her neck, holding her tight. They didn't notice that the others had come down the stairs until a cough interrupted them. When Daniel looked up, he was met with Amelia, and then Stephen as he carried in the two pizza boxes.

"Pizza is here," Stephen said, proffering them out. At Amelia's beckoning, he reached over and set them on the round table before shoving his hands into his jeans pockets and nodding towards Ellen. "Hey, Elle."

"Hey, Steve. How's Brandon?"

"Good, yeah. He asks for you sometimes." There was an uncomfortable silence as the words, and the smell of the hot pizzas, hung in the air.

"You didn't hear the knocking?" Amelia asked Daniel. In response, Daniel shook his head and stepped forward to open the lids of the two boxes. Hot, garlic bases, topped with vegetables and spices; beautiful. He tore a slice off and bit into it. Immediately, he was puffing out hot, garlicky breath as it burned the roof of his mouth.

"It's *hawt*," he warned the others with a full mouth. "CORA!" he called. The running along the upper hallway stopped and Cora trampled down the stairs with the heavy stamping of a grown man. A moment later, she appeared, pink-cheeked and breathing heavily. She scurried between

Stephen and Amelia and reached for the pizza with no inhibitions.

"Careful-"

"Careful-" Ellen and Amelia said at the same time, going to help Cora as she tore at the slice. Daniel, his gaze going from one to the other, watched as they smiled nervously at one another.

"It's hot," Ellen said, tearing a piece off and setting it aside for Cora. Scrunching her nose up, Cora waited, dancing and swinging out of the kitchen table chair as Amelia took plates from the cupboard and dished a few slices up. Daniel continued to eat from the box.

When they were finished, with not even a crust left, Daniel stacked the boxes and volunteered to carry them outside. The night had turned cool, with the sky clear and the stars peering down at him as he stuffed the cardboard into the recycling bins at the side of the house. It was unusually bright out, with the moon proclaiming its presence by casting a pale glow that lit the ground; it was almost full. Daniel shut the lid of the bin when he heard a scuttle. He turned his head to see the black cat coming out of the trees towards him. It let out a little meow in way of greeting, and sidled up next to him, rubbing its body against Daniel's leg.

"How many mice did you eat tonight, buddy?" Daniel asked, then, realising he was talking to a feline, he shook his head, wondering why they bothered to feed it when it spent most of the time in the forest, catching field mice and hamsters. It was a stray, after all; it had managed without them before now. If anything, treating it like a pet now was only going to hinder the creature in the long run - when they left at the end of summer it would go back to living outside in the cold.

Shooing him away, the cat let out a tiny hiss, making Daniel consider leaving the ungrateful bastard outside for the night. However, when he sat before him, his green eyes twinkling up at Daniel, he sighed and jogged back to the front door, the cold air biting at his exposed arms. The cat followed him, sliding in the door just as Daniel kicked it closed.

The cat disappeared into the shadows of the foyer, moving soundlessly into the dark. Daniel quickly forgot about the adopted animal when he went to the kitchen and watched as both Ellen, *'or Elle'*, and Amelia washed the plates together while Stephen sat awkwardly with Cora at the kitchen table, listening to her recite her favourite colours in order. He wondered if Amelia would soon become 'Melia' to him. Is that what people around here did for nicknames- drop off one of the letters at either end of a name? Just another reason why autumn couldn't come quick enough.

"I thought it was supposed to be summer. It's bleedin' freezing outside." Daniel shook his arms.

"Oh, hey, we were thinking we could all play a board game together?" Ellen said when she spotted him.

"Yeah, yeah, yeah! Can we, Daniel?" Cora begged, relieving Stephen at last. They were all looking at him, waiting for an answer. He lifted his wrist to check the watch there: 9: 23 pm.

"Your sister is to be in bed before nine, alright?"

Mark had been unquestionably clear about it. He glanced at Cora then. Already her eyelids were heavy with tiredness. She immediately sat up straighter and beamed at him from the chair. He would give her half an hour before she was snoring on the floor. He shrugged; maybe a little Pictionary would be fun.

"Sure."

They had settled on Monopoly for a few reasons: one, because Cora knew the basics of how to play it already and no one was in the mood to teach her to play any of the other games they had in mind, two; because it was the first one Daniel had dug out from the stuffed suitcase that was in Mark's room, and three; because it wasn't going to summon any demons, although, Daniel's competitiveness would come close.

The board was dotted with green and red plastic pieces. A car, a dog, a boat, and a thimble moved around the board, obeying the dots on the single die, the other one gone - lost down the side of a couch cushion or swallowed by a hoover hose, along with any other choking hazard sized pieces, which were inevitably forgotten about until they were needed.

"How much?" Amelia asked when her thimble landed on Trafalgar Square. They sat in the living room. They had pushed back the two floral-printed couches, pulled the cushions down to sit on, and were situated around the mahogany coffee table that Daniel remembered smelling like hamster piss when they first uncovered it earlier this summer. Now, after a spray of bleach, it mildly smelled of mildew. He had set the fire alight to take the chill from the room, but still, Amelia had a blanket over her lap which she had extended over Stephen too, who was rosy in the cheeks when Daniel shot him a cautionary glare. He had made sure to keep both of his hands above the quilt, in full view of Daniel.

"750." Ellen shot Daniel a furtive glance when he snorted as Amelia counted the last of her coloured money. She was falling short, her properties already overturned. Bankruptcy was her only option. "It's okay, you can owe me the rest," Ellen offered as Amelia handed her the last of her Dollars.

"That's okay," Amelia said, shrugging.

"I'll lend you," Stephen told her, sifting through his stack of fake money, counting out the remainder of her debt.

"No-"

"No-" Daniel and Amelia looked at each other. Her cheeks were flushed and her eyes were pinned on him. Daniel, trying to recover and conceal his competitive side, motioned towards Cora who sat in his lap, her head tucked under his chin, her mouth open wide as a pool of drool gathered on his grey t-shirt. It had taken twenty minutes before she began snoring gently against his chest. "I just think we shouldn't make so many allowances if we want to finish this tonight," he added.

"He's right," Amelia was raising her hands in a sign of surrender and sitting back from the board. Disappointed, Stephen set his stack of money to the side.

"Don't worry, we'll let you win," Ellen teased in a good-humoured whisper, winking, and gesturing towards Cora. "Just so we don't wake Cora."

Daniel raised a brow, looking at his piled cash and many properties, with their green houses and red hotels, sitting lopsided on the board. He knew she was casting out bait. He couldn't stop himself, though, and bit.

"Let me win? I would've won regardless. You three could've teamed up together and I still would've won," he told them, trying to keep the seriousness out of his voice.

"And you would've been all alone," Ellen said, rolling her eyes as Amelia began collecting the pieces from the board, separating them neatly, and putting them into the box.

"Yeah, yeah. If you were winning, you'd be the same," Daniel tried, unable to stop his irritation from tainting his tone. He tossed his pile of cash onto the neat piles and watched the notes feather out before grumbling a half-hearted 'sorry' to Amelia. He would never admit to it but tidying up the pieces before he had bankrupted the others would niggle at him. Mockingly, Ellen stuck out her tongue and sat up to help Amelia; evidently, their relationship had only grown from the confrontation earlier.

As if sensing that Daniel was gearing up to bring her to bed, Cora shifted beneath him, wiping at her mouth and making little sounds that were attempted words of protest. Her eyes fluttered open, her hands reaching for the property cards that she and Daniel shared for the game, pretending as though she were inspecting them.

"Time for bed, sleepyhead. Say goodnight to Ellen… and Stephen," Daniel said softly, kissing the top of her dark hair.

"But I'm not tired yet…" Cora moaned, whining as Amelia took the card from her closed fist.

"You'll see them tomorrow, C," Daniel assured her, getting up with Cora in his arms; either Cora was getting heavier, or he needed to get back to the gym. "Amelia, want to take over here?" He gestured to Cora's wriggling body; his job ended after transportation. She nodded, closing the lid over on the board game.

"No! Please- I want ta' stay up with you! Please, please, please- I promise, I won't be tired!" It was nearly 11. Cora should be in bed. But Mark should have been back to put her to bed. Daniel shrugged, looking to Amelia who paused with half the blanket still clinging to her as she waited for his response. Her eyes flickered to Stephen; if Cora went to bed, it was the end of the night for her and Stephen, too.

"Why don't we play one more game and then I'll bring ya's home?" Daniel suggested. Ellen, checking her watch, hesitated, but didn't object, while Stephen nodded enthusiastically as Amelia leaned in a little closer to him, their hands beneath the blanket now. With one stern look from Daniel, Stephen pulled his hands free of the cover and set them in his lap, but this time he was holding Amelia's. "Second round of Monopoly?" There was a unanimous groan of displeasure to the proposal. "Okay, what do you want to do?"

In the living room the flames from the fire emitted a warm glow onto the four teenagers as they sat around the coffee table. Their shadows danced across the floral furniture while Cora, already dozing off again, curled into Amelia, sharing the banket and evicting Stephen from it. When it had been suggested, no one had explicitly agreed or disagreed with Daniel. That had been enough encouragement for him to get the Ouija board from the basement and set it up on the coffee table.

Daniel set it up as Amelia recoiled from it, shifting herself back and tugging the blanket a little closer to her chest. Ellen watched Daniel, her eyes roaming his features when he winked at her and nodded towards Stephen, gesturing for him to move closer to the table. Stephen's eyes flashed towards Amelia.

"Are 'ya playing or what?" Daniel sighed. Stephen sat up and knelt next to the board. In the dim light, the letters were hard to discern.

"How are we supposed to tell what this says?" Stephen asked sheepishly. Daniel's brow furrowed as he pointed a single finger at the faded letters.

"You know the alphabet, don't you? Surely you can guess what comes after 'G'," Daniel retorted, pressing down on the dark 'H'. Amelia gave him a stern look that reminded him that he was supposed to be being nice to her; apparently, that included her boyfriend too.

"Yeah, Daniel isn't much of a sesquipedalian, anyway, so it should be easy enough to follow along when he moves the planchette," Amelia said. Stephen smiled at her. "It means someone who likes to use long words," Amelia said pointedly to Daniel this time. He shook his head.

"Yeah, I think we will be safe enough- the pretentious ghosts are all in bed by now," Daniel retorted, checking his watch: 11.36. "Is that your word of the day?"

"No. maybe if you picked up a book every now and again, you'd know some words with more than two syllables," Amelia countered.

"The word I want to call you only has the one. Bitc-"

"Daniel." Ellen's hand was on his arm, squeezing it. *Breathe*, it said.

"Come on, let's start this." Daniel grunted.

When Ellen sat up onto her knees, placing her hands onto the table, then one on the planchette, Daniel took her other hand and kissed the back of it before setting his atop hers, his large hand enveloping it completely. Hesitantly, Stephen let his hand hover over Daniel's as if waiting for permission. Daniel said nothing, letting him sweat; *Screw him*, Daniel thought, not making it any easier for him by glaring at him. Sensing this, Stephen set his hand atop Daniel's without looking at him.

"Okay, let's start." Daniel cleared his throat. The bulb in the corner lamp flickered. They each stared at it, watching as it threatened to go out completely. It reminded Daniel of the flashing strobe lights you would see in raves.

"Should we maybe say… like… a prayer or something first?" Stephen's idea was met with incredulous silence. "You know… for protection?" he added.

"What? Like crack out an Alive-O song?" Daniel retorted.

"That's absolutely not what I meant-"

"Is there anybody here with us?" Daniel said over him, ignoring Amelia's uncomfortable shift. With the flickering bulb still stuttering out light, they waited, watching the still planchette on the board. "Are there any spirits present with us? Any lingering dead people with nothing better to do?"

"Daniel!" Amelia scolded him. "Don't be so disrespectful," she said as Cora moved around next to her. Her lashes trembled momentarily as if she might wake, but she continued to sleep.

"She's right, you know. The last thing you want is a vengeful spirit haunting you because you were rude," Ellen noted, smiling up at him. In the flickering light, her eyes sparkled.

"Fine. How do you want to do this then?" No one spoke. The crackle of the fire was the only sound- that and the hum of the flickering lamp. "It's getting late, anyway. I should bring you guys home."

"You need to put two fingers on the… thing," Amelia told them in a breath, coming out from under her blanket and crawling to the table. She sat on her hunkers and used her two index fingers to show them. One by one, they followed

Amelia's lead until they were all sitting with their hands on the game piece. "Now, we need to do circles with it."

This is getting ridiculous, Daniel thought to himself but didn't so much as breathe deeply when Amelia started the motion in case he was blamed for something going awry. The piece slid around the board easily, moving across the peeling letters with a smooth, steady motion.

"Are there any spirits present here with us tonight?" Amelia asked just as the fire popped. Daniel's eyes shot to the embers that had flown out onto the floor. It extinguished itself to a grey piece of ash. He then watched as Amelia's eyes widened when the tear-drop-shaped planchette shifted under their fingers, sliding steadily towards the stained 'Yes' in the wood. Daniel inspected the reactions of the others.

"Daniel, stop messing," Ellen warned him as she scooted her body closer so that their hips touched.

"That isn't me."

"Answer 'Yes' again if you are really there," Amelia called out, her eyes fixed on Daniel's fingers. "Daniel, please don't mess with us," she whispered. The planchette moved away from 'Yes', to the middle of the board, and back again.

"Daniel-"

"It wasn't me, babe," he tried to assure Ellen. Under the blanket, Cora was still sleeping.

"Stephen?"

"No, that wasn't me."

"Is there more than one spirit here with us?" Amelia asked. For a moment nothing happened, then, the planchette shifted again, this time moving gently towards 'No'.

"Can you give us a sign that you're real?" Daniel asked, his fingers pressed lightly against the wooden piece. The bulb in the lamp flickered wildly, casting bouncing shadows on the ceiling and wall. Daniel raised a curious eyebrow. "Coincidental, at best," he noted when the others faced him.

The lamp light settled.

"Are you here to tell us something?" Amelia asked the spirit. There was no movement in response. Daniel, with as little effort as possible, shifted the planchette with his fingers; it was easy to do, the board was like glass, all he had to do was set it off and it continued to travel the rest of the way. It stopped over the 'No'. He kept his face blank from expression and watched as Amelia's brows furrowed as she tried to figure it out like it was one of her puzzles.

"Are you... good?" Stephen asked, shrugging his shoulders apologetically when both Ellen and Amelia shot him daggers. Daniel said nothing, trying to keep a straight face, as he gave a little push to the wooden planchette and sent it sliding to the middle of the board, where he left it sitting.

"Daniel, I don't think I like this," Ellen said in a hushed, tense voice. He would tell her that it had been him afterwards. Until then he turned his face to look at her, as if to speak, while his fingers were moving subtly, again, pushing the planchette across the board, nearly over-shooting it, to land over 'No'.

There was a collective gasp as a wicked crack burst from the lamp.

The bulb shattered.

The glass was thrown across the floor.

Cora sat up with a cry.

They were sent into near darkness. The fire, to Daniel's right, had been dying, neglected while they played their games. It gave off a low glow, barely bright enough to reach them where they sat while the rest of the room was in ominous shadows.

"Shit-" Daniel went to get to his feet and felt Stephen's hand on his shoulder. He regarded him for only a second before Stephen removed it and quickly placed his finger back on the board piece.

"You can't walk away from the board-"

"There's glass everywhere," Daniel said and stood. The shards crunched under his feet as he walked blindly into the dark corner.

"He's right, Daniel, we have to close the portal-"

What sounded like footsteps on the floor above them made them all freeze. Daniel's gaze lifted to the ceiling, as though he might be able to see through it, and listened.

Nothing.

"Did you hear-"

"Shhh-"

"It sounded like-"

"Shut up for a second!" Daniel demanded, listening still. Sitting in the shadows of the dying fire, the others all looked to Daniel as if for help, their eyes wide.

He strained his ears to listen for any more sounds of movement. When there were none, he crossed the room, quietly, to the door, and turned the cool handle. The foyer was just as dark as the living room - darker. Light slid under the door to the kitchen, where they had left the lights on.

What was that?

A long shadow moved along the floor.

Daniel started towards the kitchen, ignoring the calls of protest from behind him. He could barely see where he was going but focused his sights on the light of the kitchen to lead him. Without a second thought, he pushed open the door and stopped when, sitting atop the kitchen table, was the black cat pawing at the last of the dip from the pizza. Picking it up from the middle, Daniel carried the cat back with him. He felt the console table with his shin, wincing when he thudded against it. He bent to rub at the bare skin. He stepped through the door and set the cat down before feeling along the wall and twisting the dials. The other lamps around the room came on, the shadows bouncing back to the corners and around the wall mouldings of carved figures, which seemed to sit watching them. The others were in the same position as they had been when he had left them, holding their fingers upon the Ouija board planchette. Cora had crawled to where Amelia was kneeling, hugging her around the waist, her brows knitted together.

Seriously?

Daniel went to them, shaking his head, and tugged on the tear-drop-shaped planchette until their fingers fell away from it. He lifted it and twirled it around in his hands.

"Daniel! What're you doing?" Amelia demanded.

"Daniel!" Cora cried. Daniel regarded them in disbelief.

"It was me," he told them. At first, their faces didn't change. "I was the one moving it. And the cat was in the kitchen- he probably knocked something over."

"But that sounded like footsteps upstairs-" Amelia was cut across.

"You're such a dickhead," Ellen slumped back, her hands dropping from the table. Amelia stared at the board, chewing her lip. She wrapped her arm around Cora, shushing her tears.

"You know you terrified her with that stunt, don't you?" She said to him, hugging her sister.

Yeah, and the rest of you.

He had to stop himself from smiling.

He kicked a glass piece on the floor. Stephen stood and went to pick it up. He leered at Daniel but said nothing. Daniel went to his sisters' side and bent to look at Cora.

"Hey, it was all a joke. That's all. There're no ghosts."

"There is!" Cora wailed. Daniel took a breath, glancing at Ellen, who gave him a disapproving shake of her head.

"Hey, come here." He reached out and took her from Amelia who stood and went to help Stephen. "I was only messing, I promise. And even if there *was* a ghost, it was only Mam, giving out to me for making Amelia and the others scared, that's all." Cora wiped at her face, considering if she believed him. "But she knows that you're way too brave and I couldn't scare you. Isn't that right?" Cora looked at the others and smiled, nodding her head.

"But why did she break the lamp?" Cora asked in a small voice that struggled to be brave. Daniel shrugged.

"She didn't. That sometimes happens when the bulbs are from fifty years ago," he told her. Cora's grimace turned to a smile, and she chuckled at the thought. "Or maybe Mam was giving out because you aren't in bed yet!" After a minute of tickling, Cora was crying with laughter. "Come on, time for bed." He set her down, then thinking of the little shards of glass on the floor, he picked her back up and tossed her over his shoulder like a bag of coal so that her face was next to his head and her piercing screams of laughter spiked against his eardrum. He jumped over the pile of collected bulb pieces and, once in the foyer, turned on the few lamps there, too. They did little to light the space, however, it meant he could see where he was going at least.

Chapter 10

The keys of the 960 clinked together against the basket on the foyer table when Daniel returned from bringing the others home. He didn't bother to turn out any of the lights; Mark was still out, he could turn them out when he got in. Where he was, Daniel hadn't a clue- Mark's absence wasn't unusual; he was always out late, always inconveniently out of range of a landline, always expecting things to be taken care of by the time he got back.

He took the winding steps two at a time, skipping over the creaking set near the top, and took a trip to the bathroom to relieve himself before going to his room.

"Daniel?" He had only stepped inside his door, his unmade bed calling to him, when he heard Amelia. Her bedroom door had been left ajar. He pushed it open a little further and stuck his head in the gap; she was sitting up in bed, reading, with her lamp on next to her. Her other lamp was still crooked on her desk. Cora was in her bed asleep.

"What's up?"

"Would you mind bringing her to her room? She came in here when you left," Amelia whispered from under her thick duvet. Daniel nodded and kicked off his shoes, leaving them on the carpeted floor so that the noise wouldn't wake his sister. Cora had left a pool of drool on Amelia's pillow, similar to the one that was drying on his shirt. He picked her up in the crooks of his arms and Amelia set the plush elephant on top.

"Goodnight," he said as he carried her out and across the hall.

"Night," Amelia set her book aside, her eyes scanning the bedroom from corner to corner, and turned out her light. Cora's room was just as dark, so dark that Daniel would have plonked her down atop the nightlight sitting pins-up in the centre of her bed had the dull lamps of the hall not caught it with a glint of light. With his foot, Daniel pushed it to the edge of the bed and set Cora down. He tugged the blankets out from under her and dragged them up to her chin. On his way out, he set the night light on top of the wardrobe and shut the door.

He fell asleep, unsure if he had locked the door or not.

The Witching hour is an eerie time to be awake- when the veil of this world and the *other* world is at its finest. There is an intrusion of fears that the bravest of men push away and find themselves checking over their shoulder in a lonely carpark. It is a time when you could come across madmen, with blackened eyes and an insatiable thirsting for blood, or possessed wives wandering old country roads at 3 am, aimless, or worse, focused on vengeance. It is a time when people can be tempted to do egregious things- violent, Godless things, that they would never normally do. Shadows suddenly appear, traipsing across walls to sneer over sleeping children, attached to their fear. Invisible eyes watch as you leave the safety of your bed and escape to quench your thirst, laughing as you race up the stairs to evade their lurking, invisible fingers that tickle your ankles. It is a time when you are too afraid to look behind you- if you did, what would you see?

It is a time when anything is possible.

Mark often found himself sitting up, penning these thoughts at night. Tonight, he was standing, staring at the façade of the ugly house, counting down the minutes as that time approached, his watch's second hand ticking away the seconds, the only sound in the still night. It smiled back at him with rotted wood for teeth, stained windows for eyes, flashing the shining moon back at him as if watching *him* instead of he, it.

"Fear of the occult is nocturnal," he would tell that reporter, "A dripping tap in the sanctuary of daylight is a reminder to call a plumber; at night, well, at night it is the Devil himself tempting you to find him."

The car keys jingled in the light breeze. He closed his fist around them and started up the rickety porch steps. He was not immune to those night-time fears and doubted anyone truly was. It was only natural.

When he got to the door and tested the handle it gave way under his command and he went inside. Immediately, a cloud of warm air hit him. The lights in the foyer greeted him, leading him to the staircase, but a door left ajar grasped his attention first and so he went to it and pushed it aside.

The first thing he noticed upon entering was the remaining embers in the fireplace, still orange in colour at the centre, dying but not yet fully extinguished. The living room was alight, the floral couch cushions were strewn across the floor around the squat mahogany antique table, and atop it there lay something that Mark Owens had not seen in many years, despite his career path; a Ouija Board. A Monopoly box had been cast aside, dismissed, while the faded talking-board lay exposed to the world, for anyone to use. As exhausted as he was, Mark smiled and lifted the wooden board up to inspect it, a sort of pride filling him; he had always presumed that his children were indifferent to this side of the world- to his world, but, he supposed, if anyone's kids were to find interest in it, shouldn't it be his?

He thought back on his last experience with a spirit-board and chills of recognition and that fear of the occult gathered down his spine to tingle the hairs on the back of his neck. He set the board back down and went to the fireplace. Balancing his laptop bag on his shoulder, he pulled the fireguard around to block the exposed embers, then he went to where the dial on the wall was. A loud crunch under his foot startled him. Glass. Glancing around the room, he spotted the tiny glittering pieces of ground sand on the floor, mostly piled together but left behind, nonetheless; it was a job for the morning. He turned the dial and the lamps around the room went out.

In complete darkness, a discomforting feeling of unease teased Mark, it asked him if he was sure he was alone. He stood at the bottom of the stairs, in the disquieting darkness, and gazed at the space around him. The ticking of his watch was not the only sound now, the house an orchestra of creaks and knocking pipes, but it was the one he focused on as his eyes traced the shadows around him.

The terror of the dark, he once wrote, was a cumulative fear of the unknown, the handicap of sudden blindness and the uncanny feeling that something dreadful watched you, and that whatever that was that lived there, had been waiting for you.

"You're supposed to scare other people, Mark," he whispered to himself, turning and heading up the stairs and onto the dark landing.

He didn't look behind him.

A soft scuffle, like a cardboard box moving along the floor, alarmed him, making him pause with his hand on the banisters. His heart took an extra beat as he considered what he had heard. His other hand found the hard switch on the wall. He paused there, keeping his fingers poised as he listened to the darkness that engulfed him now, with not even a night light creeping out under a door. He flicked the switch. There was a second's lag before the old wiring brought the bulbs overhead to life.

"Jesus-" Mark doubled over when fright took hold and clenched around his stomach like a thief about to steal something and make his getaway; his reflection glinted back from the window at the end of the hallway. He couldn't not laugh, then. He flicked the switch and turned the lights out, chuckling to himself, as his stomach eased.

The Witching hour was fast approaching, it seemed. With darkness, it was encroaching on his thoughts.

Mark took another step, and then another, using the wall on his left for guidance. When he felt the ridges of a doorframe, he hesitated before setting his ear to the door. Daniel's room was silent.

Drip...

Drip...

There was a groan from somewhere in the pipes. The house was old, old enough that the washers needed to be replaced on the sink taps in the bathroom, the rubber worn away like the sole of an old runner. Mark went unsteadily to his room at the end of the hall. His fingers slid up the wall and twisted the dial there so that the little lamp, its glass shade bent over like a drooping bluebell, set a pathetic beam on his desk. With only a moment's gander, Mark noticed the slight tilt to the photo frame; it was subtle, but just as an architect would notice a line askew on his blueprints, Mark knew the frame had been moved. Cora, he supposed, had been in to admire her mother. He couldn't blame her; he admired her every time he looked at the picture.

Chapter 11

Carnival lights blurred together against the dark sky in the park. The usually peaceful space had been transformed to host the annual event. The smell of salty popcorn filled the air, masked only when passing a candy-floss stand, the sweet fumes eclipsing the scents. Screams heard over the cheerful music rolled past on metal rails and from spinning carts with arms flailing through the air.

If, Amelia thought, you looked at the carnival through the lens of a horror movie director's perspective, it had the potential to be terrifying: the children, screaming, as they ran from crazed men dressed in awful, colourful make-up and overalls, or the people being flung around, at the mercy of nuts and bolts to the sound of haunting music – if one of those screws were loose... Scariest of all, perhaps, were the smiles and laughter in the crowd of people. *How many of them were pretending to be happy?* She wondered. *At least one,* she answered.

Amelia and Stephen walked side by side through the crowded green, passing benches adorned with floating balloons and clowns with painted faces and giant, squeaky shoes.

"I'm glad you came tonight," Stephen said, reaching for her hand. Amelia smiled at him. In her other hand, she held onto the carton of popcorn he had bought for her. "I wasn't sure if you would be interested. It's just something small the town does every July. Probably seems stupid compared to anything you're used to in Dublin." Stephen set a single piece of popcorn in his mouth as Amelia shook her head.

"Not at all. I'm glad I came, too." Truthfully, she couldn't wait to get away from the house, to get outside. Unlike Daniel, who had free reign with being able to drive, Amelia was stuck at the house and was starting to feel a little stir-crazy. Stephen jerked back when a group of boys, about their age, came hurtling past, blind to anything in their path and one slammed into Stephen's shoulder. He watched after them, his jaw tightening, but said nothing. "Are you okay?"

"Yeah, I'm fine." Stephen rolled his shoulder backwards, then forwards, and shrugged. "Do you want to go on this?" he asked. Amelia stopped and stared up into the sky, the Milky Way was split by the white, metal frame of the slowly spinning Ferris wheel. "If you don't want to-"

"Yeah, I'd love to." Amelia smiled at him and stepped up onto the steep, metal steps of the ticket booth as teenagers and parents with small children were alighting from the cars, skipping, and laughing as they joined the carnival-goers in the park. Amelia passed the grumpy teen behind the plexiglass screen of the booth money for the two tickets, before they stepped through the turnstile and were ushered onboard a moving car by an older man wearing a dirty t-shirt and stained jeans. He slammed the gate of their car over and pressed down on the lock.

Amelia sat back against the cold metal frame of the ride. Stephen sat next to her, lifting his arm as if going to reach around her before hesitating and letting it sit in his lap. The Ferris wheel moved at a snail's pace, the screams and shouts of those on the more thrilling rides still loud as they rose above the crowd. The view of the whole park, and town, could be seen. Amelia took a deep breath, staring out the sides of the car, at the glowing streetlights along the main street, and then at the dark abyss that was the lake. Her stomach did a small tumble and she set her eyes on the road. Few car lights travelled along the roads and around the winding bends, before disappearing behind trees.

Beside her, Stephen shifted on the uncomfortable bench seat. "I like your necklace." Amelia's hand lifted to her neck where the gold chain dangled against her collar bones. She lifted the little 'S' pendant to look at it.

"Thanks, it was my mam's. She gave it to me a few years ago." Their car had reached the top of the wheel and was starting its descent back towards solid ground.

"Is that what the 'S' is for? Her name?"

Amelia nodded and took a deep breath, an uncomfortable but familiar lump in her throat.

"Her name is – was - Susan." Stephen's brows flinched as if he were going to frown before his face smoothed out again. "I know. Cora named the cat after her." Amelia rolled her eyes, then bit her lip in regret as a knot tightened in her stomach in regret of her crass response. "I think it might be just her way of dealing with it - I don't know how much she understands, really." Stephen offered a gentle bob of his head.

"When did she pass?" Amelia's gaze moved out towards the lake and she chewed on her lip, dropping the necklace, and picked at the popcorn that sat on her lap.

"It was nearly a year ago, but it doesn't feel like it. Especially because of how much it was in the newspapers. With my dad being who he is it made some headlines. It was just before school started."

"That must've been hard."

"Yeah. It was. What makes it harder is that like no one really wants to talk about it- to talk about her. Sometimes I wonder if Daniel and my dad are trying to forget her, you know?" Of course he didn't, she knew. It wasn't something that happened to every family.

"Well, you're more than welcome to talk to me about her." Stephen took her hand just as their car door was yanked open by that same dirty man, now shouting for them to stand before waving aggressively at them to exit. Stephen held her hand as he stepped out and lead her onto the wobbly stairs.

"There's Daniel and Ellen," Stephen said as he pointed with his free hand. Amelia's gaze followed his extended fingers and watched as Ellen and Daniel stood, legs shoulder-width apart, shooting water guns at stacked bowling pins - trying to knock them down - at a carnival booth. As they walked towards them, furrowing her brows, Amelia scanned the booth for sight of Cora.

"Daniel," Amelia called. He ignored her, instead he pushed against Ellen's shoulder playfully to knock her off balance. The two of them laughed. "Daniel!" This time he looked over his shoulder and his eyes flickered to her, but he continued until the centre of his stacked pins collapsed inwards and the entire pyramid fell. The man working the stall clapped unenthusiastically and raised a wooden hook up to reach a stuffed animal. He pushed it to Daniel's chest and went about restacking his pins.

"Daniel!" Amelia was almost shouting his name as panic started to nudge its way into her mind. Daniel handed the stuffed bear to Ellen.

"For you," he kissed her cheek.

"Cheater," Ellen teased but hugged it, nonetheless. "Hey, guys," Ellen's grin faltered and she frowned as she met Amelia's frazzled stare. Amelia pushed Daniel's shoulder. He took a step back, scowling.

"Daniel, where's Cora?"

Daniel frowned, looking to his side, then at the ends of the booth before his eyes went wide. "She's not with you?"

"No- you said she could go with you!"

"Shit!" Daniel swore and searched the immediate space around him.

"I'm sure she hasn't gone far-" Stephen tried.

"Or she's with some absolute Pedo from this inbred town."

"Daniel!" Ellen swung her arm into his.

"That helps," Stephen grunted.

"We should find some security- get them to make an announcement," Amelia said, her fingers finding the chain at her throat.

"No, we'll find her. She's here somewhere," Daniel told her, his eyes wide, his tone resolute. "Let's split up and meet back here in about fifteen minutes."

"What if we don't find her?" Amelia could feel a cold sweat coming on.

"We will," Daniel told her, confidently. "Let's go." Daniel started towards the colourful carnival booths with Ellen in tow.

Daniel only ran, pushing through disgruntled carnival-goers, for about fifty feet before he spotted Cora. Standing and staring longingly at the stacks of stuffed animals piled high next to a game booth, was his little sister, her hands twitching at her sides as she watched the teenage boys kick soft footballs at the giant, inflated game of x's and o's. Her shoulders were rounded, her lips in a pout as she watched the boys cheering with every shot, whether they had hit their mark or not.

Ellen's hands came to rest on his shoulders, her gaze shifting to where Cora was slouched.

"Oh, thank fuck," she sighed and squeezed him. "I'll get Amelia and Steve and let them know." She turned and left him. Lingering at the side of the booth, Cora was leaning from side to side like a begging puppy. Daniel was only feet from her when the booth owner caught sight of her, his brows furrowing in concern. With one eye on the teenage boys and the other on Cora, he leaned over the stall to talk to her.

"Are you okay, pet?"

Daniel reached her, the booth owner's eyes followed him now as he knelt next to her.

"Hey, Cora, we're gonna have to start calling 'ya Dora if 'ya keep exploring." Cora's eyes moved to Daniel. A mixture of relief and guilt filled her face. "You okay?" She bobbed her head, her eyes wide.

"Everything okay here?" The man asked, his attention going back to the boys. Daniel stood.

"Yeah, thanks." Daniel reached his hand into his pocket for cash. "Can I buy one of the toys here for her?" Cora slipped her tiny hand into his.

"Sorry, buddy, you gotta play to get one." The man was moving towards the teenagers as they started kicking the inflated game with their feet instead of using the soft football. Daniel sighed and looked down at his sister.

"If I get this teddy for you, you've to promise to not wander off again." Cora nodded vehemently. Once the man in the stall had finished shouting at the locals, Daniel approached him and passed him money in exchange for four small, soft footballs. Behind him, Ellen returned with the others in tow. Amelia stood next to Cora and took her hand.

Standing at the bright green tape that stood as the penalty line, Daniel kicked the first ball at the inflated game and knocked the 'X in the top left corner down. The second one he hit was in the centre. His third ball missed completely, but the last one hit the 'X in the bottom right corner to make a diagonal line across the board. Behind him, Ellen and Cora cheered as he lifted his arms in victory. The man behind the stall nodded when Daniel picked Cora up to choose her prize and handed the giant elephant over to her.

"Hey, Daniel." Daniel turned at the sound of his name and spotted the pretty brunette he had met at the store and had helped him shop.

"Oh, hi..." he struggled to remember her name.

"Kate," she offered. Kate was wearing a different top to the tight, homemade V-neck Westlife shirt now. It was a baggy one, with shorts that went high enough for Daniel's imagination to attempt to betray him. He reeled it back and cleared his throat, forcing his eyes to her face. She was joining the group of rowdy teenagers.

"Hi, Ellen." She gave Ellen a small wave.

"Kate, yeah. Kate helped me in the shop one of the days," Daniel quickly explained. Ellen's brows raised in mock concern. He shook his head as if to silently squash her worries - and shake *that* image out of his head. One of the boys next to Kate turned around, his eyes glassy, his words slightly slurred.

"Who's this, Kate?" he asked with a burp. Daniel eyed him. He looked like a dope, Daniel thought. He imagined him, his small-town worries, spending every weekend at the stupid lake, doing the same shitty things with the same shitty people, and he was glad. He would bet that this crap carnival was the highlight of his summer. Daniel set his shoulders back and met the boy's glassy eyes with a confident stare, one that said *"None of your fucking business, you culchie."*

"This is Daniel, you know, that author guy's kid." She turned away from them to say this in a whisper to him. The boy wobbled on the spot for a moment as he took in her words. Daniel's jaw tightened when his eyes roamed over Daniel from head to toe, a smirk spreading across his ugly face.

"Oh, shit, yeah. I know all about him." Daniel frowned, shaking his head, and almost managed to pull himself away from the scene. "We looked you up. Is it true? What they wrote about you." A rush of hot blood travelled to Daniel's face. "That was a wreck, wasn't it?" The boy laughed, then, turning to his friends, "Do you get it? A wreck?"

His pathetic friends snickered behind him.

"Daniel!" He heard Amelia call out, pushing forward to grab her brother, knocking Cora's new elephant onto the mucky ground, but she wasn't fast enough. Daniel had the boy by the scruff of his t-shirt, and shoved him against his friends, knocking them down like bowling pins. From somewhere on his right, one of the others came towards Daniel, his arm already pulled back, and swung his fist at Daniel's face. Thankfully, he was just as drunk as his friend and his fist only skimmed Daniel's cheek. Daniel tasted blood as his teeth closed on the inside of his cheek. Before anything else could happen, tall security men appeared and pushed Daniel in the chest – hard - so he had to step backwards. He put his palms outwards in surrender and turned to the others. Cora was crying, her new elephant ready for the bin.

. For the entire journey back to the house, Cora cried about her elephant. The inside of Daniel's cheek was swollen, making it hard to eat his hot dog, eventually forcing him to throw it from the window of the car on the way home. Ellen gave Cora her own stuffed bear, but it did not suffice or console her. By the time they got back to the house, after dropping the others home, her cheeks were as puffy as Daniel's swollen one and her eyes were red.

When the front door swung open, Mark appeared from the living room, a tumbler in one hand, his laptop in the other, as if they were both extensions of his limbs.

"What happened?" Mark asked. Daniel shrugged, taking a deep breath. Cora ran to him, wrapping her arms around his legs.

"Nothin'," Daniel muttered, at last. Mark stared at Amelia then, who dropped her eyes to the floor.

"What happened to your face?"

"Nothin'."

"Nothing?" Mark sighed. "Everywhere you go 'nothing' seems to happen." Daniel stalked to the stairs. From behind, he heard Mark call out, "I hope you were taught a lesson."

He headed straight for the shower.

Cora's hand was sore, her fingers closed firmly around her grey crayon, her nails covered in the waxy colour as she pressed hard on the page. She wished she had her teddy there in front of her so she could remember if he had had green or blue eyes, but he had been thrown away after Amelia shoved her last night and he had fallen into the dirt.

She hadn't cared if her teddy was dirty, she still wanted him, but Amelia took it from her and put him in the bin before she even had the chance to say that she would give him a bath. As she filled in the lines of the elephant's ears, her elbow knocked her other colours - which had been set up in perfect order. They rolled away from her before falling onto the floor.

Cora twisted in her seat, her hair flying over her face, and watched the crayon roll across the floor, towards the kitchen door. She wiggled free from her booster seat, which wobbled beneath her, and scooted so she could hang her legs down while she lay on her belly, before scooting down and touching the floor with her tiptoes. Just then, the door opened and both Amelia and Daniel came in.

Neither of them noticed Cora's colours on the floor and Daniel even almost squashed the blue, which Cora had finally decided in that short moment was going to be her elephant's eye colour. She shouted out. He stopped walking and looked at his feet, where the crayon had rolled against his foot.

"Sorry, C." He kicked it and sent it flying forwards, hitting the back of Amelia's leg. When she turned around, her eyes rolling upwards the way she does when she gets annoyed, Daniel pointed at Cora. Amelia knelt and collected the crayons, ignoring Cora's outstretched hands as she reached for her colours, and set them on the kitchen table, next to her drawing. Daniel lifted Cora and brought her back to her seat, sitting her on top of her booster seat without even asking what she was doing with her crayons. Neither of them took a single second to look at her picture. Cora went back to her drawing as Daniel leaned against the counter, his arms crossed. Cora could only see the red, swollen part of his face, the side that he had been hit in just after her elephant had been ruined.

"So?" Daniel was watching Amelia as she opened the door to the room where all the clothes went after they wore them.

"So, what?" Amelia had her back turned but Cora bet she would be frowning.

"Have you any of my shorts sorted?" Daniel was opening cupboard doors, looking inside, and closing them again. For a moment, Cora hoped he would pull out something tasty to eat, something he would share with her – he would have to share because he was the reason her teddy was ruined. Her dad said so. But he didn't pull anything out, not even some crisps.

"No, why would I? I don't do your washing."

Daniel paused his idle searching and stood facing Amelia. "That's hardly fair. You do everyone else's."

"What's not fair? Cora can't do hers and Dad gives me money for his, so if you want me to do yours then pay up."

"You're joking." Daniel had crossed his arms again.

Amelia shook her head, "no, Daniel, I'm not Mam and I'm not your slave."

"Did I say you were?" Daniel's brows were coming together over his eyes. Cora could feel a tingling in her belly as their voices rose. "I do all the shopping and loads of other shit for you."

"Oh, let me get my tiny violin for you," Amelia copied Daniel, her arms over her chest, as she stood in the doorway to the room filled with clothes. If he was playing 'Simon Says' he would win, Cora thought. Except that he wasn't going as red as Amelia was. For a moment, they didn't say anything, then, just as Cora changed colours from blue to green for the eyes of her elephant drawing, Daniel stormed towards Amelia, losing the game.

"Fine. I'll do it meself', like absolutely everything else round here." Cora watched from her seat as he bent next to the washing machine, taking handfuls of his clothes out of the really full basket, and shoving them into the machine until it was so full that he had to press his hands in to keep the clothes from falling back out.

"Daniel, you're going to break it! You can't over-fill it that much!" Amelia was yelling as Daniel kicked the door to the machine closed and grabbed the hose to push into the drawer at the top of the machine. Water spurted out the end of it, covering Daniel in water and making Cora giggle aloud, but Amelia and Daniel definitely didn't find it as funny. She would bet that if Daniel was sitting with her when it happened he would have laughed, too. Now though, he was wiping his hands on a stack of folded clothes.

"Those are clean!" Amelia shouted at him. Daniel pushed the whole pile over so that they fell off the counter and into the pool of water beneath the machine.

Cora was so busy laughing now that she didn't see when her dad came in, his hand rubbing his head while he held a short glass in his other hand. He stood at the other side of the table and watched Amelia and Daniel for a few seconds before he stepped over to the door of the washing room – Cora knew there was another name for it.

"The you-til-a-t," she corrected herself in a whisper..

"What are you two fighting about now?" From where Cora sat, she couldn't see into the room anymore but could see Amelia's hands waving around as she rushed to tell on Daniel. "I don't want to hear it. From now on, Amelia, sweetheart, you do the washing, and Daniel, you can carry the baskets up and down the stairs when they are needed. Ok?" There were huffs and muttered words and maybe even some bad words said then, but Cora went back to her colouring, choosing the orange crayon in the end for her elephant's eyes because she loves orange, and her teddy is in the bin so no one will really know that they weren't orange at all.

Chapter 12

Amelia couldn't move when she woke up. Her body felt like setting cement spread thin to cover the mess beneath, her breathing a gasping cry lost in a chasm. Her body was rigid, her eyes wide. No matter how much she tried to, she couldn't lift even a solitary finger.

Her room was dark, without even a sliver of silver light poking through her window. She stared at the ceiling above, at the old damp spot that stained the wood.

Then, a creak from the corner of the room, startling her, sounded. Her gaze travelled slowly across the ceiling before dropping to the dark space at the end of her bed where she stared at the void as it threatened to swallow her whole.

There was some movement around her, she was sure of it, but couldn't bring herself to look for the source, to bring her eyes away from that space.

There was silence, her breathing the only sound, and yet her ears rang with the absolute certainty that there was something lurking in the shadows of her room, something watching her with bated breath.

Her breathing became ragged, her mouth dry. An all-consuming fear was taking over her mind and body; something was watching her.

A breath tickled her stiffened neck.

What was happening?

Why couldn't she sit up?

She slowly scanned the darkened room, wishing she had left the light on like she had promised herself.

Her breathing was loud, her throat was too tight. Her chest was heaving up and down in terror, like an accordion, squeezing her chest of all her oxygen so only a tuneless whimper escaped.

What was happening?

Her blinking became rapid, too fast for her to keep her focus - making her light-headed.

Her body began to tremble, shaking uncontrollably when she spotted the tall, dark figure watching her from the corner of the room.

Without seeing its face, she knew it was sneering at her.

Her bones rattled from within.

It stepped forward, the shadow, moving like a curtain blowing in the breeze, flowing towards her.

Amelia's heart was almost sore from the thumping.

The floor creaked.

She couldn't look away.

It stood over her bed, its blackness petrifying.

Then, chilling her to her core, it sank, out of sight.

That was worse.

Her mind was frantic as her eyes searched to find where it had gone, when, chillingly, she watched a single, crooked hand creep over the end of her bed. It was no longer pure shadow, but a tangible, touchable hand, tugging at her blankets in the dark. Still frozen in place, Amelia watched as a second hand reached up and gripped the duvet with a clenched fist and pulled on it.

The cover moved slowly, sliding down her chest and body like a seductive partner, exposing her to the cool, tepid air of her room. Her scream was stale, caught in her throat, clogging her oesophagus as terror pinned her eyes open, forcing her to watch as a head of white hair appeared at the bottom of her bed, slowly making its way to her. A downturned face turned up and uncovered a most gruesome feature; eyes wide, round, and pinned on Amelia, a snarling, wide-toothed grin under a flattened nose. The head of the creature twitched in a circle as it crawled statically towards her.

She felt the weight of the thing on her body as it crept closer to her, salivating with the scent of her sweat. It crawled over her, its long, ripped nightgown trailing behind until it was above Amelia, over her, staring at her- into her.

Amelia thought she might die. Her heart was beating too fast. Her screams caught in her throat. She tried to push them out, could feel them choking her. She was utterly immobile. The tears came down her cheeks as the old hag tucked her legs up onto Amelia's chest and she crouched there, hungry.

The black iris's hovered over her, and there Amelia felt she *really* might die- that her heart would suddenly stop its frantic beating as the crushing weight of this hag sat on her chest, strangling her, smothering her. There was nothing but ragged breathing and then, as white-hot horror filled her, the old hag cackled menacingly in her face.

Amelia could not look away, as hard as she tried, she could not.

"Amelia..." Her name came from someplace in the distance, distorted and quiet. It sounded as though she were underwater, as if she were drowning. "Amelia..." Her body was shuddering, the fear too much for her to comprehend, a visceral reaction coming out through her shaking limbs.

"Wake up..."

Amelia bolted upright, her head colliding with something solid. Pain scorched her brow. There was a loud thud, and suddenly, there was light from the hallway streaming into her room, the yellow strips leading from the door to her bed. She was panting, gasping for breath, feeling her chest with her palms, grasping – clinging - to her jumper. Her eyes darted around the room, moving too fast to stay focused, searching for the hag.

She was okay.

On the floor next to her, Daniel was rolling around, holding his hand to his nose, his bare arms tense. He was swearing. Amelia, still shaking, searched out her duvet. It lay crumpled at the end of her bed. A cold sweat trickled down her neck.

It had felt so real. She could still feel the resonance of the old hag on her chest now, a terrifying reminder.

"Are you okay?" she asked her brother, her teeth chattering together, from fear or the cold, she couldn't tell the difference. She pulled her blanket up from the end of the bed and tugged it close to her, as if for protection- the little girl in her resurfacing, hoping that a duvet was enough to hide her from the monsters under her bed.

"Yeah, are you? You were screaming the bleedin' gaff down," Daniel said, standing up and checking the ends of his fingers for blood. "And you were crying," he added. Amelia touched her cheeks. They were still wet. "Bad dream?" he asked. Amelia couldn't find her voice, her words, the terror she had felt inexplicable. She nodded.

"Well, you woke Cora up." Amelia could hear the whispered voices coming from the other room, her father's gentle tone. She got from her bed on shaky legs and followed the sound.

Her toes clenched when they hit the rough carpet in the hallway, her exposed feet hating the way the fabric felt against her bare skin. She crossed the hallway, feeling dizzy, and caught her reflection in the glass at the end of the hall; her face was startlingly pale against her auburn hair. She pulled it over one shoulder and stopped in the doorway of Cora's room. Her father sat on the edge of the bed, a look of consternation on his tired face. Cora was shuddering with tears, inconsolable with upset. Her blankets, like Amelia's, were leaning off the end of her bed in a pile.

"You just had a bad dream, pet," Mark assured her. His eyes were dark with tiredness. He looked like he hadn't slept – had he been up already? Working on his book? If he she had been screaming like Daniel had said, would her father have heard her before Cora had? How long had he left her to scream before Daniel had checked in on her? If Cora hadn't woken up, would anyone have cared? There was a thick feeling in her throat, a stinging behind her eyes.

Her dad glanced up at Amelia but said nothing. She felt his silent blame. Beside her, Daniel leaned against the doorframe and crossed his arms over his chest.

"I felt it pull my blanket away!" Cora told him, her face red with anguish, her eyes blurry with tears. Amelia, her hands still a little shaky, listened with a strangled breath. "It wanted to get me!"

"Now, calm down, Cora. It was just a scary dream." Amelia had many memories of those words being said to her. It was 'just' a scary dream, it is 'only' in your imagination. *Don't be silly.* Always slightly dismissive, minimising her fears.

Did that work? Well...

"Nothing is pulling your blanket. You must've kicked it off." Amelia watched as her father scratched the underside of his chin, growing more tired as the seconds passed. Peeking at Daniel's folded arms, Amelia glimpsed the time: 3.58 am.

"I felt it!" Cora cried. Her dad took a deep breath, his eyes closing as he gathered his thoughts.

"Listen, sweetheart, there's nothing scary in this house," his tone was growing impatient.

"But the ghost-"

"Remember what I told you? The only ghost that would visit you would be Mam, checking in on you," he told her. Cora wiped her eyes with the back of her hand, chewing her bottom lip. For the first time, she noticed Amelia and Daniel standing at the door. Amelia gave her an agreeable bob of the head and the smallest smile- the biggest she could muster at that moment.

"Where's your night light?" Mark twisted and turned, searching for the light. Cora was shrugging.

"Where is Susan?" Cora asked, checking the floor next to her for the black cat. In unison, Amelia, Daniel, and their father all searched the floor for the stray. The cat was nowhere to be seen. Amelia checked over her shoulder, her gaze landing on her bedroom door while a shiver shook her spine.

"He must be outside, pet."

"But why would Susan go outside in the dark?"

"Well, he probably has friends out there and wants to see them; you know how Daniel likes to go out at night to see his friends, even when he should be in? I bet... Susan... does the same." Amelia looked at Daniel, apprehensively. He stood still, his jaw clenching and unclenching at the snipe. When Mark turned to beckon towards him, Daniel lifted his chin in defiance and turned to stalk back to his room. Amelia watched him go, his fists tight by his side, and then as he closed over his bedroom door, blocking them all out.

"But what if he's scared?"

"Why would he be scared? That's where he lives."

With Cora snuggled close to her, Amelia felt a sense of security, as if whatever had happened before would not happen now that she had her sister there. But... what did happen? She felt ill thinking about it.

It had felt too real for it to have not happened. But she had awoken, drenched in sweat, with Daniel next to her and no sign of the old hag to be seen.

A lucid dream, perhaps, plagued by some soulless ghoul.

Not able to relinquish her senses to sleep, in fear of what might happen if she did, she lay awake for a long time.

She stared at the wall, the darkest corner, afraid to blink, her eyes drying up like snails rubbed in salt, stinging until she could not bear it. She blinked. And repeated the process many, many times over.

A sinking feeling struck her as if a medieval rat had been burrowing a tunnel to her stomach before gnawing at it from inside, when she noticed how the Virgin Mary statue atop the deep-stained wardrobe sat facing her, twisted towards her so that her unholy eyes were glaring down at her, instead of away as she usually did.

Amelia left the light on all night.

"If you want, I can try and move this lamp into the corner of the room," Stephen said, one hand holding the lamp on Amelia's desk, the other holding an extension lead. She shook her head.

"No, it's fine. I kind of just leave it on," she told him, pulling the sleeves of her jumper down over her hands and crossing her legs in front of her on her bed. He set the lamp and the extension lead down before kicking off his runners and sitting across from her, shifting uncomfortably before swinging his legs over the edge of the bed and sitting sideways.

"Are you having a lot of nightmares?"

Amelia tightened her lips, tasting the sweet gloss she had used earlier, and nodded. "Every other night." Her voice was shaky.

"That's crap. I'm sorry I haven't been over in a week or so. My dad is building a dog pen and said I had to help him if I wanted some money. Is there anything I can do to help?" Amelia was shaking her head when Daniel appeared in her doorway, carrying a wash basket under one arm, and dragging a second one behind him. He bent, dropping the one in his arm onto the floor and sliding it over the threshold with his foot, and sighed.

"Laundry service," he grunted and picked the second basket up into his arms.

"Thanks." Amelia got up from her bed and pulled the basket towards her.

"Hey, ya' haven't seen a navy bra in the wash, have you?" Daniel asked. She shook her head. "You sure? You haven't picked it up and worn it, by any chance?" Amelia frowned at this.

"No, Daniel. I haven't seen Ellen's underwear in my washing, and if I did, I would hardly wear it," she said, pointedly.

"No need to be narky. It was a simple question."

"Maybe if you did your own washing for once you would find it." Before Daniel could respond, their father called out.

"Daniel, you need to go to the shop!"

"For fuck's sake..." Daniel's jaw tightened, his eyes closing over as he took a deep breath. Without a word to Amelia, he stormed off.

"Things seem a little tense around here," Stephen said quietly, watching the doorway in case Daniel returned.

"It always is."

It took three attempts for the flame to ignite on the little blue lighter. Amelia's thumb was stinging from the abrasive wheel as she lowered it to the awaiting candle. The wick didn't catch at first and so Amelia held the lighter on it for a few moments more until the orange glow separated and rose to a pointed flame as it caught on fire. The cake was sponge with thick chocolate icing, topped with an orange elephant that Amelia had tried to shape with some shop bought fondant, but looked more like a lopsided snowman with an unflatteringly huge nose.

"Happy birthday to you, happy birthday to you."

Behind Amelia, the others began to sing as she lifted the cake up and spun. Daniel and her dad were standing either side of Cora as she wriggled in her seat. Her eyes rounded and her little hands shot into the air when she got her first glimpse of the cake, the number five candle glowing brightly against the chocolate.

There was a flash of bright light as Daniel snapped a photograph with the disposable camera while he belted out the words of the song.

"Make a wish," Amelia said. She set the cake down in front of Cora and stood back, watching as Cora crawled up onto the tabletop, her hair dangling over the candle and swinging over the flame. Daniel reached over and held her hair back from her face so that she wouldn't catch fire. Close enough that her lips could have been scorched by the candle, she blew it out and sent spit onto the table. Together, the three of them clapped and cheered with smiles on their faces and glee in their voices; if Amelia didn't know any better, she would have believed them herself, but to her they looked like they were playing charades, acting out a happy family scene from a movie.

There was the click of the camera as Daniel took a couple of pictures of Cora with her cake and then of Amelia as she cut it into slices. They sat together at the round table and each took a piece – saving the fondant elephant for later. Amelia held her fork in the cake but couldn't bring herself to take a bite. Instead, she pushed the sponge around her plate for a few seconds before letting the fork stick up from it like a beacon. Her mouth was dry, her jaw tired from smiling.

"Which presents are you going to open first?" It was her father who asked Cora the question, his own slice of cake only nibbled at. He was wearing a blue party hat, the string cutting into his chin, splitting the hairs of his beard. Both Daniel and Amelia had matching yellow cones on their heads, while Cora looked like a traffic cone with the orange hat. Cora shrugged so that her birthday sash fell down her shoulder; the dark frosting was smudged at the corners of her mouth.

"Ehhmmm…. Probably the one from Mam," she said. Amelia's gaze darted to her father; his lips were in a thin line, his brow fighting against a frown. Her eyes shifted to Daniel who had stopped himself in the process of getting his second slice of cake. There was a beat of silence.

"Cora, Mam couldn't get you one this year," Amelia said softly, her tone gentle, when no one spoke.

"Yeah, but there's *loads* of others from us for you upstairs," Daniel added, dropping the second piece of cake back onto the tray and leaning away from the table. Cora wavered from side to side in her chair and nodded, as if accepting this instead.

It had been a last minute effort – the birthday party – to make Cora more comfortable after her recent nightmares. Apparently, Amelia's didn't matter, though.

Amelia had sent Daniel to get balloons and banners adorned with colourful animals wrapped around the number five, and ingredients for the cake that they were now eating. The gifts that they bought were all from the local shops, not that they thought Cora would mind; Amelia had gotten her an art set with over thirty colours, and a colouring book with the thick black lines around the drawings. None of them had thought that Cora would ask about their Mam today. *Foolish, really,* Amelia thought to herself. *Why* wouldn't *she?*

"Okay." The crumbs fell to the floor.

Daniel's chair squeaked as he pushed back from the table. He stood and Amelia watched as he let his eyes roam the scene in front of him. They landed on Amelia, who met his stare. She waited for him to say something, but he didn't, and instead he headed for the utility room and disappeared behind the door.

"I'm going to have to head off for a little while," her dad almost whispered to Amelia, as if it were only a mild inconvenience and not him leaving his daughter's fifth birthday party – and a measly one at that.

"But-" Amelia let out a loud sigh when her father stood and turned his back on the table, his focus shifting to Daniel as he came out of the utility room dressed in a pair of shorts and t-shirt, one runner already on.

"Where're you going?" Amelia watched as Daniel shrugged and continued undoing the laces of the shoe he had in his hands. As they stood next to each other Amelia could see the resemblance – other than their hair colour, her dad's softening jawline and his rounding middle, they were almost mirrored images of one another.

A twist in her stomach told her that the charades were coming to an end, and an abrupt one at that.

"Out for a run, why?"

"You're going to leave your sisters here alone? Today?"

Daniel's brow creased, his fingers paused on his laces, "yes," he said, simply.

"And you weren't going to ask if it was okay, or say anything?" Amelia glanced at Cora. She was busy playing with the elephant fondant, using it to walk the edge of her plate and dipping its poorly shaped trunk into her glass of milk.

"No. Why would I? I'm hardly disappearing into thin air. I'm going out the back." Daniel was almost smiling as he spoke, *almost*. His eyes were fixed on his father's, his shoulders sitting forward, but his mouth was somehow relaxed enough for him to seem nonchalant.

"Oh right. But if you were going to disappear you would ask, would you?" Amelia's twisting stomach clenched as her father spoke. The atmosphere in the room thickened and she wanted nothing more than to look away, but she couldn't.

"Ah, here. I'm going out. I'll talk to ya's later." Daniel shook his head, bent to shove his foot into his shoe, and pushed by their father. He barely paused to take the disposable camera from the table and to ruffle Cora's hair, before jogging out the door, letting it shut loudly behind him.

Amelia stared at her slice of cake, at the fork that was sticking up from it like the newly installed Spire in town, and listened as the back door closed against the frame, barely making a sound, as her dad left.

"Do you want to open some presents now, Cora?"

Cora was determined to redeem herself- to prove she wasn't a scardy-cat, although she wasn't sure where that idea came from because her cat, Susan, was probably one of the bravest creatures she knew; Susan wasn't afraid to go out into the woods at night alone, or afraid to sleep by himself, even when he felt someone touch his leg when he slept, which is something Cora *loved* doing because his fur was just so soft. Anyways, she wanted to prove that she wasn't afraid of... well, anything!

She only got spooked that night – when she was sure she felt someone pull her blankets - because she had been younger, then. Now, she was a little older and understood things. Like sometimes when you feel someone stroke your leg it's because they like you – like Cora loves her cat - and that even big people sometimes sleep with a night light - like Amelia - which meant she could keep hers on too, or that sometimes things that might seem scary at first aren't really very scary at all- like the wee-ja game that she had found.

Daniel and Amelia had played with it before, even though it's really *her* game, even though *she* found it under the couch, but she didn't want them to make her go to bed when she wasn't even tired, so she let them play with it. Now she can play with it herself.

Cora sat crossed-legged on the floor in the basement, staring at the wooden board. She was certain that she was brave enough to play with it by herself, now that she was older and wiser and didn't scare as easily. And it is a game, isn't it? It's supposed to be played with by kids. She liked the idea of being able to talk to her mam, too- of asking her if she can fly now- and if she wouldn't mind, if those things were possible, not pulling her blankets down at night anymore because sometimes Cora got cold in this house and she sometimes thinks that Amelia doesn't want to share her bed, even though Cora shared her game with her.

She wanted to be brave enough that she didn't need to sleep with Amelia anymore.

On the rug in the very downstairs room, she fidgeted with her feet, tapping them with her hands, her hair swinging to-and-fro as she wobbled on the spot. She also wanted to ask something that she felt a little bad asking but figured it was okay seen as her mam was her mam and she wouldn't get mad at her.

Cora wasn't really sure how to play the game, though. She sat forwards, up onto her knees, and put her hands onto the other piece that she found under the couch. She pushed it around, the wood slippery. Absent-mindedly, she watched the piece skate around, wondering how to start.

"What colour is my underwear?" Cora asked, feeling a little silly, but looking at the ceiling, just like Daniel did. Nothing happened.

"Just STOP eating it!" Amelia had woken up in an even worse mood than usual. Cora wasn't sure why she didn't like sharing her snacks with Daniel, but she was glad that she didn't mind giving Cora some.

Cora leaned in close to the game board, trying to watch it without blinking in case she missed something. She stared so long that her vision was fuzzy. Cora pressed her fingers on the tear-drop-shaped wood as she scooted her legs back behind her so she was lying on her belly now.

"Come on, Mam, move it…" Cora gasped when the planchette trembled as if it might shift. A thrill of excitement ran through her when it slid over several spaces, landing on 'i'… no, 'j'- Cora always got those confused, they just looked the same- except for the curly tail at the bottom.

There was a rattle from over on the wall. It sounded like someone shaking rice in a plastic bottle. "Do it again!"

"Cora..." Her name sounded funny, like someone was talking through a paper cup phone but she didn't hold the other end and so she could barely hear it.

"Mam!"

Chapter 13

Despite it being the end of July and only 3 pm, a dark fog had been creeping in from the lake, blanketing the house in a dank, dreary atmosphere. Amelia felt the dampness seeping into her skin, drenching her bones and setting an unstoppable chill that rattled her to her core. She was on edge, every creak in the old floorboards making her jump, every draft through the uninsulated windows a sinister force trying to trick her to allow them in.

The night had been long.

They were all long now.

She was spending endless hours in the dark, lying awake, fighting sleep. On the nights she did sleep, she saw vile images behind her lids, scratched there like the finger marks scratched on the walls of the house.

She sat in the living room, the fire alight and crackling as the embers danced about, with her duvet wrapped around her for warmth, and a book upon her lap, however, she only stared at the coffee table before her wondering if they had made a mistake in playing with the talking board that night a few weeks ago; if that was what spurred on her intense dreams.

As much as Amelia liked to pretend to have a logical view of the paranormal, she often found herself questioning things, second-guessing noises, interpreting shadows as hallucinations and, here in this house, she struggled to find reasonable answers. Sometimes there just was no explanation.

Daniel had sworn responsibility for the movement on the board, but what if they had inadvertently taunted whatever else was with them in the house?

Was it a coincidence that both she and Cora had had some form of terrible, ghostly experience that night a couple of weeks ago? Or was it the result of the mocking of some ethereal deviant? The thought gave her chills.

Her eyes were heavy where she sat, her mind tired, but if she allowed herself to doze off for even a moment, she would see the cruel smile of the old hag leaning over her again. Each time she felt consciousness slipping, she would recover it by pinching her inner thigh so that now there was a series of red welts there, splotchy and sore when her trouser legs touched off of the raw skin.

Atop the mahogany table, Amelia had set the statue of the Virgin Mary so that she could watch it, daring it to shift in place, but praying silently that it would not. It had moved from its place in her room, more than once, each time to face her, and she would turn it away only to wake up and see it staring down at her again. It had happened again last night. But she knew what she was thinking was fit for her father's stories. Inanimate objects can't move.

Then, does that mean *something* moved it?

Amelia pinched herself again.

The feeling had been undeniably real, indisputably palpable. She had felt something there in her room with her that night.

The idea that something watched her, *interacted*, with her, petrified her.

"Woah, you look terrible. Are you sick?" Daniel appeared in the doorway. Amelia sat up, shifting her duvet around her shoulders, and shook her head. "Right, okay." Daniel picked the statue up and rolled it around in his two hands, his brows coming together as he examined it, confused.

"Did you move that?" Amelia's question came out as an accusation. One of his brows rose.

"Now?"

"No, last night- any night?"

"Hey, Amelia, are you feeling alright?" Ellen came through the door, holding her shoulders as though cold. How did she go about answering such a question?

"No, I've never seen this before in my life."

"Are you sure? It was on the wardrobe in my room upstairs."

"I'm positive. Is this what is giving you nightmares? I mean, I can understand why- there's something a bit off about the face, isn't there?" Daniel twisted the ornament around, his features turning down as he scrutinised the face of it. "Where's Cora?"

Ellen shook her head when Daniel offered the statue to her. Amelia's eyes followed the ornament as Daniel set it on top of the tall mantle.

"She's... ehm... downstairs- down in the basement, I think."

"Is Mark home?" This made Amelia frown at her brother.

"No, Dad's not here."

"Great, we are going upstairs, alright?" Daniel gave her a look that alluded to more than he was saying. "Alright?"

"Yeah, I don't care." Amelia's lacklustre response made Daniel pause. He beckoned Ellen to the door. With a moment's hesitation, he followed her, stopping in the doorway, and watching Amelia as she stared blankly at the figurine. She felt his eyes on her, like she felt that presence in her room, as clear as day.

"If you need me, I'm just upstairs." Daniel lingered for only a second more before his steps faded in the foyer, the carpeted stairs muffling them even more so that it was only the rhythmic base of his footfalls that could be heard before the loud bang of his door demanded privacy.

They lay on his bed, Daniel leaning over Ellen, one hand placed on her hip, the other around her neck as he kissed her. She purred under him. Having an absent father had its ups and downs - this was one of the more advantageous aspects of it.

One of the downfalls, however, was the fact that he was more often than not near his sisters.

Daniel rolled over and got up off the bed. Ellen sat up onto her elbows, watching as he crossed the room to his door, pulling his white t-shirt back on over his head, and fixing his jogging shorts so he looked a little less dishevelled. The footsteps had been constant. He just knew that Amelia sent Cora up to disturb them, he would put money on it.

Typically, when Daniel got up, the running steps had ceased, a childlike giggle coming from the hallway now, as if hearing his approach. Irritated, Daniel reefed the door open and stepped onto the carpeted floor. The hallway was dull, with no lamps on and the dark fog blocking the dismal light from coming through the window at the end of the long hallway.

Daniel was alone on the landing.

"Come on, Cora. Out you come." Daniel rested a hand on his doorframe, waiting impatiently for her to come out. There was only silence. "Go back down to Amelia." He delayed a moment longer, expecting to hear a giggle, but none came. He closed over his door and retreated to where Ellen lay, her brow creased.

"Is she not out there?"

"Nah, but I'd say she's hiding. She'll go back downstairs."

"Are you sure that was her? It didn't really sound like her." Ellen brushed her hair away from her skin, her flushed cheeks cooling to a more natural complexion.

"Yeah, of course. Who else would it have been?" Daniel stretched over her, kissing her neck, tracing her jaw with his lips, but she gently pressed against his chest, and he sat back from her, confused. She looked worried.

"You okay?"

Ellen chewed her bottom lip, taking a deep breath, and shook her head. She met his gaze.

"I just… It's the house."

Daniel slumped his shoulders, sighing. He let his head drop.

This again.

"I know you think it's dumb, but I just can't get it out of my head about what happened here, like it's crazy to think it was in *this* house, and now you and I are... about to... you know..."

"Fuck?" he offered with a teasing smile. Ellen rolled her eyes.

"Charming."

"Come on, you know I don't mean it like that."

"Yeah. It's just, like, we said we were going to hang out at mine and-"

"You said your parents would kill you if you brought me over there," he reminded her; he had been happy to spend all their time at her house, delighted even. Any reason to get him away from here.

"I know." Ellen looked torn.

"Look, you don't even know if those stories are true. Most of it is probably whispers and rumours. That's what happens everywhere. We once rented a place that had rumours about the owners draining the blood of orphans for satanic rituals. They had apparently let their Doberman chew the limbs of the kids afterwards while they were still alive." Ellen's bright eyes widened, her brows etching together while she chewed her lower lip.

"What *actually* happened was their Doberman got rabies and bit their foster kid in the face. Mark wrote a novel where demons were kidnapping foster kids and sending Hell Hounds out for blood payments. Stories change all the time."

"Really?"

"Ye."

"But what if parts of the story are true? Like, people don't just come up with this shit in their heads, do they?" Daniel smiled at her, thinking of his father's entire career; where would Mark be without his embellished nightmares? Home might be one place he'd make an appearance. Then, he had another thought and shrugged, falling back to land on his back so he was staring at the unstained slats of wood on his ceiling.

"I mean, I'd say it's *possible* that he buried the kid in the walls of the house; it is huge and wouldn't be *impossible* to do," Daniel said with a mischievous grin.

"Stop it, Daniel. You're freaking me out!" A glint of glee shone in her eyes as she said it, her voice high-pitched with some excitement.

"I'm serious; there could be a hiding place for a dead baby. Will we try and find it?" Daniel was already up off the bed, extending his hand out to Ellen as she squirmed at the idea. Did he mean it? Probably not, but who knew – the house might be boring enough to drive someone to murder if they were living here long enough.

"Oh my God, will we?" Ellen's eyes were wide, her brows nearly touching her hairline. Her expression was a mix of horror and thrill.

"Well, I'm going to go look for it." He was only out of his door a single stride length when he heard Ellen clambering to follow him out. He hurried down the stairs, tapping the banisters on either side of the wide staircase with his outstretched hands. At the sound, Amelia appeared in the kitchen doorway. She no longer had the duvet draped over her shoulders and instead carried a cup of steaming coffee. She brought it to her lips slowly and sipped. Her eyes followed Daniel's movements lazily, as though she had just woken from a nap.

"What are you doing?" she asked, dispiritedly. She looked as though she might collapse with the slightest push on the shoulder.

"We're looking for the hollow wall," Daniel called over to her, not stopping to explain further as he began knocking on the walls of the foyer and pressing his ear to the panels.

"He's being ridiculous," Ellen said, laughing and following him around the large foyer.

"What're you talking about? Be careful-" A second too late, Daniel stepped back and knocked into the lamp atop the old console table that sat next to the basement door. It wobbled before toppling over and smashing on the floor. "Daniel!" The already dim area was sent into shadows.

"It's grand. I'll clean it," he said, kicking the clay pieces to the side before continuing. He stopped and set his hands on his hips, facing the two girls. "Amelia, you love this shit, where do you think there could be a hiding place?"

"You're joking?" Amelia's coffee cup was paused halfway to her mouth.

"No. I'm actually deadly serious," he said. He waited as Amelia took a sip of her coffee. She turned, setting it down on the counter in the kitchen, and took a deep breath.

"The library."

―――

Amelia led the way to the small room behind the corkscrew stairs. The others followed her excitedly. The door blended into the shadows of the hallway, barely noticeable in the dark. She touched the cool wood with the tips of her fingers on both hands and pushed. With a loud creak, the door gave way and swung inwards, revealing a room about half the size of Amelia's bedroom, with walls covered floor to ceiling with dusty books. It was a tomb of work, uncared for and forgotten.

The outside lamps, staggered along the porch, sent a sinister yellow glow through the looming fog, and cast ugly stripes of light into the room and across the old carpet, which had been stained by something dark. It smelled musty and as though some of the shelves on which the books rested upon might be rotting. Dust motes lifted into the air at their entry, swirling airborne in an attempt to cling on to any surface. A cool draft billowed in through the cracked frame of the window, sending fresh shivers across Amelia's skin. She longed to have her coffee back in between her palms for warmth.

"I didn't even know this was here," Daniel said, standing in the middle of the room; if he widened his arms, he would not be far from touching both bookcases on either side of the library. This didn't surprise Amelia. He spent that much time absorbed by his own reflection he didn't have time for anyone else.

"We used to dare each other to come in here alone at night - when the place was still empty. It still gives me chills," Ellen told them, running her fingers along the shelf closest to her, wiping the layer of grey powder away between her two fingers.

"You used to come here?" Amelia turned to look at her. She nodded. "Did you ever... you know... hear or... see anything?"

Ellen hesitated, glancing at Daniel. Amelia twisted just in time to see his expression of apprehension before he busied himself with trying to cover the crack in the wooden window frame, blocking almost all of the light coming into the room. Ellen gave Amelia a tight grin and shook her head.

"No, never. We were just kids messing around in an old house. We just freaked each other out if anything."

Amelia stayed in place; her arms wrapped over her chest for a moment longer before she went to the bookcase in the centre of the right wall. Her dad had shown her it in the first days they had arrived at the start of summer, when she had been excited to see the new house, hear about his new story. With packed suitcases and cardboard boxes still filling the foyer, her dad had been excited to drag Amelia away from unpacking to show her this. When he had opened the door, revealing the secret behind, Amelia had shrunk away immediately, an unnerving amount of unease appearing in her stomach. She hadn't been able to explain it then, and still couldn't, but since then she had struggled to shift that sense of uncanniness she felt while in the house.

It was as if by pulling back the false case, you were unveiling something dark about the house, looking at the diseased guts of it; like she had taken a peak at house's secrets without ever knowing the truth.

There was a distinct difference in the level of dust on the shelves on either side of the one she stood before. They were undisturbed, their surfaces stacked with powdered, grey skin mites, where this one had finger marks smudged in the dust. She set her hands on the books, feeling for the ridge in the shelf, made more difficult with the light almost completely blocked behind Daniel's silhouette. When she felt it, she dug her fingers against it and pulled.

The bookcase moved outwards, silently, opening to a shallow alcove in the wall, like a disguised door that might lead to a private speak-easy behind a rack of coats in a café.

"This what you're looking for?" Daniel was staring, his mouth agape, over his shoulder. He stepped away from the window, the dirty yellow light pouring back into the dull room and went to stand next to her. She leaned back, allowing him to step in front of her and distanced herself from the renewed eerie feeling that washed over her yet again.

"Holy shit," he muttered, regarding the space behind the bookcase. There was nothing to be seen in the alcove, just three empty shelves.

"How have we never found this before?" Ellen whispered, more to herself than to them. She stepped forward, past Amelia, as Amelia began to shrink back, away from them. She couldn't put her finger on it, couldn't quite articulate what it was she was feeling, but a sense of foreboding swirled around in her stomach like a gathering storm.

"Amelia?" Amelia met Daniel's waiting gaze.

"What?"

"How did you know about this?"

"Dad showed me it a couple days after we moved in."

"This is so crazy. I bet this is where he left her-" despite Ellen's hushed voice, Amelia heard.

"Who? What're you talking about?" Amelia's palms were sweating.

"Nothing." Daniel squeezed himself into the alcove, hunching his shoulders and ducking low to fit. His frame filled the entire space behind the bookcase.

"What're doing?" Ellen was laughing at him, but Amelia was starting to feel overwhelmed – claustrophobic - as if she were the one trying to fit into the tight space. She had to turn away to regulate her unsteady breathing.

"I think there's something else behind here." Daniel's voice was strained. He was pushing against the back panel of the alcove, knocking against it, rapping on the wood. Amelia turned around and watched as he started driving against it with his shoulder. When nothing happened, he set his palms on one of the shelves and started to kick against the bottom. Through a cloud of dust, Amelia started coughing, fighting off the dust with her waving hand.

"Careful, Daniel." Ellen watched with intense curiosity, taking a step backwards to avoid inhaling the rising dust.

There was a loud *crack* and Daniel stepped back, taking a cautionary inspection of the panel. There was a split in the wood where Daniel had kicked a hole in the panel-board. He knelt and touched the splintered wood, pulling the broken pieces away, hissing and examining his fingers.

"I don't think that's a good idea, Daniel." Amelia took a tentative step forward, watching as he went back to pulling the wooden slats away, exposing a black hole. There was a bundle of wires moving with the commotion. "You could get hurt."

"She's right, Daniel. This house has really old connections, you don't know what you might do if you touch off bare wires."

"There's space behind here, I wanna see if I can fit." He was out of breath. Amelia looked, wide-eyed, at Ellen.

"You struggle to fit through turnstiles, Daniel. Just leave it." Ellen touched the back of his leg, coaxing him away from the hole. The debris lay haphazard on the carpet. He retreated, closing over the bookcase and wiped his hands on his shorts, poking at a splinter in his fingertip.

"Why did you ask about that?" Amelia's head was starting to pound now, exhaustion making it hard for her to focus on their answer.

"Eh, Mark said something about hiding his whiskey there. We wanted to find it."

"He keeps it in his room," Amelia told them, too tired to wonder why they were lying to her.

"You look a little pale, Amelia. Maybe you should lie down?" Ellen chewed her bottom lip, offering her concern.

"Yeah, I think I might nap on the couch." She could hardly stand to fight it any longer. Without listening to what they said to her, she turned and started out of the room, towards the living room, her body desperate for sleep. Behind her, she heard the distinct sound of slapping and Daniel's exclamation, which was followed by Ellen's warm laugh.

"Do you mind?"

"Couldn't help myself when you were bent over!"

Their voices drifted off as Amelia went, feeling as though she were floating, to the living room. She lay on the floral couch, set her head against the back of it, and closed her eyes. Her mind fought to keep her awake for a few minutes, but the allure of sleep was too strong, and she started to doze off. At some point, while she was in between a sleeping and waking state, she heard movement around her, but too tired, she let herself slip into unconsciousness, hoping that like the eerie alcove in the library which she had not thought of in weeks, she would forget about the noise.

Chapter 14

For an uncertain amount of time, Amelia slept there, in the living room on those old couches. When she woke, she sat up, pushing her long, unkempt hair away from her face. The fire had been kept alive whilst she slept and now cast a flickering glow in the room, creating long, shifting shadows crawling up the warped walls, sick with water damage. The lamps had been turned out, leaving her in near darkness. But she was warm. At last she could feel the heat. Seeing the flames flicker, she considered if she was too harsh on Daniel sometimes, if he was more thoughtful than she gave him credit for. Maybe.

Her breath caught, her eye catching the shadows of the wooden carving of a cloaked figure on the opposite wall, and morphing it into a hooded shadow, alive and peering at her. It had been a selling point for her dad- those carved figures. They watched you move throughout the house like gatekeepers, their eyes glaring at you no matter where you went in the room. Her heart leapt, racing uncomfortably. She slouched and slinked back in her seat when her mind orientated.

The fog outside had become so thick that the last of the evening sun was but a hazy illusion - like a pool of water in a desert mirage - and could not pierce the gloom at all. A shiver ran over Amelia and she clutched the duvet closer to her.

She had slept peacefully, with no ghouls or ghosts waking her, and felt unexpectedly well-rested. She stood, leaving her blanket behind, and sauntered to the fireplace. The mantle sat back against the wall and was as tall as she was, with bulging cherubs and wooden carvings of ivy vines and leaves protruding along the surface. The breast above the fireplace was bare, the paint peeled off from years of heat exposure and never redone.

It was funny what sleep can do for the mind, Amelia thought. Tired and sleep deprived, she had been almost delirious, scared by shadows and cool draughts. The heat warmed Amelia's palms as she placed them outwards. She stayed there, feeling silly then, that she had been so frightened.

She had heard of sleep paralysis before when listening to podcasts and reading of the occult. It was ironically quite a perspicuous occurrence that many people experience. It was a state of dreaming- scary, but a well-studied state.

The situation of the figurine moving was something she found harder to determine, however – she shook her head, thinking- it was not paranormal. It couldn't be.

The house is old. It is cold. It is quite possibly teeming in black mould.

Amelia, a self-proclaimed horror fan, refused to be frightened by anything lesser than an apparition. And yet...

These thoughts were refreshing to her but fleeting.

The basement door slammed shut, followed by the loud, urgent steps across the foyer, muffled once they reached the stairs. Amelia snapped her head around, the closed living room door blocking her from seeing what was happening. The grandfather clock next to the moulding in the wall chimed. 4.30 pm.

Crack

The fire snapped at her, a spark leaping out of the hearth and clinging to Amelia's grey trousers.

"Shit-" she pat at her leg, singeing her palm and leaving a red mark on her skin.

Inspecting her palm, Amelia paused when a booming clatter from above sounded. There was a clangourous commotion, mostly muffled to Amelia. Her immediate reaction was to take to the foyer, to check on Cora.

In the lightless hall, Amelia went to the basement door, which she opened hastily and jolted when only blackness faced her. She took a single, hesitant step inside the vestibule and leaned against the staircase; the lights at the bottom of the stairs were off, revealing only darkness where her shadow monsters lurked.

"Cora...?" She meant to call for her, but her voice faltered and came out in a shaky whisper.

It is just a house.

Angry voices travelled down to her from behind, from up the twisting stairs. Perhaps, she considered, Cora had intruded on Daniel and Ellen. Amelia turned and went to go upstairs, wetting her lips and readying herself for a confrontation. The stairs creaked near the top, and the hallway, like the rest of the house, was dull and cold. Why, Amelia wondered, does no one like to turn on the lamps?

A blonde strip of light escaped out into the hall from one bedroom, across which shadows moved back and forth. When Amelia got to Daniel's room, she stepped inside and immediately blanched.

"Cora?" Amelia gawked when she peered in. She saw Daniel wearing only a pair of tight boxer shorts with his back to the door as Ellen bent her head between her legs, hissing and crying, clutching the blanket to her bare chest with one hand, while the other was set firmly against her head. Daniel was holding a grey t-shirt to her temple. Little dots of red were on the bed covers. Cora, twiddling her thumbs together with etched brows, stood at the end of the bed, saying nothing. On the floor, with a bloodied base, was the figurine of the Virgin Mary.

"You're okay, you're okay. I think it's stopping," Daniel dabbed the t-shirt against Ellen's scalp, tilting it to check the blood flow. His face was set in a scowl.

"Wh- what happened?" Amelia took another step forward. Daniel, realising she was there for the first time, glared at her.

"You were supposed to be watching her! For fuck sake, Amelia!" It took her a moment to respond as she absorbed the scene.

"We *both* should be watching her-"

"You knew we were up here - you should've used your head."

Incredulous, Amelia scoffed, narrowing her eyes. "Cop on, Daniel!"

"You cop on! You're fucking sixteen and you still need to be looked after like you're a child. Just fuck off, I need to take Ellen to the doctors." He left Ellen to hold the shirt to her bleeding scalp and started picking through the clothes in his drawers. "I said, fuck off," he said, pointedly. Amelia reached over and took Cora as she cried and led her out of the room. She guided her down the stairs and back into the living room.

When Daniel jogged down the stairs, Ellen in tow, he collected the keys to the Volvo and slammed the front door behind him, so roughly, that the glass in the living room trembled.

"Cora, why did you throw that at Ellen?" Cora sat on the couch, her legs swinging out, kicking the air. She shrugged, her little shoulders touching her ears.

"Because Mam said I had to if I wanted my present."

Amelia felt cold.

The mist was thick, the headlights bouncing off the dense fog, the roads full of the bright red bulbs of the slow-moving cars. They got to the GP office with only four minutes to spare before they closed for the evening. The secretary had a wide-eyed glare behind her round glasses when Daniel barged through the door of the narrow lobby with Ellen in tow wearing one of his t-shirts and shorts, holding another to her forehead. With a sigh that said that this was the last thing she wanted to deal with, her hand already holding her handbag as she readied to leave for the day, she called for the nurse. The nurse was a friendly-faced older woman who *cooed* and *awed* when she saw Ellen, greeting her by name before turning to Daniel.

"Sorry, son, I can't let you come in since you're not family." She gave him a tight grin. Gently, she pulled the t-shirt away from Ellen's forehead to get a glimpse of the gash in her scalp. Ellen gave a small whimper and began to cry again. The nurse gave her a sympathetic pat on the arm before handing the bloodied shirt to Daniel. "Well, the bleeding has stopped," she said, and guided Ellen towards the little room at the end of the corridor. "Let's get you sorted, chicken," Daniel heard her say cheerfully to Ellen. For a moment, Daniel wasn't sure what to do and spun on the spot in search of the waiting room.

"You can just wait outside. I'm sure they won't be long," the secretary said to him. He paused, took a deep breath, and went to reply, but she had her back turned to him, her hands busy with paperwork. He bit his tongue and left the doctor's office, crossing the road as yellow headlights neared on either side, the body of the cars invisible in the fog.

The car came to life and hot air flowed freely from the vents. Daniel sat, watching the dull lamps on either side of the door to the GP's, his hand tapping against the steering wheel, his foot bouncing on the carpet. With his other hand, he reached over and turned the heating off before winding down the lever anti-clockwise to let some cool, foggy air in. His eyes flickered to the stained t-shirt then, and he gritted his teeth, thinking. His breathing was still deep and fast.

It had happened so fast; he didn't even hear Cora creep into the room.

This wasn't how he had planned to spend his evening.

He sat waiting long enough that he dozed off, his mouth wide open, the engine still running.

He woke with a start when a car horn blared. Daniel's eyes opened and he sat up, looking out the window and watching as Ellen crossed the road towards him, a thick bandage covering her forehead, a paper prescription in her hand. The car that had come to a sudden stop when they spotted her, stared after her, the disgruntled driver waving at her angrily. Daniel checked his side mirror before opening the door and stepping onto the road.

"I hope they prescribed ya something fun," Daniel teased, but couldn't bring himself to smile with it. Ellen only glanced at him before she walked around the bonnet of the Volvo 960 and sat in the passenger side, not closing the door. Daniel hesitated before he climbed back in and pulled his seatbelt over his shoulder and clicked it in place. "So, where to? Which chemists?" he asked, knowing already that there was only the one. *I wonder if they still have those photos,* Daniel thought to himself, thinking of the disposable camera he had left in after Cora's pitiful party.

Ellen was sitting, holding the prescription in her lap, the doctor's illegible scribble scrawled messily on the paper, her head bowed. She chewed her lower lip before looking at him.

"My dad is coming to collect me," she said. Daniel's jaw tightened while the hand that rested on the wheel now clenched around it.

"Oh. Do you want me to drop over later?"

Ellen was shaking her head, her eyes welling up with tears. Daniel felt a tightness in his stomach, his breath catching.

"I can't do this, Daniel. It's too much."

"Do what? What do you mean?" There was a pause then, and Daniel felt as if the fog was pouring into the car through the open door, coming to choke him.

"*This*. Us. It's just not working out." She was waving her hands between them, in the space above the gear stick.

"Hey, I'm sorry. And I'm sure Cora is too. I'll talk to her about it. She was probably just messing-"

"No, Daniel. It's... just the house- I *told* you that I didn't want to be in it. I *told* you that I don't like it there. It's weird and... and scary... and I just can't spend another minute there." Her voice was shaky, her tears flowing freely.

"Alright, well we can just go to yours-"

"No, Daniel. Look at my forehead! I'll be lucky if it doesn't scar." She took a deep breath. "It's... it's over, I'm finished." She met his eyes with unwavering finality. He didn't speak, didn't reply. What was he supposed to say? There wasn't much to say. "There's my dad." She pointed out the window lamely to the other side of the road, where her father had parked his Mondeo. Daniel didn't look. Ellen waited a minute longer – wiping the tears from her cheeks - before she silently climbed out of the car. She stood at the door, lifting her hand to her father in a polite wave, and hesitated.

"I'll see you, Daniel."

Daniel didn't respond verbally, only met her eyes, and nodded. She shut the door over and walked across the road. Daniel didn't watch, just sat, staring at the gearstick with a tight jaw. He stared at it for so long that he felt a stiffness in his neck and eventually stared out the window, across the road to where the empty parking space disappeared in the fog. There was a lump in his throat, a stuffy kind of sensation that he tried to force away.

It was just some summer fun. Something to get you out of the house.

Only it hadn't gotten him out of the house enough, apparently.

And maybe it was something more. Maybe.

The others had it easy here; Cora didn't understand what was going on half the time, and just played with her dolls and cat. Amelia had her books and puzzles, and Mark, well he had his *work*, if that's how you wanted to phrase it. Daniel had Ellen.

And now he didn't.

It was a strange feeling; one he had never felt before. It was like his arm had been taken away from him; he could survive perfectly well without it, but he felt as if he were missing something vital.

A once familiar idea crept into his mind, one that he couldn't remember the last time having thought about it, but it was once a regular occurrence and gave him comfort, like an old jumper or his first pair of proper runners. It wasn't as potent as before, but it gave him a sort of comfort that he knew he couldn't get from anyone else. It was past 6 pm, so the cafes wouldn't be open, but Daniel knew his father well enough to guess his other haunts.

―――――

Dark wooden doors opened into a smoky pub, making it look as though the fog had spilled through the cracks and filled every space. A long bar ran along the wall on the right with old, four-legged stools topped by green cushions, sitting beneath it, while tables were scattered around the remaining space. A man was standing at the other end of the bar, a dartboard on the far wall, pointy flights glinting in the dull downlights as he readied to throw another one.

Daniel dug out his wallet from the depths of his pocket and fished out his ID, approaching the bar where an older man pushed three pints of settled Guinness towards an even older man who looked as ancient as Arthur Guinness himself, a lit cigarette held firmly between his lips. At the bar, he set his hands down and leaned against it. He checked over his shoulder, in the dark corners, but there was no sign of his father.

"What can I get you, son?"

Daniel turned back and pointed with the hand he held his ID in at the shelf of whiskey behind him. "Give me a Jameson, please." He offered the man his ID. In return, the two men laughed.

"Desperate for me to take it, aren't ya'?"

Daniel frowned.

"The biggest giveaway to being underage is having the bloody thing ready!" The old-timer chuckled and wrapped his hands around the three pints.

"Well, I'm not underage," Daniel told him and went to put his ID back. The barman clicked his fingers and waved for him to take it back out, smiling.

"Come on, let's see it then." He took it from Daniel and leaned against the beer taps as he pulled a tumbler from beneath. He read over it, his brows raising. "Ah, the apple doesn't fall too far from the tree. Your old man does be in here drinking the same thing." He handed it back to him and poured him a drink.

"Was he in here today?" Daniel took a sip of his drink and passed the barman cash. Then, for a split second, the barman and the old man shared a look of co-conspirators who harboured a nasty secret.

"The day of the week wouldn't end in 'Y' if he wasn't," Arthur Guinness mumbled as he toddled away, limping to a table of men in their golden years. Daniel watched him hobble over without spilling a single sip of drink.

"You missed him by about forty-five minutes, son. Might be in The Harvest now." He wiped at the countertop. "You want me to call Jimmy for you and see if your old man is there? He might not be in the best shape at this time, though." He twisted his wrist to check the time. Daniel considered this. There was a nostalgic part of him that undoubtedly wanted comfort from him. But nostalgia is a lie we tell ourselves to make the past better than it was. It was wishful thinking and so was his father's presence.

Daniel shook his head and downed the rest of his drink in one. With a mutter of thanks to the man behind the bar, he left and got back into the car. Just once he had thought Mark might be helpful.

Just once.

Chapter 15

"And you're sure that's what she said?" Stephen sat opposite Amelia at the kitchen table. He mirrored her, holding his mug of tea in his hands. He had arrived, not long after Daniel had stormed off, and found Amelia shivering in the living room, despite the heat from the fire. Hours had passed since then, and Amelia had put Cora to bed, and she sat there, in the kitchen with Stephen, nursing her tea. She had told him what had happened once she was sure that Cora was sleeping.

"Yes, positive. She couldn't have said anything else."

Stephen took a sip of his hot drink and set it down, leaning back in his chair.

"That's crazy. Where do you think she got that idea?"

After speaking with Cora, Amelia had forced herself to go down to the basement, to where Cora had been playing before she had thrown the little figurine at Ellen's head, and had felt a brush of cold air hit her when she reached the bottom of the stairs. There on the floor, set up as if waiting for Cora's return, was the Ouija board. When she told Stephen this, his brows knitted together.

"What if something happened when she was playing with it? What if something did tell her to do it?"

"But, Amelia, Cora can't read yet. She said so herself."

Amelia closed her eyes, pinching the bridge of her nose. Of course she knew it was ridiculous - Cora couldn't read, or at least, not very well. She knew only words that she had memorised which consisted of a handful of colours and names.

"I know." Amelia sighed. "I just, I don't understand why she would've done it."

"And what did your dad say about it?"

Amelia's eyes fixed on the cup in her hand, on the steam that rolled from the hot tea. She gulped. It occurred to her how strange it was that when it happened – when Cora threw the figurine at Ellen's head and split open her scalp – the last thing any of them had thought to do was get in touch with their father, to seek his advice. It was stranger still that this wasn't strange at all.

"He's been out all day. We haven't seen him to tell him."

Stephen took a quiet sip of his tea. "Oh, right." He set his mug down and sat back in the kitchen chair, thinking.

"So, do you think it's possible? What I said about the Ouija board?" Amelia asked.

"I mean maybe-"

The front door opened, and Amelia turned to look through the gap of the open kitchen door to see a shadow, stopping first at the living room, before crossing the foyer and coming towards the kitchen. Daniel pushed open the door, too hard so that it banged against the wall before swinging back to close over. His face was dark, his eyes heavy with tiredness. He had muck on his new runners and dirt splashes on his legs as if he had been out for a run. He went to the stove, where Amelia had left the remnants of dinner. The cutlery in the drawer clinked together when he retrieved a fork. Without a word, he lifted the pot of pasta and ate straight from it. After only a couple of bites, he set it back down and got himself a glass of water.

"What's he doing here?" He had his back turned to them, tilting his head back and drinking his water down in one. Stephen's eyes shot to Amelia.

"Don't be so rude." Amelia eyed her brother up; he was more lugubrious than usual. "How is Ellen?" He didn't turn when he answered.

"She broke up with me." He shrugged his shoulders. Amelia gave Stephen a pitiful look. "She's fine, though." Now Daniel turned to face them both, leaning against the counter with his arms folded over his chest. "Did Cora say why she did it?"

Amelia hesitated before speaking. "Yeah, she uh... she said that Mam told her to do it."

Daniel's jaw muscles were tense. He looked away, out the dark window, his reflection staring back at him.

"Was she aiming it at me, or something?" Daniel's voice cracked on the words. Amelia felt a flutter in her chest. She shook her head. "So, she thinks she's talking to ghosts now?" No one said anything to this. It was a moment before Stephen shifted in his seat, the sound bringing their attention to him.

"This is going to sound stupid, I know," he prefaced, particularly to Daniel, before speaking again. "And I know that it's just a game, or whatever - that we all played with it - but," he paused. "What if, and it's only a suggestion," he said, his eyes on the tabletop, his hands up in a surrendering sign, "but, what you said, Amelia, what if the Ouija board is real-"

"You're joking-"

"Daniel, let him finish."

"All I'm saying is, *what if* it is real. I mean, after all, there's gotta be some spirits or *ghosts* around *this* house, if any, right? And if by some chance that we, or Cora, somehow contacted them, maybe they did tell her to do it in some way?"

"What do you mean? What happened here?" Amelia's heart was speeding. She heard Daniel scoff from behind, but he didn't interrupt this time.

"Wait, that's not why your dad brought you here?" Stephen looked genuinely perplexed. "Because of the murders here, no?"

Horrified, Amelia twisted to look at Daniel. He glanced in her direction but said nothing.

"Did you know about this?"

He only shrugged, staying mute.

"Tell me what happened." She faced Stephen again. He leaned forward, his elbows resting on the tabletop, and began.

"I don't know how much of this is true, there's always a different version being told. But this is what I heard: so, apparently like 35 years ago an American family moved into the house after it was left to them by their family, and supposedly the wife was into some weird satanic things. She practised some rituals with a local coven and things went really bad one day and they ended up contacting some pretty... nasty things, supposedly. From that point on, nothing was right with the couple. The Guards were constantly being called to the house, no one really knows why, but someone - Adam McGown - said that his granddad, Eoghan, is a part of the Gardai and that when he went there one night - when he was only on placement - that he found that Mrs Evans and her husband were standing in a circle lined with salt, saying they were being chased. It was messed up."

"Another person- Eddie Richardson - he actually lives on the other side of the lake - said that one night when he was out walking, he heard a sort of *wailing* coming from the house - like a really high-pitched scream - even from the end of the laneway!"

Amelia was rigid in her chair.

"It started getting worse when Mr Evans started coming into town and started arguing and falling out with people when they would ask how he and his wife were settling in. They ended up losing his hardware store down the town because of it- it's still boarded up because people think it's bad luck or something but it all came to a head when-"

"He killed his wife?" Daniel asked. Stephen shook his head in response, growing more animated and sitting forward, waving his hands around as he spoke.

"No, at least that's not what I heard." Stephen took a mouthful of tea before continuing, "I heard that the Guards got a call from the house phone, a fuzzy kind of call begging for help. Saying something about how it had all gone wrong, that *'it was coming for them'*." Stephen was looking directly at Amelia now, her skin tingling with apprehension. "When they showed up, they found that Mr and Mrs Evans were both hanging from the rungs in the staircase, rigor mortis already set in, making it impossible for them to have called the Guards."

"What about the baby?" Daniel asked. Amelia gulped, wondering how much of the story Daniel knew.

"So, you have heard this before?"

"A version of it, yeah. What happened to the baby?" he asked, more pointedly. Stephen met Amelia's wide gaze and considered his next words. When he said them, however, he was looking at Daniel.

"They didn't find her."

Amelia's heart threatened to stop. She felt the air come out of her. Her palms were slick with sweat, her mouth going dry.

"That sounds just as far-fetched as the other version; how do babies go missing? How do dead people ring the Guards? It sounds like bullshit to me." Daniel was adamant in his opinion and seemed like he might continue with it if they hadn't been interrupted. Amelia startled when her father appeared in the doorway, his laptop bag over his shoulder and a thick folio in his arms.

"Hey guys, how's it going? Did you sort you and your sisters for food, Daniel? Oh, Stephen, how are you? Good to see you." His words were blurring together. Deaf to the atmosphere of the room, Mark kissed Amelia atop her head and collected a glass of water for himself, spilling some of the water down his shirt and onto the floor.

"Did you drive?" Daniel asked, watching his father with a tightened jaw. Mark took a second to answer, eyeing Daniel up, looking like a scolded child before he shook his head.

"No. I got a taxi." He sniffed at the leftovers in the pot before pushing it aside, smiling at them all, the hairs of his beard were shiny with the water he had spilled down his front. Amelia turned in her seat and watched as Daniel's jaw clenched once more. "Where's Ellen, Daniel?"

"At home." Daniel stalked from the room, disappearing into the shadows of the foyer and up the stairs... *the stairs*. Amelia fought hard to get the image from her mind.

"What happened?" Mark asked, watching after Daniel. Amelia, unsure if Daniel would appreciate her telling their father about the day's events, decided to shrug. "Right, well, I'm off to bed. You okay getting home tonight, Stephen?" Stephen bobbed his head in response and Mark headed back out of the room.

"I should probably get going."

Amelia felt a weird shiver shake her at the realisation that she would be alone now. "You don't want to stay?"

"I think that's a bad idea- especially after the last time. I think Daniel is starting to warm to me." He smiled as he said it, standing and collecting his jacket.

"Okay," Amelia murmured, and walked him to the door, wondering if there was a way for her to ask him to tuck her into bed without sounding laughable or infantile. If she were at home, in her own house, and had been told such a story, or watched a particularly frightening movie, she would simply stick on a light-hearted comedy to lighten her mood. Here, however, she was unable to do that, stuck with only her thoughts, and worse – imagination - for night-time entertainment.

"I hope I didn't freak you out. I mean it's all just gossip, and people like to exaggerate things, don't they?" She nodded, holding the door open for him. The fog was thick and ominous, almost blinding with its density.

"Safe home." He leaned over and kissed her on the lips, the warmth of his mouth the only sunshine in the choking fog.

"Thanks. Goodnight, I'll see you tomorrow." With that, she shut the door over and turned to face the darkness. A feeling of unease came over her, and Amelia suddenly became intensely aware of herself, as though she were being watched. Her skin prickled, her heart began to race and an urge to run away at full speed, came upon her. An uncanny alarm in her head told her she was not entirely alone here. Frozen in place, she imagined the something that might be with her as her fear spiked, her mind toiling with the idea of a creeping hand reaching over her shoulder, or a breath touching the nape of her neck.

She scurried to the wall where she felt for the light switch and eagerly twisted the dial. A couple of seconds later, she was no longer in complete darkness, but the shadows were still a threatening abyss.

She ran for the stairs and took to them like a rat scurrying up a drainpipe, away from predators. She imagined a hand, outstretched, grabbing her by the ankle and dragging her down.

She did not turn around.

Chapter 16

Amelia tossed and turned all night. She dreamt vivid dreams of satanic rituals and of rooms filled with thick fog where she watched women huddled in a circle, bowing to lit candles, and of shadowy monsters, lurking at the bottom of the winding staircase, crouched, and waiting to reach out. The image of such a monster came to a terrifying climax when it sat, grinning, under the swaying feet of Mr and Mrs Evans, who hung by the neck from the rungs of the twisting banisters. The squatting creature was cradling a crying baby as it glared at Amelia before pulling its swaddling over the baby's face, muffling its cries as they grew in intensity and fear. Amelia was crying, reaching her hand out to the creature, but did not move towards it out of terror, and watched as the Demon showed its forked tongue before quietening the baby for good with its firm grip. It tilted its head towards Amelia, an invitation of a challenge, but when she didn't attempt to move, it floated backwards, disappearing into the shadows, and taking the silent infant with it.

Amelia awoke panting, her entire body drenched in sweat, and unnerved further to find the lamp beside her, which she had left alight, had been turned out. Moonlight crept through her window, its pale glow a lonely reminder that like the moon, Amelia too, was awake and solitary while others slept. She untangled herself from her blankets and set her face in her hands, feeling her wet skin. She caught her breath and wiped at her face, checking her wristwatch: 2.37 am. It would be a couple of hours yet before the sun was set to rise. She sat up in her bed, listening to her heartbeat, and tried to banish the residual images that flashed across her eyelids each time she shut them.

She hadn't had this many nightmares in a long time, nor had any as unsettling before, ever. She feared that they would only increase in both ardency and frequency until she was driven insane, and the pit in her stomach sank deeper.

The moon, she realised then, had pierced the fog outside. With the hopes of clearing her mind, she stood and went to the window. Immediately upon leaving the warmth of her bed, Amelia noticed the drop in temperature and walked across the wood on her tip-toes to avoid the cool floor. At the window, she peered out; the fog had not fully dispersed, however, it had settled on the ground, like a blanket atop the soil and stones. From her room, you could see nothing but the trees of the forest and the stars in the sky, with the moon's face glaring down at her. Other than that, all she could see of the house was the railing of the veranda which was cast in darkness with the lamps turned out. She wondered how one came to the conclusion of wanting to live a life in a house like this; away from everyone. It was a daunting thought; to be so far away from help. Staring at the trees in the dark made her long for home with an ache in her heart.

Home is where the heart is.

The ache was homesickness, but even when she was home- where all of her things were, where she had been raised, where she had fond memories enough to fill a library, there was still a dull ache of homesickness in her chest.

Amelia remembered the flashing lights outside her bedroom window when they came to give the news of her mother, and how as they spoke, she felt as if she were understanding less of what they said; their words blurring together as if she were in a pool and her ears were filling with water, her grief drowning her. It had felt like going into anaphylactic shock after being stung by a bee, her throat closing so she couldn't breathe. She was still waiting for that epi-pen. What was left behind felt like her guts had been removed, leaving only an empty space that seemed to grow larger with the passing time.

A distant sound pulled her attention from the window. A quiet banging somewhere in the hall- similar to the one she often hears in her room. She listened, straining her ears, not noticing the cold floor when her feet went flat against it as the noise neared. She stayed by the window, not wanting to move, and tried to discern if it was the same sound as before, in case she needed to wake her father. It continued on, nearing her steadily, the sound getting a little louder, reaching a crescendo outside her door. She waited for it to pass, for the noise to continue down the hall, but it stayed there as if knowing she was standing on the other side and listening.

When it stopped, Amelia exhaled, her chest tight from holding her breath. She began to breathe normally and walked back to her bed, making a mental note to tell her father of the noisy pipes. When she had tucked the blanket up to her chin, her blood turned icy as the muffled, but quite tangible steps, started on the landing. They were slow at first, as though someone was taking a casual, leisurely stroll in a park. They passed Amelia's door, without falter, and continued on, making her wonder if it was simply Cora sleep-walking her way towards the bathroom, but when they turned back, walking at a slightly faster pace, she knew that it could not be her younger sister.

Images of masked burglars flooded her mind, causing hectic thoughts to panic her, but, she soon came to justify: they had begun on the landing. She waited, her heart in her throat, as the steps passed by her door again and turned to walk back the way they had come. Her father, perhaps, pacing through his thoughts? She had never heard him up before, though.

The steps continued on, speeding up going in one direction, and slowing down again when going the other.

Then, running.

It sounded as though somebody was sprinting back at forth along the hallway.

Tears sprung from Amelia's eyes and rolled down her cheeks. Her staggered breath was caught in her throat. She barely realised what she was doing until she felt the hard switch of the lamp under her fingers. Light burst from the lamp.

The running came to a sudden stop. Outside her door.

Amelia was trembling. What she saw next was something she was certain would stick with her for the rest of her life; there was a shadow under her door. It stood, hovering there. Amelia felt nauseous when she spotted it. She felt her blood turn cold when she heard a faint whisper through the door.

'... *Amelia...*'

She barely recognised her own name. It sounded strange- as if the letters were not sounded out properly.

'...*Amelia...*'

It was more of a hiss than a word, contorted so that she couldn't hear the 'l'.

She didn't keep track of how long the shadow stood there, but when it retreated, disappearing - along with the footsteps - Amelia felt a shaky sense of relief wash over her, a heavy weight had been lifted off of her chest and she could breathe again.

It took her quite some time before she garnered enough courage to stand, her legs shaky, and approach the door. With a hand that still shook, and a heart beating too fast, she slowly turned the door handle and opened it. She gasped when she spotted the ugly little doll on the floor outside her bedroom, and recoiled from it at first, expecting some monster to jump out at her. When none did, she reached down and plucked the doll from the carpet, using only two fingers, and twirled it around in the dim glow of her lamp. It was old and tattered, with a torn dress and a droopy eye that looked downwards instead of straight ahead. Its hair was cut short and spiked out in different directions. Without hesitation, she put the doll down and retreated into her room, closing over her door.

She left her lamp on.

———

Ready for a new day, a day closer to the end of this ridiculously shitty summer, Daniel finished his bowl of porridge and was about to head out for another day on the trail – alone - when Amelia slammed the box of Frosties onto the counter and rounded on him, looking wild and angry. Instinctively, he took a step back.

"STOP taking *my* cereal, Daniel! If you want to eat something with flavour, you should've asked dad to get you something other than shredded cardboard for breakfast!" Amelia huffed, glaring at him.

"That wasn't me," he shrugged, kneeling to tie his laces up. Did *no one* consider that *he* did the shopping? If he wanted shite food, he would pick it up for himself. Just then, Cora wandered in, spotting him, and dipping her head in a bow without a word.

"It *was* you. Cora can't reach it, and Dad doesn't eat it. And STOP trying to scare me, too! I know that is you at night."

Daniel stood and began stretching out his limbs.

"Haven't got a clue what you're talking about. Maybe it was the ghost you and Stephen keep talking about that ate your cereal?"

"Oh, shut up," Amelia growled, turning, and sticking her hand into the box. "When are you moving out, again?"

"Oh, not soon enough," he replied under his breath and went to shake out his legs. He had overheard Amelia and Stephen talking about that stupid story again when he had visited her yesterday evening. No wonder Amelia couldn't sleep in the dark.

Cora pushed her cereal around with her spoon. Daniel frowned before sliding a chair out and sitting next to her. "Hey, what's wrong?" Cora shrugged, not lifting her head. "Cora?" Amelia sat down opposite him, but said nothing, picking at her cereal with her fingers but did not eat any.

"Are you going to be running with... Ellen...?" Cora's words were mumbled together so that Daniel had to lean in closer to hear them.

"No. You know I haven't been running with Ellen for a couple of days, C." He tightened his laces some more. "I don't think Ellen will be hanging out with us anymore," Daniel said, coolly- he was over the whole thing now, just ready to get through the last of their stay here and then get home where he can begin to forget this whole season.

"But... I like her..." A tear fell into her bowl. Daniel sat back in his chair, meeting Amelia's curious gaze as she dropped the cereal she was playing with back in her bowl.

"Well, that's what happens when you throw shit at people's heads. They don't particularly like you after that."

"Daniel!"

"I'm sorry," Cora cried. Daniel took a moment to breathe. Maybe he wasn't over it after all.

"Listen, I liked Ellen too, but sometimes shit happens." His motto.

"Can't we say sorry?" Cora looked up at Daniel from under her lashes. "Please?"

Daniel sat, tapping his foot, thinking. He wouldn't mind seeing Ellen again.

"I guess we can try again. But you've to promise to not throw anything else at her head, deal?" Cora nodded her head vigorously. "Okay, fine."

"What are you going to say?" Amelia was sceptical, watching him with that gloating expression she always had when he did something she didn't approve of or looked down on. Daniel shrugged, glancing around the kitchen for inspiration, and stood. He reached into the cupboard and slipped the clear bottle into the waistband of his shorts and covered it with his t-shirt.

"Sometimes you must think beyond words, Amelia. I bet you don't have a pretentious saying for that in one of your journal scribbles." She rolled her eyes at him and went back to playing with her cereal.

"Dad is going to notice that's missing."

"Yeah? And what is he going to do about it? Bring me away from civilisation? Oh, wait."

"You're an idiot-"

"Hey, hey, hey, no name calling in this house." Mark came through the door, clutching his laptop bag and chewing on a piece of toast. He set his plate down. "You feeling okay, pet? You look tired." With his father's entrance his cue to leave, Daniel left backwards so that the bulge in his waistband could not be seen.

"Can I talk to you, Dad?"

"Sure, pet-"

Outside the sun was warming the garden, drying the moisture another foggy night had left behind. Daniel made his way to the side of the house, where the bins were kept, and balanced the shoulder of vodka there while he knelt and dug around in the dirt until he found the flask he had stashed.

"Good morning, beautiful," he said, jumping back up and twisting the cap of the vodka off with his teeth and spitting it out onto the ground before doing the same with the flask. He poured it carefully, not letting a single drop escape the neck. When he finished, he collected both lids and tightened them, noticing now the cat food pebbles that had been scattered around. He began kicking them close together, creating a mound by the food bin and made a fleeting mental note to come back and clean them before any more strays decided to live with them. When he was done, he placed the vodka bottle, which was near empty now, in the space behind the bin and tucked the smaller square flask into his waistband. Without another thought about it or the loose cat food, Daniel started into a jog towards the forest trail.

The study was in the belly of the house; closed in on all four sides by adjoining rooms, there were no windows. It was crammed with boxes overflowing with papers and was covered in a thick layer of dust which had even coated the dustsheets that were covering the furniture when they arrived at the beginning of summer. Now, the chandelier still had the grey deposits, but the desk and giant armchair that accompanied it had been wiped down for use. Mark had filled the remainder of the floor space with boxes of his own so that a narrow gully was the only pathway from the door to the desk.

When he had happened upon the study, he initially imagined himself behind the oak desk, and finishing his novel there in that room, where melancholy seeped from the pores of the house and the walls seemed to edge slowly closer to you so that claustrophobia strangled you before you noticed.

"Do you believe in the things you write about?" the reporter would ask from across the desk, shifting uncomfortably whilst imagining the terrible things he wrote to have happened there. He would sit, his hands linked together on the cold, oak antique table, and shrug, relishing in their unease.

"I believe in horror," he would say.

"So, you believe in ghosts and monsters?"

"Those are two very different things."

But as all things go, he spent very little time here, using it more for storage of his research papers and first drafts than anything else. He found that instead of here, he mostly spent time in the local coffee shop in the beginning, and now he would sit in the dark pubs; becoming a fly on the wall was the best thing to do to get a real picture of the locals, of his characters - to write, you must first know.

It was difficult to write in a house full of children - he needed peace, he needed space, and he needed his muse to stay as horrifyingly gruesome in his mind as he could manage to keep it. To terrify his readers, he first must become terrified himself.

"What can I do for you, Amelia?" He was flicking through a rough draft of his manuscript. It was decorated with red lines and colourful highlights. Amelia was standing on the other side of the desk, in the narrow space of the alley. She was pale, with dark bags under her eyes. Suffering again from anaemia, perhaps. Mark made a small note to ask Daniel to sort out a doctor's appointment for his sister on his notepad - and for himself to make a wide enough gap on the other side of the desk so that a chair might fit for interviews.

"Have you read the chapters I left for you?" Amelia tugged her jumper sleeves over her hands, her fingers fidgeting with the papers on his desk. "Honey, be careful with those." Her hands stilled over the papers.

"Sorry."

"That's okay, what's up, pet?" Amelia was reluctant to speak, her eyes darting around the room, looking at anything but Mark. "Are you okay?"

"Dad, how would you know if a house was actually haunted?"

"Metaphorically speaking, aren't all houses haunted in one way or another?" Amelia chewed her lip. Mark checked his watch – the one he had bought after he sold his first novel to his publisher – he was running late for a coffee date with a local who claimed to have heard a banshee the night before the house's previous occupants'… untimely departure. He sucked air between his teeth. "I suppose that it just depends on what you consider haunted."

"Like, with harmful spirits. Angry spirits."

Mark took a moment to answer her. "I imagine that it would start with a sense of unease, an uncanniness in the atmosphere, even. Typically, people say that it progresses from there. But, honey, you know that these things are rarely- if ever- real. Ghosts can't hurt us."

"But, if they could, and we were being haunted, you would take us away from it, wouldn't you?" Her eyes were glassy. He frowned.

"Amelia, are you okay?"

"Please, Dad, just tell me, would you?" There was a pregnant pause left hanging between them.

"Honey, you know I'd never put you guys in danger. What's wrong?"

"It's just... Dad, it's this house." Her bottom lip was trembling, her voice shaking. She waited, cleared her throat, and composed herself as Mark waited for her to go on. "I just *feel* something here, all the time. And the sounds - they wake me up. I keep hearing footsteps outside my room at night."

Mark unfolded his arms and sat forward in the seat, leaning his forearms on the desk.

"It is probably Daniel going to the bathroom, Amelia."

"No, Dad, I don't think it is. And... I *know* what happened here. Stephen told me." Mark scratched the underside of his chin; his beard had grown long and unruly. He picked up a pen and scribbled a note on his pad as a reminder to get to a barber's soon for a trim.

"And what did Stephen tell you?" Amelia's eyes followed the pen's movement, like a hawk staring at its prey. She began to retell the story. Beside his note on the barber's, Mark scribbled Stephen's name. He was always getting more and more impressed with his kids' stories. Amelia was her father's daughter, he thought proudly.

"I think I can feel whatever presence that was here then, now. Especially since Cora has been playing with that Ouija board she found."

"Can you tell me exactly how you feel when you feel as though you are being watched? Like, explain how it begins- in your own words." He was leaning over his pad of paper, now, his pen moving furiously across the page, making notes and annotations on their conversation thus far. When Amelia didn't speak, he tilted his head up to look at her. She was staring, unblinking, at his notepad. She was rigid, her mouth in a tight line to stop her moving lip, but her chin shook. She must be feeling quite ill, Mark surmised and took to underlining his previous note on the call to the doctor. *What date is it? Is it that time of the month again?*

"I actually... I... never mind." Without saying anything else, she turned, knocking in to and toppling over a box of papers, and went hurriedly towards the door.

Skittish. Anxious. Tired. Nervous. Irritable. Pale. Cold.

Mark wrote the words at the end of the page as his daughter left the room before signing his own name at the bottom. He needed to practise his signature.

Chapter 17

Daniel knocked a nursery rhyme on the freshly painted doorframe. He took a step back, the forest swaying gently behind him. There was a shadowy figure behind the frosted glass and Daniel set his hand on the flask in the waistband of his shorts, ready to reveal it. A moment later, the door lock clicked open and the door swung inwards. Ellen stood before him. When she met his eyes, she hesitated, but did not close it over again and instead leaned against the doorframe. *Not a bad sign*, Daniel thought. Her forehead, where the figurine had connected with her scalp, was no longer red and swollen, but still had the white stitches peeking past her hairline. She tilted her head sideways, expectantly.

"Hey."

"Hey. What are you doing here?" She checked over her shoulder and turned back to him.

"You didn't show up for our run." One of Ellen's brows rose without humour. Daniel shrugged, slipping his hands into the pockets of his shorts. "I wanted to check on you- to see how you were doing and if you were feeling alright. And to say sorry, again." Ellen took a deep breath and folded her arms. She stared into the trees of the forest as if contemplating her response.

"Thanks. I'm sorry, too. I was pretty upset that night. I guess I was just taking it out on you." She chewed her lips, her eyes following his hands as he reached around and revealed the flask. He twisted the cap and extended it out to her. With a coy smile, she took it and sniffed at the neck.

"An olive branch," he told her. She took a sip of the vodka, wincing as it burned at her throat, and handed it back to him. "Does this mean you accept my apology?" She didn't answer immediately, just stared at him as a smile tugged the edge of her mouth upwards. When she nodded, a slow, reluctant nod, Daniel grinned and stepped closer to her. He leaned down and pressed his mouth on hers. She didn't reject him and instead pulled him closer to her where their kiss became something more, something urgent and necessary, but when Daniel took her by the waist and stepped through the door, he felt her pull away from him and press her hands against his chest. He retreated a step.

"You can't come in. I'm babysitting," she told him, smiling. Daniel's brows furrowed, confused.

"Babysitting? Who?"

"My sister."

"You have a sister?" Ellen scoffed theatrically and pressed against his chest again until the threshold of the door separated them.

"Maybe if you ever listened to me-"

"Come on, don't be like that. I was just kidding- I think that statue hit me in the head first and then bounced to you. It must've made me forget..." he teased as Ellen shook her head and rolled her eyes. "How old is she?"

"Six."

"Perfect, let's get Cora and her and we can all go get some ice cream or something." Ellen's eyes narrowed, her lips a tight line, but nodded in the end.

There was no such thing as an ice cream parlour, and Daniel doubted if they even had an ice cream van in the town, so he brought them to the garage where they were served 99's by a grey-haired woman. Cora and Edel were becoming fast friends and busied themselves by tossing stones into the water of the lake.

The town lake spanned for several kilometres in each direction. It was the heart of the town, the main attraction, which, to Daniel, put into perspective just how shit the town actually was. If a body of water is the only interesting thing in the place, then it is not an interesting place to be. No wonder they made up stories about haunted houses.

The lake was dead, besides from a couple of joggers and them, reaffirming just how tired the whole town was that not even the most popular location was busy on a sunny day in summer.

Daniel and Ellen were seated on a blanket that he had found in the boot of Mark's Volvo, which, like his children, he seemed to have abandoned for the summer for the newer rental he had organised when they got here. They sat watching the two girls as they finished their cones.

"You look like your sister," Daniel said.

"No I don't."

"Wow, you're really making me work for this, aren't ya'."

"Uh-huh." Ellen was doing her best to not smile. "Amelia and Cora are very similar, but you look different." Daniel nodded and wiped the dribble of ice cream off his hand and onto the blanket.

"Yeah, I look more like Mam."

"I don't know, I can see how you look like your dad with certain expressions." Daniel's brows rose.

"That's probably because you've never seen Mam. I don't look like Mark, everyone says I look like her." There was a finality in his tone, followed by a long pause. Daniel could feel her eyes on his face as he stared across the water. He knew what she would ask when she spoke next.

"What happened to your mam?" Daniel didn't go to answer straight away. Reason number five hundred why he missed home: no one asked him questions like this, they already knew the answers. Whether they were right or wrong, it didn't matter, he didn't have to correct them if they never spoke to him about it. He watched the sun bounce on the water's facade, its reflection shimmering when the stones broke the surface.

"She eh… she died. Yeah, it was a car accident last year. Her car – well Mark's – that is… was… Mam's," Daniel motioned towards the car behind them, "Mark's was totalled by a drunk driver in a van." Daniel's breathing was uneven, like when you realise that you are breathing and suddenly forget how to do it naturally, unable to find the rhythm as his foot tapped against the stones. He ran his tongue over his teeth and tilted his head to the sky. The trees cast shade over them, but Daniel still used his palm as a visor to protect his sight when he stared into the clouds. His stomach tensed as if he were holding a heavy boulder on it, making it difficult to function, to breathe.

"Shit. I didn't realise. Did anything happen to the driver?"

Daniel's breath eased when Cora scurried towards him, waddling from side to side, her face scrunched up. He got to his feet, the conversation ending before they could discuss the slap on the wrist that the driver got in comparison to what had happened to his mam.

"Daniel, I need to pee!"

"You're in a lake, the whole thing is a toilet."

"No! I need to go!" Daniel glanced at Ellen and shrugged. She bent her legs under her and got to her feet. She started folding the blanket up.

"Alright, let's go. Do you mind if I swing by the house and drop her off first before we head back to yours?" Ellen was reluctant. She had warned Daniel that in no uncertain circumstances was she going to take a step inside the house again. She looked at Cora, dancing on the spot, and sighed. She bobbed her head in agreement.

Buckled and belted into car seats, Cora and Edel chatted in a language of their own. Daniel felt Ellen's glances every so often, but she did not press him on their previous conversation.

"I had a cat, but she's missing now," Cora told Edel. "Her name is Susan."

"Susan is a boy, Cora. And he is probably gone home," Daniel interrupted the conversation, looking in the rear-view mirror to spy Cora making a face. He stuck his tongue out at her.

"Girls can be boys too, you know." Daniel shook his head.

"Sure they can." He said nothing more, choosing instead to flick through the radio stations. There was only static noise sounding through the speakers. You couldn't even get a radio signal out here. Great. He wondered then, where had the cat gone? He hadn't seen the little bastard in a while and wondered perhaps if he had lost a fight to a forest creature on one of his night adventures; after all, he was being fed and even had a damn bed in the house. Cats may not be the most loyal of creatures, but they weren't dumb, either.

"I haven't seen my friend in a while," Edel said. "I think they got lost when they were at the lake." Daniel turned to look at Ellen who mouthed 'milk carton kid' to him. Taken aback, Daniel faced the road and said nothing else on the drive back, only listened as Edel and Cora moved quickly onto the topic of fruit, and why oranges are the best.

Her father's book sat on the table in the basement. On the cover there was a masked figure, the façade wasted in blurred colours being dragged towards the bottom margin. It was his latest release, focused on the house they had stayed in last summer, wherein a man had been tortured by his teenage children after they had been possessed by a dark force that had been terrorising the family with flying chairs and slamming doors. It was a thrilling read that touched on teenage angst and ongoing abuse within the family. It had soared to the top of the charts last October.

Amelia remembered that house well. It had been a bungalow on a country road, in the middle of nowhere, with not a single radiator installed. It was old, cramped, and full of mildew. The trees around it had been chopped down, rumoured to have been attacking the walls of the house when an exorcist that been introduced to rid the family of the threat. It had been eerie, desolate, and Amelia had felt completely comfortable there, in comparison to how she felt in this house.

Things had been different then, she supposed. It hadn't just been her and the others. Her mother had been there, too. Perhaps, Amelia thought to herself, that was the difference now; she was alone. It was her… and them, and maybe it always had been, but her Mam had blurred the edges, been the buffer so that Amelia felt a part of something, of family. Now, she felt she was apart from it. Take today, she thought, she was by herself, expected to be alone even here, in this place.

Beside the newest release, the loose pages of her father's most recent draft were stacked with annotations poking out the sides. The pages were glaringly white in the cold fluorescent light. It had been days since Amelia had picked it up to read. The pages taunted her, daring her to read through them, to read about the horrors that happened in the house she was in.

She had never felt like this before.

Nothing quelled her night-time worries. No number of blankets or thick hoodies, or burning fires warmed her bones. Something had wriggled itself into her mind and burrowed deep into her brain and refused to leave even with rational thoughts and explanations pushing at it. It only clawed deeper, clung more determinedly in an effort to terrify her. And it was winning.

The feeling was of oppression, of aimless horror, or gasping for air when something invisible was pressing on her chest. She felt watched, felt the hair on her neck rise as she walked alone through the house, walking carefully to avoid making a sound in case she provoked whatever it was that watched her to come forth from the shadows. She was becoming sick; deluded. She could no longer muster an appetite. Dread filled her to her core when she thought of nightfall and if she would hear her name whispered to her as she lay in her bed.

A creak from the floor above made her start. She turned, slowly, in her chair to look at the dark stairwell, praying in her mind that she would not see a figure poking its horrible, tilting head down at her, a wide-eyed smirk on an ugly face. When the light appeared at the top of the stairs from the opening door, Amelia thought she might pass out. It was only a sliver, a shard, even, of blonde light breaking through the darkness and coming to join the white light of the overhead fluorescents, not malignant in nature but horrifying here. She imagined a creature crawling on all fours down the stairs, backwards, its face rotating in stunted circles. Its arms would be bent backwards, its waist contorted and facing downwards so that the torso was twisted. It would breathe through its mouth, its breath catching on the lump in its throat, whistling through the gaps in its broken teeth, so that it made gurgling sounds. Its lids would be peeled back from the eyes, so it was forever watching.

No movement, nor sound, nor any creature followed this noise.

Daniel, maybe home early with Cora. This idea gave her some fleeting comfort; however, it was only temporary as footsteps from above sunk fear deeper into her stomach.

They wouldn't be home for some time, Daniel telling her to sort dinner for herself when he collected Cora. She had felt an inkling of resentment when he took Cora out and left her here, to be left alone in the house, as if he had left her to thread water in a tumultuous sea or to wade through treacherous waters that tried to engulf her, but the idea of him coming back was like being thrown a buoy ring.

Not wanting to move but knowing that she definitely didn't want to be waiting there to be found, Amelia got to her feet, her heart pounding, her breathing the only sound to her ears. She crossed the basement, and stalled at the foot of the stairs, afraid to round the corner in anticipation of what she might see. Her hands shook by her sides; she tried to still them and couldn't. She took a step and went to the foot of the stairs. She didn't look to the top but faced down, the light at the top falling on her now like a vail. Amelia took the stairs slowly, but steadily. She held her breath until she got to the top and was blocking the light, afraid that if she exhaled her nerve would be lost with her breath. As she stood there, face down, she imagined a gruesome eye staring at her through that gap in the door, watching her. When she felt ready, she pushed lightly against the door. The hinges cried an unnerving scream.

The foyer was empty.

Silence surrounded her.

She was alone.

She looked to the front door then, her mind fighting against being consumed by horror, but the door was firmly closed, the colourful glass panes dull as the sunshine disappeared to be replaced by encroaching rain clouds. To her right, the kitchen door was also closed, and then across the foyer, the living room's double doors stood sentinel. The other rooms - the study and library, were too far from the basement for a draft to interfere.

Sounds from upstairs alerted her. It sounded like boxes being dragged along the floor. She listened, barely able to concentrate, her fear was so intense, and edged towards the winding stairs. She stood at the bottom, her hand resting on the balustrade, and when she fought past the tightening in her chest, the lump in her throat, she called out, "Daniel...?" Her voice was low, but the movement above stopped suddenly. Whoever- or *whatever*- was up there, had heard her.

A sinking feeling in Amelia's gut told her she had made a grave error in calling out. Her face drained of blood and her whole body shivered. She heard footsteps, like the ones at night, coming towards her and she prepared herself for what she might face.

When the noise happened, it sounded like it was inside Amelia, inside her body, her bones, her head. It sounded like it was a part of her. It was guttural. It was grotesque and it was loud. It was a scream that she had only ever read about. There was a loud BANG that followed, and Amelia nearly collapsed when she heard the running steps.

She didn't wait to see what caused them.

Too afraid to scream herself, Amelia bolted for the door, not looking behind her to see if she was being followed. She slammed the door shut, the old glass in the door trembling as it bounced against the frame before swinging open again, and she rushed down the porch steps, tripping on the way and scrambling forwards, the dirt and stones scraping at her skin.

Tears sprung from her eyes; her entire body was shaking. She could go no further. She curled her arms around her knees and lay there, sobbing.

She could go no further.

———

When Daniel pulled into the driveway, he was too busy looking back at Cora and Edel, tickling them with his left arm, to notice that the door to the house was wide open and that his other sister was lying in a ball at the foot of the porch steps. Ellen tugged on his arm, sitting forward in her seat, and already taking her seatbelt off. Daniel twisted in his seat, his smile fading as Ellen reached for the door handle of the still-moving car.

"Daniel, stop! Stop!" The car tyres skidded in the stones. The passenger side door shot open and Ellen sprinted across the drive to kneel next to the trembling ball of fabric. It was only then that Daniel realised that it was Amelia who lay, huddling her knees to her chest, on the ground.

"Stay here," he said, and unbolted himself from his buckle. His door flung open, the hinges clinging to the heavy arm of the door. He ran, almost slipping on the gravel, and went to the porch. Ellen had taken Amelia by the arm and helped her to stand. Her face was void of colour, apart from her reddened eyes. Her palms had been cut and were bleeding. When she saw Daniel, she almost collapsed into his arms. He caught her and held her head against his shoulder. Ellen stared at him in shock, her head shaking from side to side. From behind, another of the car doors opened.

"Amelia, what happened? Are you okay?" Amelia was shaking her head. Ellen set her hand onto her shoulder and squeezed it. Her eyes drifted down to Daniel's side then. Daniel twisted his neck as much as he could and spotted Cora there.

"Go back to the car, Cora," Daniel told her, firmly.

"But I still need to go," she whined, bouncing from foot to foot. "Is Amelia okay?"

"Ellen, can you bring Cora to the car. Cora, go. Now." Cora cried out but did as she was told and allowed for Ellen to lead her back to the jeep. "Amelia, tell me what happened." Amelia rubbed her face against his chest, leaving wet streaks across the fabric, and leaned back.

"There's something in there! Something... inside!" Daniel's brow's stitched together. She looked wild, he noted; her hair was coming out in messy strands, her eyes were unfocused and blurry with un-spilled tears. There were red marks down her face from where she had rubbed the skin with her bloody hands.

"What do you mean? Was there someone in there?" Daniel demanded, taking her by the shoulders and steadying her. He shook her when she didn't look at him. "Amelia- is there someone in the house?" Amelia's gaze settled on him. She nodded. Daniel had no time to react.

"Is it Mam? Is she bringing me my gift?" Cora shouted from the car. She was smiling a brilliant smile, all concerns over her bladder forgotten. She ducked under Ellen's arms and ran for the house, crawling up the steps like an excited puppy. When Daniel let Amelia go, he was afraid she might fall again, however, she stayed standing, and more than that, she pushed past Daniel and ran after Cora, yelling.

"Cora, wait! No! Come back!"

Ellen didn't go after them, instead stayed outside, looking helplessly after them. She caught Daniel's eye and stared at him apologetically. He turned, going after his sisters.

He took the twisting stairs two at a time, landing on the creaking set near the top, then onto the landing where he watched the wispy strands of hair disappear through Cora's bedroom door. There was a cry of panic and Daniel lunged to the other end of the hall, using the doorframe to fling himself around the bend and into the room. Cora was crouched on the floor, smiling a huge grin, and holding a ragged-looking doll in her two hands, like she held Simba up to show the pride. Beside her, the Ouija board was poking out from under her bed. Amelia was standing over her sister, her two hands held over her mouth, her eyes watering.

"What's wrong?" Daniel went to his sisters and bent next to Cora. She only stared at the doll, barely noticing him there. "Did you give her this? It's disgusting," Daniel said, examining the dirty toy. Its hair had been cropped short and it had seen better days.

"No! That's the one that was outside my door before. I thought you had left it there!" A thudding sound from downstairs grabbed his attention then and Daniel was on his feet, heading into the hallway. He glanced down the hall, towards Mark's room. Through the window, the afternoon was slipping into the evening, dragging the last of the sunny day with it. It looked as though it might begin raining.

Daniel walked along the centre of the floor, knowing that it made the least amount of sound there, and stopped outside Amelia's room. He pushed open the door and careened his neck; it was empty. The bathroom was next. He pushed open the wide door. The claw-footed bath was large enough to hide in. He checked it, and the tight shower, and found nothing.

His bedroom was just as he had left it, the blankets tossed to one side of his bed, his runners paired neatly at the foot of his wardrobe.

As he walked down the stairs, he peered over either banister, checking for movements, but found none. Ellen was standing in the doorway, keeping her promise to never enter the house again, but waiting eagerly for his return. When she saw him, he pressed his finger to his lips and went to the living room. He pressed firmly on the handle and pushed the door inwards. Only silence and shadows awaited him. He stepped in and felt a cool breeze rush past him, making his skin prickle. He took another step and went to circle the room, checking beneath the couches, behind the curtains, and taking a poker from the fireplace in his hands. He hesitated when he came to the carved figure in the wall, wondering why anyone would ever think to have something as horrible as that carved permanently into their house wall. Back out in the foyer, he headed for the basement. As he passed the stairs, an image presented itself unexpectedly in his mind; two hanging bodies from the banisters. He paused in his search and looked up at the dark railings of the stairs before shaking his head and continuing on.

The basement stairs were dark. He moved down them quickly, knowing that the element of surprise would be on his side if he came across an intruder down here. What he found, however, was just the old, musty furniture and scattered pages on the floor. The kitchen offered no sign of disturbance, leaving only the study and the library to check. He started with the study, the door barely opening against all of the piled boxes. As soon as he stepped into the dark room, it was evident that an intruder would have no room to hide in the cramped space. He shut the door over and went to the library. Daniel stood at the door, his hand ready on the handle, his other clutching the fire-poker in anticipation. He could feel his blood hot in his veins, his heart pounding in his chest; if he found an intruder inside then the intruder would not be leaving whole.

The door opened and Daniel was in near darkness, with dusk fast approaching and no working light in the room. He rushed in, swinging his weapon, but cut only air. His chest was heaving, his muscles rearing to go. He felt almost disappointed when the room was found empty. He turned on the spot, going in circles as if he might find someone in the shadows around him.

But he was alone.

A noise, like scratching, sounded, and Daniel listened out, trying to find the source. He felt that cool breeze again, and this time he shrugged his shoulders as if trying to shrug off a blanket. An eerie sense of having someone watch you through a window irked him, and he spun to check the window, almost sure he would see someone peering in at him, mocking him as if to say *'Hah! I got away'*, but only dark clouds forming above the forest stared down at him. He felt a little light-headed and reached out to the closest shelf to steady himself.

Sktch... sktch... sktch...

There it was again, that sound of scratching.

An idea occurred to Daniel and he felt along the bookcase until his fingers found the ridge in the shelves. He pulled it. The alcove behind the shelves was just as empty as before, with a piled mess of splintered and split wood at the bottom from Daniel's attempt to break through. Among the mess, however, there were little brown stones... no...pebbles. Kibble, even. He knelt, squinting in the dark, and picked up one of the pieces. He felt it in his hands, curious. He set the poker down and shifted so he was laying on his stomach. If he had a torch he would have been able to see, but for now, he just stretched his hand through the hole in the wall and ran it along the floor and wall. His fingers grazed something wet and his stomach turned as images of dead mice or badgers... or the cat... crossed his mind. His skin crawled when he felt the warm, slimy sensation of being licked. Then there was movement behind the wall, and he jerked back, bouncing to his feet. Then, out from the hole came a ball of black fur.

The cat. Alive.

"You have a fat tongue." Daniel let out a heavy sigh and picked the cat up. "You were nearly skewered," he said, rubbing the cat's back. He kicked over the bookshelf door, and left the room, feeling considerably lighter. The fire poker was left behind.

Daniel passed Ellen, showing her the cat as if it were a prize, and rolling his eyes. Ellen, however, did not look assured by this and turned to sit on the steps. He carried the cat upstairs, where he heard Cora's soothing tone to Amelia, and he smiled. When he entered, Amelia jumped up from where she sat on the edge of the bed, eager for answers. Cora, however, was happy to play with her doll.

"Here's the culprit," he announced, dropping the cat without bending. He landed on his feet and sidled up to Amelia's legs, purring. "Found your friend."

"No! There's someone here. I heard them scream!" Amelia demanded, recoiling from the cat. Daniel lifted his shoulders, setting his hands upon his hips.

"I think you might be going crazy, sis."

"Susan! Where were you?" Cora dropped her doll and reached for the cat.

"The cat was in the house. Must have found a crawl space and got stuck. I got him out of the library." His words did nothing to calm Amelia.

"Daniel, you have to believe me! There was *something* here with me. I know it wasn't the cat. And look," she shoved a crumpled piece of paper towards him. He didn't take it. It was scribbled words, nearly unintelligible, in a child's writing.

To Cora Love Mam

"This was with the doll. I think the Ouija board-"

"I'm going to drop Ellen home." Daniel didn't even pretend to humour her. "I'll be back soon. Will you be alright?" Amelia was starting to cry. She turned to hide it from him. "Amelia?" She didn't respond. "Cora, will you look after Amelia while I'm gone?" Cora giggled.

"Sure. Me and Mam and Susan will make sure she's okay." Amelia saw him flinch, he knows she did; he hated the damn cat's name. She regarded him with a sense of disdain and righteousness but did not speak.

"I'll be back. Just... don't fucking read anything scary while I'm gone," Daniel whispered to her, hesitating before he walked out, regarding Amelia. His jaw tightened as he considered staying as though it was him that had caused her to become paranoid. But it was not. It was not his fault, and it was not his problem.

She is sixteen, for Christ's sake.

Chapter 18

"**Writing unlocks a world of possibilities**. It's a place where anything can happen. It just so happens that in writing horror, you write about things you hope never do happen," Mark would tell the reporter.

"Why do you think people like to read it?"

"I think we all have a morbid curiosity with these things-that, and I believe in reading it we can minimise the horrors in our own lives."

"Is that why you write it? To forget about-"

Mark tilted his head back, the whiskey burning his throat. The tumbler touched the desk with a thud. He pinched the bridge of his nose, wincing as the fiery golden syrup expanded in his belly, warming his guts. When he opened his eyes, they fell on the photo frame. His wife smiled back at him, her eyes glinting in the sun, her hair shiny with life.

Sometimes it helped to sit with her when the writer's block hit, like he used to do before. He could pretend he was brainstorming again, firing out plot points like throwing darts at a board and seeing which stuck bullseye. During that time, she didn't even respond to him, only nodded her head every now and again, understanding his process. Now, though, she never responded. Not even a furrow of a brow, not even a tilt of her head.

The cold light of his laptop exuded from the screen, covering him in that teasing glow, the glow of a blank page that said he wouldn't get it finished in time, wouldn't have a draft ready to hand over by the end of the summer. It was fast approaching, his deadline and the end of his time here. He would be expected to return home then, return to that house where nothing he wrote about compared to the fears he felt. Where the crashing waves of a stormy night felt less lonely than his own bed, or whiskey did nothing to numb the pain in his chest.

Houses were like books, he supposed, full of characters and their stories. And that was one he had no longing to open the pages of, because as soon as he did, as soon as the front door opened, he would be reminded of what he could never experience in any way other than memory.

That story had ended.

"I wish you were here, Susan." He lifted the glass to his lips, the whisky burning the back of his throat.

Daniel was spooning the last of his sticky porridge into his mouth when Mark pushed open the kitchen door and crossed the room to pull open each of the cupboard doors, rummaging around for a couple of seconds, before closing it over and moving onto the next, each with growing intensity. Daniel knew what he was looking for, and he knew he wouldn't find it there; the last of the vodka was still sitting out behind the bins.

With a knowing glance from Amelia, Daniel got to his feet, set his empty bowl into the sink, and headed towards the door.

"Where are you going?" Mark's question came just as Daniel got one foot out the door. He hesitated before turning around.

"I'm meeting Ellen," he replied. Mark's nostrils were flared, his hands set firmly on his hips. He looked at Daniel, then at Amelia and Cora sitting at the kitchen table, and put his hand out towards Daniel, expectantly. There was a long pause before Daniel shrugged. "What?"

"Give me the keys to the Volvo," Mark said. Daniel met his eyes.

"What? Why?"

Mark moved the fingers of his outstretched hand in a 'come here' motion.

"You know why."

Daniel broke eye contact first, fixing his gaze on the cupboards, breathing deeply. He stuffed his hand into his pocket and fished out the jangling keys. He slapped them into Mark's palm and left on foot.

Chapter 19

Sitting on the floor of her bedroom, surrounded by all her toys, Cora set about carefully examining each one and sorting them into a line. If Cora had to choose one thing, just *one,* as her absolute favourite thing to play with right now, it would be her new doll. It wasn't very pretty, not at all, and she wished that it could have long hair so she could brush it and tie it up to match hers each day. Maybe she could cut her hair to match her dolls…

She would also probably get it a new pretty dress or some dungarees- probably in orange or green, or maybe even in blue. She had thought about asking Amelia to wash her doll's dress with her clothes, but Amelia looked at her doll the way she looks at Daniel sometimes, just before she shouts, and so she didn't want her to touch her doll. Really, she didn't want anyone to touch it because it was hers, and it had been a present, and her dad always said that if someone gave her a present then it was hers to keep. You don't have to share your presents, especially if it's a Christmas or birthday one.

This was a birthday present. It was very late but that was okay with Cora. She didn't really mind when her presents were late because that meant she had less time to wait before the next ones. Besides, this was a special one. It was from Mam.

Cora missed her mam. Sometimes she forgot that she missed her and when she remembered it made her feel funny- like her belly had bugs crawling around inside of it. She didn't think her mam would mind though if she knew about it. Her mam didn't mind anything.

And now she didn't have to miss her at all.

Cora would do almost anything for everything to stay as they were. *Almost* anything. If she had her new elephant teddy from the carnival she would give it away, that's how much she wanted things to stay the way they were.

But she *couldn't* do what her mam asked her to do. She just couldn't.

Cora had suggested that her mam talk to Amelia too, because maybe then her and Daniel would get along a little better, maybe she would be as happy as Cora was to see her. But even still, when Mam said she didn't want to, that she liked watching Amelia at night but didn't want to talk to her, Cora had been happy, because it was like Mam was just for her, just like her doll and her new game; a present especially for her, and she was just for her mam which is exactly what she wanted.

When the grandfather clock in the living room struck 3.04 am, Amelia awoke with an immense amount of pressure upon her abdomen. She lay there for a moment wondering just how much she had drunk before bed and couldn't quite recall having drank any. Nocturnal polyuria came to mind, burned in there from a homework assignment on bladder infections, but she dismissed it almost immediately and put it down to the increased amounts of coffee she had been ingesting; it must be irritating her bladder. She squirmed in her bed, rolling onto her side so that her back faced her lamp, and shut her eyes, trying with all of her willpower to doze off. No matter how hard she tried though, she could not ignore the feeling of urgency.

She sat up in her bed, keeping the covers tight to her body, and watched the darkness beneath her door for any signs of nefarious activity. Should she have seen any she probably would have no need for the bathroom, only a spare set of sheets. However, there was no movement under the door, no waiting monsters that she could see - in fact, it had been days since she last felt a presence around her at all - perhaps it had gotten enough of a thrill out of her near mental snap the day Daniel had gone to the lake.

She stood, her shadow creeping along behind her, and went to the door. It was an odd feeling- the crushing anxiety at opening a door at night, afraid of what could be lurking on the other side.

"It's just a house," her voice was hoarse. She had barely used it. When the door opened darkness enveloped her, sucking her out into the hallway like a blackhole. However, like a beacon to a lost sailor, there was light coming from under another door; her father was still awake. This offered some small amount of comfort and she found herself walking briskly towards the bathroom, telling herself that no monster would dare expose itself when there were other souls awake in the house.

Step on a crack, break your mother's back.

Amelia pushed the childish rhyme from her head for it to only be replaced by two more.

One, two, he's coming for you.

Hell is empty. All the devils are here.

Amelia got to the bathroom and closed the door. She rested her face against the wood, her breath coming in quick rasps. Her mind whirled, scanning through images of masked murderers sweeping through the house, swinging an axe from side to side as they travelled up the hallway; of creatures from hell, shaking the door handle- all like slides on a projector screen, flashing by.

"Stop it..." she moaned, wiping her face with her hand, feeling perilous to the fear that seemed to breathe from the walls like poison from a smoker's cancerous cigarette. "If I scream, he will hear me." This, at least, was true. If something vile was to happen, all she was to do was scream and her father would come to her aid. She thought of what it had been like when she had been Cora's age, to know that she could seek refuge from her father at all hours, could ask her mother to bring her to the bathroom because she was scared by the shadows. Now, though, she couldn't dare ask such a thing. When exactly did that extended hand of help retract?

Amelia could hold on no more. She turned and relieved herself without looking up. She touched the handle to flush the toilet but paused, considering if the noise would be too loud, if it would shatter the silence of the night - and then, wondering if she had ever wondered this before coming to this house.

As suddenly as you notice that your rollercoaster safety belt is not tight enough, did Amelia notice that the light from under her father's door had gone out. Her stomach plunged and she was tempted to turn around, barricade herself inside the bathroom. What convinced her otherwise and spurred her to scurry across to her room, was the tiny outline of a figurine sitting outside of Cora's bedroom. With the little sliver of moonlight that crept through the hall window, the face was alight, watching Amelia. The Virgin Mary statue had disappeared since Ellen had been hit with it, only to reappear now. She made eye contact with it and a shudder ran through her body. A thud from down the hall sounded and she hid for the night.

Amelia, before conscious of the loud flush of the old toilet, was not at all aware of just how hard she had slammed her door.

While Daniel's foot fell through the rotten slats of the porch roof, snapping loudly and falling with a tremendous thud to the decking, Amelia's door slammed shut, disguising some of the racket from his fumble.

"Shit," Daniel hissed and pushed hard on the windowsill so that he could lift his leg out of the hole. He dragged himself through his window and landed on the floor in a heap where he stayed, frozen in place in the dark room, listening for any sounds to indicate Mark's approach. Only silence met him. With a groan, he twisted around to inspect his bare shin. In the little light from the moon, he spied a trickle of blood rolling down his leg. He would show Ellen it tomorrow, as proof of his commitment to her.

She had stayed steadfast in her decision to never enter the house again, and so Daniel had been spending most of his evenings at the Hadley residence. Mark had been just as stubborn with the keys to the car. Whether in defiance or not, Daniel had become fond of walking through the forest at night now, not even bringing a light along. Having to climb through his window since Mark had started locking the door on him, well that wasn't his favourite thing to do. "All in the name of love, eh," he mused and got to his feet.

A rustling from outside stilled him; he crossed to his window and stuck his head out to inspect, expecting to see Stephen escaping. Whatever caused the sound was hidden by the porch. It was by the bins, knocking into them. A badger, Daniel presumed - or perhaps the cat digging its way back into the house to its favourite hole. Either way, Daniel lost interest in the creature and pulled his shirt from over his head, his shorts down his legs, and dressed in a pair of tracksuit bottoms and a fresh t-shirt.

He fell into a deep sleep almost immediately.

When he felt a hand touch his neck, a breath tickling his ear, he jerked awake to find it was still dark out, the moon lost in the clouds. And that he was alone. He sat up, his breathing slowing and his chest coming to a steady rhythm of up and down, up and down. He gazed around the room, looking at the shadowy outlines of his furniture, his pile of clothes, and his paired shoes, and lay back down to stare at the ceiling for some time. There was a knock from the wall above his head, coming in sets of three taps, then silence, then three more taps. With a closed fist, he reached up and banged on the wall, louder than he meant to. The knocking stopped. And he went back to sleep.

The next time Daniel woke was not until the morning. 9.55 am. Daniel shot out of bed, already reaching for new shorts and shirt, uninhibited by the overcast sky and forecasted rain. Something fell to the floor, clunky and noisy, rolling to the end of the bed and bouncing off the bed frame. Daniel hesitated when he spotted it, pulling his legs through his shorts slowly as he considered it. The doll that Cora had been playing with was lying on his floor, its ugly face staring up at him. He lifted it to examine it. It smiled at hm through lopsided eyes and a puckered mouth. When had Cora come in to his room with it? And why had she left it behind? Taking it and his runners with him, he pushed Cora's bedroom door open.

Unexpectedly, a smell that reminded Daniel of the bottom of a dirty bin forced him to take a step out and cover his nose with his forearm.

"Jesus, Cora, it smells like something died in here," he said, holding his arm firmly across his face. Cora, however, did not budge. She lay, sleeping, in her bed. She looked like a tucked chicken fillet wrap, and a part of Daniel's imagination dragged him back to school lunches. He crossed the threshold once more, scanning the room for any evidence of the smell's origins without finding any, and set the doll next to Cora while she snoozed, her mouth open wide so that a pool of drool had collected on her pillow. He gently rocked her until she stirred, checking over his shoulder - Amelia's door was firmly shut.

Where was she? He needed to get going - wasn't this her job as big sister?

"Time to get up, stinky." In response, Cora groaned and rolled away from him. "Come on, up you get." He pulled her blankets down and shook them like a fan so that the wind blew the hair around her face. She chuckled. "Grab your pillow and we can go downstairs. You can sleep when you're dead!" Through the window, Daniel watched as Ellen came through the trees, standing on the crest of the hill. She checked her watch and set her hands on her hips; he was late. Her arm lifted into the air then and she began waving at him, spotting him through the glass pane. He waved back.

"I don't think you sleep then either," Cora mumbled, rubbing at her eyes. She dragged her pillow along the floor, dropping it completely when she got to the door.

"What're you doing?"

"My doll!" She bounced to her bed, grabbed the dirty little doll, and ran back to collect her pillow.

"What has you sleeping in so late, anyway?"

"Just playing, I guess," she wiped her hair away from her face with the palm of her hand, struggling to hold everything at once. Daniel pulled the pillow from her, carrying it under his arm.

"By yourself?" In response, Cora giggled at this.

"No! With Mam!"

Daniel gave her a gentle push on the shoulder and a teasing smile before he raced her to the stairs.

Amelia passed by the bottom of the stairs, heading to the kitchen, without even a glance in their direction as Cora yelled and laughed, sitting on her pillow, and hopping down the stairs one bump at a time. Daniel found the activity a lot less fun, and much more uncomfortable, however, he grinned and cheered, nonetheless. He left her at the bottom of the stairs, guiding her towards the kitchen while her pillow stayed, forgotten about momentarily, at the bottom of the stairs. And just as he would forget about the pillow, which Amelia would eventually bring back upstairs, he forgot about the stench in Cora's room.

Chapter 20

Midday came and passed, the clouds darkened and eventually spilled over. Daniel returned to the house drenched through and shook off like a dog at the door before kicking off his muddy runners and leaving them on the porch. His stomach was growling. He walked to the kitchen, past Cora's forgotten pillow on the steps, doing nothing to minimise the water that fell from him and onto the floor as he followed the smoky scent of frying bacon. Only Cora looked in his direction when he came through the door. He paused when he stepped into the kitchen and took in the rare sight: Mark sat at the table, his head down and his hand moving in repeated motions across the front page of a book. He closed over the cover and set it atop the pile on his right before taking one from the shrinking stack on his left. Amelia was standing in front of the stove as the frying food sizzled, her eyes glazed over. Without a word, Daniel took a plate and fork and reached around her. He stabbed a burning rasher with the fork prongs and then a second and third one and set it on his plate. Only when he turned to butter some bread did Amelia jerk back, her eyes rendering on him and her brows knitting together when she realised what it was that he had done.

"That's mine," she demanded and went to take the crispy bacon back. Daniel moved the plate out of her reach, smiling.

"What? I'm just making sure it's not poisoned." She was not impressed, however, and scowled.

"For once could you not be an arsehole?"

Daniel's brows rose and he scoffed.

"Jaysus, what's gotten you in such a bad mood?"

"You. You're always taking my food. You aren't even trying to hide it anymore."

"Okay, first of all, this is the *only* time I've taken any of your shit food. And secondly, fuck you, have it back," he flung the pieces of bacon from his plate back onto the pan. Amelia's cheeks flared. She turned to look at Mark, her hair knotted at the back of her head, but he was oblivious. Daniel pulled a chair out from under the table, not lifting the legs so that it squealed on the floor and set his plate with its single slice of Brennan's bread on it down with a bang. Cora's swinging legs stilled. Mark looked up from his books.

"Good afternoon, Daniel," he said and set the final book atop the pile.

"Mark," he nodded. Mark regarded him, his eyes shifting to Cora, and took a breath.

"Amelia, Stephen's books are all signed for him. Daniel will drop them over-"

"Daniel will not be dropping them over. Daniel has his own shit to do."

"Daniel," Mark's voice was steady.

"Mark." Daniel shrugged. Mark reached over and pulled his plate away from him. Daniel set his palms flat on the table, his stomach groaning.

"What are we doing here?" Mark asked, their eyes locked like two animals about to fight.

"You tell me."

"What does that even mean, Daniel?" There it was again, Daniel thought, that mocking tone that he used with him a little too often these days.

"It means, why don't you do it? Or do anything around here, instead of making me do it all." Daniel's voice betrayed him with its shaking. His fist closed over, stopping that from doing the same. Mark's gaze flickered to his hands, spotting the motion.

"I'm working Daniel. I have a job; you know, one of those things that you can't seem to keep?" *Once*, Daniel thought, *he got fired once.*

"Fine. I'll bring your shitty books over there. But give me the keys to the car back." Mark leaned back in his chair, outwardly composed, but Daniel knew that his anger was writhing around inside him, he could see it in his eyes, almost hear the words he wanted to spew at him. After a moment, with the bacon burnt black as smoke filled the kitchen while Amelia watched them, Mark reached his hand into the pocket of his jeans and pulled out two sets of car keys; one was much shinier than the other. He held the older set out to Daniel, dangling them on his finger like bait on the end of a hook. When Daniel reached across to them, Mark pulled them back and took a breath, not dropping Daniel's glare for even a second.

"I saw the hole in the porch roof. What time did you get home at?"

"About three."

"Hmph. So, nothing has changed then, not even after everything." Daniel felt his entire body tremble. Red tinted his eyes. He leaned over and snatched the keys from his finger, hearing his knuckle crack. The bag he filled with the books had only one strap. He pulled on it, swinging it across the table, knocking the coffee mug over. The hot liquid spilled out onto the table, covering Mark's lap. He collected his runners as the smoke alarm in the kitchen blared and stormed to the car as thunder crashed overhead.

Nobody answered the door when Daniel rang the bell at Stephen's house. A dog that was being kept dry and warm inside the house barked each time the chime sounded. *Where the hell would Stephen be in this shitty town*, Daniel thought, his frustration only exacerbated as the rain pelted down on him. He returned to the car - his knuckles white as he shook the steering wheel, the bag of damp books on the seat next to him. He considered dropping the bag by the door and leaving. *Fuck them*, he thought, *let the books melt to mush*. Instead, though, he sat with the heating turned up full blast.

His body was shaking, his mind dizzy. Reaching over, he pulled on the glove box door and retrieved the protein bar that had been left there as a reserve. He ate it in four chomps, then started the second one. This solved his blood sugar levels. He was surprised he didn't find a flask in there and then supposed that Mark would keep it in the newer model he rented. A flash in the sky illuminated the forest. His pulse quickened, his foot bounced on the floor, close to the pedals. He needed to burn off the energy building in him.

Leaving a trail of dust behind him, Daniel sped out of the driveway.

Daniel didn't know how long the trail ran, nor where it led.

He felt hungry for the numbness of the trail, thirsty for the freedom from all things Mark. He parked the car and stretched before heading out, welcoming the noisy thunder above him, and the cool shower the rain washed him in. Nothing could touch him here; not the lightning, not the blame. He felt it. Felt it in his bones- to his core. But here, here he felt nothing other than the soil beneath his feet and the air pumping in his lungs.

He followed the pathway, the lake on his right, until it narrowed and led him through a wooded area that veered away from the lake edge. When he came through to the other side of the trees, there was a line of houses on his left, facing the lake, with long jetties and small rowboats tied at the end of their driveways. Stapled sporadically across the poles and trees were flyers with water-downed ink, some becoming close to transparent against the bark as the rain lashed down. He didn't stop to investigate, but caught the word 'Missing' in runny, bold letters, a blotchy picture beneath in black and grey splodges. The child in the photo was just a mess of dark colours blurred into one puddle.

Chimneys coughed out smoke under the grey sky as the cold rain seeped into his bones, but he didn't stop running. Only when he felt like his lungs might explode, did he slow to a jogging pace before stopping and walking with his hands on his hips. Lightning exploded above him, and he bent over, leaning his hands on his thighs, panting as the light split the clouds apart.

"You need some help?" Daniel stood up. A man with a white beard and balding head had called out to him from his porch. He was standing in the porch, out of the rain; a woman of a similar age was in the doorway behind him. Daniel shook his head.

"No, I'm fine, thanks." He set his hands on his hips and shook out his legs. The cut on his shin had reopened and a dribble of blood ran down, mixing with the rainwater and dirt.

"You sure? You look like you were running from something - seems like the only reason you'd be out in this weather." His words were muffled in the overhead thunder. Barking dogs responded to the storm. Daniel took a few steps towards the man and his wife.

"I'm grand, honestly. Just out for a run." The man regarded him for a moment longer than was customary for polite conversation.

"You that author's kid? The one living in the old Evans' house?" Daniel hesitated before nodding. The man's wife reached out to take her husband's arm. "Those Yanks came over and built that house out of sticks and wonder why it wouldn't sell. If I had it my way, I'd set the thing on fire and let it burn to the ground." He smiled then, more to himself than Daniel. "Maybe even do it on the fourth of July!" He chuckled, then, to Daniel, "What do you think of it?"

"Eddie, leave the boy alone."

"He's hardly a boy, Deirdre." He shook her away and faced Daniel. "Anything weird happen over there?" His voice had lost all the mirth with this question. Daniel could feel his adrenaline slowing. He would start to feel the cold if he didn't keep running.

Ignoring the intrusive thoughts of Amelia's delicate sanity, Daniel shook his head, "No, why?" Daniel's heart rate was slowing, his breathing coming easily now.

"You got any young wans' living there?" Daniel took another step towards the house. He was standing close enough to the couple to see the burning fire in their living room, a framed Gardai hat resting on a hook above it. The woman's brows stitched together in disapproval of her husband's prying.

"Yeah."

"You keep an eye on the little gersha, won't you?" The man said it without blinking, his eyes fixed on Daniel's.

"Is there something I should be looking out for?" Daniel looked to the woman now, watching her as she stared at her husband. He parted his lips as if to say something to Daniel, but then let his gaze move out onto the lake, staring in the direction of the house.

"You just can't be too safe these days," he said. Daniel didn't respond, unsure how to in this instance.

"That have anything to do with those flyers I've seen?"

The man took a moment to think, his eyes resting on Daniel, sizing him up.

"It's a good town, son. I hope your da won't be telling people it's not."

Daniel met his stare with a blank one of his own, the water running down his face with cold slaps.

"Have a good run." The man turned and went to go indoors once more but stopped and faced him again. "They're felling trees up ahead; you won't get much further than these rows of houses. You should turn back soon enough."

"I will, cheers." Daniel watched him and his wife go back inside, closing over the door and pulling a blind down over the glass pane. A crack of lightning whipped across the sky. He turned to go back.

Ellen's eyes widened as she took in Daniel's soggy form at her door. His t-shirt and shorts clung to him like a cold second skin, his light hair darkened to look more like the rest of his family, and his runners were covered in a thick layer of mud, which had also been spread over the carpet of the car. He tried and failed to conceal his shivering until Ellen laughed and fetched a large beach towel. She didn't invite him in, instead, she joined him under the cover of the porch roof as he dried himself off.

"Did you go for a swim in the lake?" she asked mockingly as he shook the towel through his hair. When he pulled his shirt over his head and squeezed the water from it, holding the towel between his legs, Ellen checked over her shoulder and at the door.

"I went for a run." He scrunched his shirt up in the towel to try to dry it, before drying his bare skin and pulling it back on. His skin prickled when the cold fabric touched his chest and shoulders.

"A second one?" she asked, incredulous, and then stared out at the lashing rain.

"I'd to blow off some steam-" The front door opened and a boy, about his age, stepped out onto the porch. He looked familiar, yet Daniel had never met him before. The boy stalled, his hand still on the door handle. The three of them stood in silence, the rain pelting down on the roof the only sound.

"Hi," the boy was the first to speak, closing the door over. His eyes darted to Ellen and back to Daniel.

Shit, Daniel thought. *This is awkward.*

"Alright, what's the story?" Daniel said, and quickly finished drying his legs off, smearing red streaks from his bloody shin across the towel. "I'm Daniel." He reached across Ellen to shake his hand.

"Brandon," he replied before setting his hand into his pocket.

"This is eh... this is Stephen's older brother," Ellen told him then, swaying from side to side.

"Oh right, yeah, I thought you looked familiar."

"Yeah."

"Me and Daniel run together." Daniel scoffed unenthusiastically at this.

"Oh right." There was a weird, uncomfortable silence between them. Daniel wasn't an idiot, regardless of what some people might think. He also wasn't interested in this.

"Am I interrupting something here?"

Ellen began shaking her head, while Brandon said nothing. Daniel shrugged, inwardly regretting not punching Stephen a second time when he had had a chance. "Okay, well, I'm going to head back to the gaff. Tell Stephen he'll have to call to mine if he wants to collect his books, yeah?" He said it a little too harshly, his words crass. He took a deep breath and set the towel over the railing of the porch before skipping down the steps, back into the downpour.

"I'll call over later!" Ellen called from the end of the porch, not stepping into the rain. Daniel didn't respond though, climbing into the car and shutting the door so that all he could hear was the roaring rain on the windscreen.

Daniel returned home and left the backpack in the corner of the foyer, where the soggy books collapsed in a heap. He took the stairs in several leaps, already undressing. Amelia was wavering from side to side in the corridor at the end of the landing, her head turning towards him and her eyes widening when she took in his sodden form. She said nothing though, and stood, staring into Cora's bedroom.

The shower spurted out hot and cold water in intermittent intervals, spewing scalding water onto Daniel's scalp before freezing him with sub-zero temperatures. It wasn't until he had almost finished that there was a steady stream of hot water. He stood under the rush of water, letting it pound on his shoulders before rolling down his back, hoping it would wash away the last eight hours, if not the last eight months. He didn't much believe in karma or cosmic intervention, but if ever there was an argument for it, this past summer was it.

He shouldn't let it get to him, but he couldn't help it. What had been happening between them before he arrived, soggy and cold on her doorstep? He must have looked pathetic.

It doesn't matter.

He would be gone in a matter of weeks.

And if it came to it, Daniel could handle Brandon.

He took a deep breath, turned the faucet to the 'off' position, and pushed open the shower door.

As he dried off - for the third time that day - Daniel felt queasy and had to hold onto the edge of the large claw-footed tub to steady himself. His stomach rumbled ferociously to match the thunder outside. He wrapped the towel around his waist, blinking past the dark spots in his vision, and made his way out, almost slipping on the puddle of water his clothes had created on the floor. He dressed and headed downstairs.

In the kitchen the remnants of lunch had been left in the pot on the stove, cold and sodden, looking how Daniel felt. He stirred the mushy vegetables lazily, before dropping the ladle and going in search of something else. He reached into the press and retrieved a poppyseed bagel from between some granola bars and half-eaten tortilla chips on the shelf marked 'A'. After buttering it and stacking it high with spinach, turkey, cheese, and mayo, he sat at the table to eat it.

"Don't eat my food, Daniel."
"It wasn't me, Amelia."

Except this time, it was him. His revenge didn't taste sweet, not one bit. But he did feel his mood lift almost as soon as he finished his bagel.

Amelia barely noticed him as she wandered into the kitchen, her eyes two dark holes in her face. She still wore that same baggy jumper with her long, knotted hair sticking out over the hood of it. She walked past Daniel and the mounting piles of dirty washing that escaped from the basket by the utility room door, without even a word of complaint towards him.

"What's wrong with you?" Daniel finished off his bagel and shook his hands above his plate, nearly all the crumbs falling from his palms and missing the plate to land on the table instead. "Amelia...?"

"Nothing. I'm tired." She hit the button on the kettle so that the room filled with the noise of boiling water.

"Up late with Stephen?" Daniel teased, twisting in his chair to look at her. She didn't say anything for a long time then, just stood before the kettle, her hands wrapped around her coffee cup, watching the steam billow out the spout.

"It's this house."

"What do'ya mean?" Daniel was using his fingers to fish out the seeds from between his teeth.

"This house- it wakes me up at night. Whatever it is that lives here with us-"

"Amelia, what are you talking about?" She wet her lips and poured the boiled water into her mug. The smell of coffee filled the room.

"Just..." She hesitated, stopped herself from finishing her sentence, and took a breath, "nothing." She lifted the cup to her lips and sipped from it. Too hot, she hissed and went to set the cup back down, misjudging the counter space and setting it too close to the edge. Daniel got from his seat, the chair squeaking loudly on the floor, as the mug toppled, spilling its hot contents all down Amelia's front. There was a second's pause before she realised what had happened and let out a tired yelp. She pulled the fabric away from her skin with the tips of her fingers and stepped away from the sharp pieces of the shattered mug.

"Shit, are you okay?" Daniel stood in his socks, trying to avoid any pointed edges of the clay, beside Amelia. She seemed dazed or disorientated, as if she hadn't quite comprehended what had just happened. "Here, be careful- take the jumper off." Daniel handed her the tea towel and helped her pull the hoodie from over her head as she held it out from her body. She was wearing a thin string top beneath, her collarbones protruding out from her chest. Daniel hesitated, regarding her, as she pat herself down with the towel. The tracksuit bottoms she wore were his and so naturally they hung loose on her waist, but now, now they had been tied so tightly that the fabric was scrunched together and a thick knot held them in place.

"You should probably put some cold water on your skin."

"I'm fine," she muttered, tugging her vest away from her stomach, the wet patch staining the white fabric.

"No, really, you nearly scalded yourself-"

"I said I'm fine." Amelia's tone was firm. She stared at Daniel - her eyes sunken and dark - for a few seconds longer before she pushed past and left the kitchen. He watched her go, dragging her feet behind her as she went up the stairs until she disappeared in the twist of the banisters and went out of sight. Daniel knelt and began scooping up the loose pieces of the mug in his palm, cutting himself once, and emptying the pieces into the bin.

Chapter 21

The house had once been home to a loving family- to people who decorated it with care and who chose perfect drapes to frame the wide windows and had hand-picked matching cushions to accentuate the colourful throws on the back of the couches. Then, that loving family had been killed. Or died. Killed, or died, it was close to being the same. Their time had been ended in this house, Amelia was sure of that much, and whatever it was that had led them to that untimely departure from this world was perhaps - no, undeniably - still lurking. Amelia knew it; it was the only reasonable explanation for what was going on.

Now it was inhabited by a dysfunctional family on the verge of collapse with every conversation, every interaction becoming a point of debate, and the house enjoyed it, *devoured* it, relished in their misery as if it were a savoury snack.

The sounds in the house at night, the shadows that crawled along the wall, following her, and the shapes she would see, morphing in the dark corners of the house. Either she was experiencing something macabre or else she was losing her mind. Both, at this point, seemed as likely.

She had fought the idea off at first, refusing to believe in such things, blaming her night-time reading or her inclination towards the paranormal - but too much had happened now. The house, from the beginning, felt off, then there was the matter of the Ouija board.

But then Cora's obsession with the thing and her claims to be speaking with ethereal beings was too much of a coincidence.

There was the case of the dirty doll that she carried around with her.

And then the noises from within the house.

And the fact that the previous residents had experienced something sinister within these walls to only succumb to its malignant powers.

And the screaming creature; she had heard it. She could not be convinced otherwise, no matter what. She had not been alone here that day and had begun doubting that any of them ever were. Something in Amelia's gut had known from the very beginning.

From Cora's doorway, Amelia stood watching her sister playing. She danced her doll along the surface of the Ouija board, mumbling and muttering to herself in sweet, musical tones. The window had been unlocked and pushed the whole way open, letting a stiff breeze in and blowing the loose sheets of paper that were on the floor around in circles. Scribbled drawings of their family, with the addition of the cat and doll, in a variety of colours flew around in the breeze.

Daniel moved past her and went down the hall, his form hazy in her peripheral. He knocked gently on their father's bedroom door. When there was no answer, he disappeared behind the door and returned a moment later with a bottle of whiskey in hand.

"It's a bit chilly, isn't it?" Daniel stopped next to Amelia and spied the open window. His nose crinkled from the lingering smell.

"You can smell that, too?" Amelia asked, straightening her shoulders, her voice rising.

"Yeah, it stinks. Know what's causing it?"

"No," Amelia shook her head.

"The cat probably dragged a dying rat behind the wall. I reckon there's enough space for it." Daniel knocked on the wall with the end of the whiskey bottle, his eyes slowly following the scratches on the wall to the ceiling. They looked like desperate marks of someone being dragged along the hallway in the deep-stained wood. "Isn't it mental how tall the house is, but the ceilings aren't that high?" Amelia had zoned out.

"It's him - the spirit that haunts the house. I've read that it can cause a house to smell. It's in all the movies, too." If the house had a VCR or TV, Amelia would show it to him.

"Amelia-"

"I'm serious, Daniel. I've seen things here - heard them. I feel like I'm being watched in this house." Daniel didn't speak, only stared at her with suspicion.

"Nothing is watching you." He unscrewed the cap on the bottle and drank from the neck without even a grimace. How much was he drinking these days, she wondered for a split second.

"I think it has something to do with that Ouija board and the doll. Cora shouldn't be playing with it."

"It's a lump of wood with the alphabet carved into it," he said, harshly, and then a little softer, "You're the only one experiencing these strange happenings. Maybe it's time to lay off the coffee, sis." He took another swig.

It was textbook oppression, Amelia surmised. It happened in all the horror stories; the entity would target the most susceptible person in the house and drive them insane.

It's the house, Amelia thought as Daniel disappeared around the curve in the stairs, it was coming for her.

"Writing Horror is like being a magician; to do it well you need to make your readers focus on the trick in your right hand - that being the monsters and the gore, only for the real magic to be happening in your left hand," he would tell the reporter. Her brow would crease a fraction while her mouth would tilt to a smile.

The desk drawer rattled on the hinges, singing out protests on old rails. He stopped it halfway, his brow furrowed, and slid his hand in to fill the empty space within. With a deep breath, he pushed back his chair and walked down the hall, past the banisters, pausing when he caught sight of his reflection in the dark window inside the bathroom. His stubborn stomach was only growing, spilling over at the hips. He had been doing everything he could to shift it... *hadn't he?* He had tried more running, but each time he went for a jog he tasted blood in his throat, the tiny capillaries leaking blood into his lungs as his body gasped for oxygen. He needed to get his draft finished. There was no time for exercise. Less whiskey? *No,* he shook his head at the very idea, *that wouldn't do.* With a quick movement of his fingers he unbuttoned his jeans and fixed his t-shirt so there were no lumps or bumps in his reflection. *Done.* It was his jeans that was the problem. *You're no longer a growing boy, Mark,* he heard the voice in the back of his head, the voice of a younger, fitter version of himself.

Undoing his button didn't solve his softening jaw... He shut the bathroom door and brushed his hand through his beard. When the final draft made it to the editor he would get back on track.

Mark made his way to the last door. Without knocking, he turned the handle and pushed the door inwards. From his bed, Daniel glanced up at him but said nothing. The bottle of whiskey, the cap untwisted and balancing atop the neck- hanging on for dear life- was missing a fifth of its contents.

"I didn't realise I raised a thief." He spun the lid on the bottle, his mouth watering already. Daniel didn't move from where he lay, barely acknowledging his father at all.

"You didn't raise any of us," Daniel said plainly.

"I'm sure your mother would be proud if she could see you now, son." His tone was sharp, too caustic. He would regret it later.

"Yeah? And what would she say about you, *Dad*?" Mark stood with the whiskey in his hand, staring at his son. Daniel's eyes were fixed on the ceiling, his hands clenched by his sides.

"I'm going out from early tomorrow. You need to stay here with your sisters. I told you that you need to be looking after them."

Daniel's eyes darted towards him for a fraction of a second, his jaw muscles tightening.

"You know Ellen has a little sister. Her friend went missing recently." There was an insinuation and a question in there. "Did you know about that?" Mark took the lid off the whiskey and hesitated before taking a mouthful straight from the neck. Daniel did not watch.

"That Ellen had a sister?"

"That a kid went missing in the area."

Mark took another gulp of whiskey before leaving.

Daniel woke in the same foul humour he had fallen asleep in. He had woken once in the night, that loud banging above his bed waking him up again, and his mind had then filled with things he fought hard to keep out of his head. Things that needed to be forgotten about.

When he had dragged himself out of bed that morning, Amelia had been staring in at Cora again, her arms limp by her side, her eyes blankly staring at their sister. He said nothing but silently reminded himself that summer would end, and this house would too be forgotten.

Daniel considered himself good at many things with that at the top of the list.

Ellen was waiting for him outside when he went to leave for his run. She sat on the crest of the hill, in a pair of jeans and a t-shirt with two coffee cups in hand. She sipped from one, offering the other out to him. At first, he didn't take it, stretching his legs out one at a time, before accepting it.

"I don't think you are going to get too far in those," Daniel told her and took a mouthful of the steaming Americano. It tasted burnt. She got to her feet, rubbing the grass from the backs of her trouser legs.

"I wanted to come and explain," she told him, rolling her eyes at him. Daniel felt his jaw tighten and busied himself with shaking out his ankles in turn. He took another mouthful, reminding himself that he was only going to be here for another couple of weeks anyway.

"No need." His jaw was sore from biting down.

"Daniel, please," she set a hand on his forearm.

"No, really. It's grand. I just would've appreciated a head's up, is all. So I don't look like a gobshite-"

"You don't! I promise. Brandon is an old friend. But that's about it." She shrugged. Daniel considered this, meeting her eyes, and took another mouthful.

"Yeah?"

"Yes." A smile spread across his face and Ellen let out a loud laugh. "Let's go for a walk."

Amelia spent the guts of an hour brushing her hair through with first a comb, and then a paddle brush, untangling the nest of knots she had let accumulate in her hair. She flipped her hair over her head, kneeling forwards on her bed, when she realised that there was something amiss. Her hand grappled at the neck of her jumper, through her brushed hair, to feel for it. It usually dangled against her chin when she brushed the underside of her hair, tickling the nape of her neck as it slid against her skin. A bubbling of apprehension simmered in her stomach.

She stood and turned to frantically toss her cushions aside, to tear her duvet off of her bed. She tugged her base sheet up from the corners of the old, uncomfortable, spring mattress and flung it to the floor, but still, she did not find what she was looking for. Her hand went back to her neck, feeling the bare skin with cold fingers and a shiver spiked down her spine as a lump formed in her throat.

Exhausted, she couldn't remember taking the necklace off, but that was not to say that she didn't do it, or that it had possibly unlatched itself in her sleep, maybe caught on something and was pulled off her throat; it was an old chain, after all. But it wasn't here.

Panicking, she turned and knelt next to her duvet, lifting it and shaking it out from the corners, hoping to see a glint of gold in the folds, but to no avail. Her shoulders slumped and she shut her eyes, silently crying.

There were a couple of reasons that Cora wanted to stay in this house: firstly, she liked the house, and she liked that Susan was here, too. She had heard her dad telling Amelia that he would have to stay here once they went home, and Cora hated that she might have to leave him behind. Secondly, Cora was afraid that like Susan, Mam would be left behind once they left here, too.

If Cora had been a little older she would have told her dad that she wanted to stay here forever, even if that meant being here alone. But, as it was, and as she was still quite small, she knew that she would have to go with her family back to their old house. Knowing this, she planned on asking her mam to come with them; after all, it wouldn't be all that hard for her to do it, she used to really like that house, and while her dad had put all of her clothes into the space above his bedroom ceiling, all of her other things were still there, like the pictures that Cora had drawn for her.

What crossed her mind though, was that if they all went back to their house, maybe her mam would have less time for

Cora than she did here. There, she might have to do the things that she used to do and wouldn't be able to stay with Cora all the time. Wouldn't let Cora play when it was really dark outside, or with whatever toys she wanted to play with.

If it was up to Cora she would choose to stay here forever.

Chapter 22

A murder rose on the wings of darkness with a disconcerting harmony of caws and squawks. There was a noticeable change in weather today. Daniel zipped his jumper up to the neck and found himself wishing he had changed from his shorts before driving with Ellen to the lake. He dropped his empty coffee cup into the green bin and started walking along the lake edge, a lonely duck waddling along behind them in search of food.

"When do you go home?" Ellen asked, rubbing her bare arms with her hands to warm herself up when a biting breeze cut through the trees. Daniel unzipped his hoodie and offered it out to her. She took it without complaint, pulling the oversized jumper on and zipping it up.

"I think we've got another week or two here before we head off. We have to get the girls back for school."

"What about college for you?" Daniel had been thinking more and more about going away for college. Once exciting, the idea weighed heavily on him now. What did he want to do? Where did he want to go? Had he even gotten accepted to his courses?

"Yeah, that too."

"You don't sound convinced about it."

"I'm not. I mean I want to go, obviously. Anything to get away from my family. I just…"

"Feel guilty?" Daniel stopped walking and watched the duck following them. He reached over to Ellen and pulled the half-eaten protein bar out of his jumper pocket. He broke off a small piece and threw it to the duck's webbed feet.

"Something like that." He wasn't sure what it was if he was honest. It was a feeling of weight that rested on his mind, like a headache, whenever he thought about leaving – abandoning – his life with his sisters, and hung above him as if the thought had sprung from his mind and manifested physically above him as a dark cloud tethered to his shoulders.

"Well, you could always get a job around here." Daniel scoffed and smiled at Ellen's glare. "I mean, I'd like it if you were sticking around." She reached up onto her toes and kissed him. They started walking again, the duck toddling behind in hopes of more food. Daniel tossed it the remainder of his bar. "By the way, any sign of my bra in your house?"

Daniel frowned. "Hmm?"

"The navy one?"

"Oh, eh, no. Sorry. I'll probably find it when I'm packing."

"That's okay. You can keep it." Daniel took her hand in his, kissing the back of it, inhaling her perfume. He would miss her.

"I ran this way yesterday. Came across one of the gaffs that face the lake - some old boy came out to me. I think he thought I was nuts running in the rain." Daniel was quick to change the subject.

"Oh, yeah?"

"Yeah, I think he said his name is Eddie." Daniel tried his best to sound nonchalant but he couldn't quite tell if he had succeeded.

"Eddie is a sweetheart. He used to be a Guard for years. Nice guy." Ellen was walking with her face turned towards the lake, looking out towards the jetties on the far side. "He used to let us away with murder!"

"Oh right. He said something weird at one point, actually."

"What?" Ellen faced him. The wind blew her blonde hair into her face.

"He said to keep an eye on Cora. I just thought that was a strange thing to say." Daniel shrugged, purposely omitting his question on if Daniel had witnessed anything strange in the house.

"It's probably because of the kid that went missing around here," Ellen said after a moment of consideration.

"Edel's friend?" He stopped walking now and stared out at the water. Ellen nodded.

"Yeah, and I think there are maybe one or two other kids that have gone missing in the last few years."

"You're joking?" Daniel felt a wave of familiar impatient anger rise in him.

"No, why?"

"So, you're telling me that there have been young kids going missing, and you still believe that there's a haunted house? Sounds like this town has a trafficking ring more than a ghost infestation," Daniel said, shaking his head.

"They're not mutually exclusive, Daniel," Ellen replied, matching his scorn. "Come on, let's keep walking."

Daniel's jaw was tight as he looked out at the lake and watched the birds flying. Ellen tugged him by the hand and wrapped her fingers through his, leading the way.

By the time Daniel had dropped Ellen home the day was starting to darken, with the trees swaying in the wind and the sun slipping behind gathering clouds.

He set the car in neutral and pulled the handbrake up to its fullest. The porch steps creaked in protest as he climbed up them and pulled the front door open with force. It slammed shut behind him with a loud clatter.

Lamps illuminated the foyer, flickering with the resonating bang and casting shaky shadows along the wall. Daniel went to the living room, where one of the doors was ajar, and found his two sisters inside in front of the fireplace where orange flames licked the coal and wood in the grate.

"Where's Mark?" Daniel asked. Amelia was sitting on the couch with a blanket over her legs and a Sudoku book open next to her. She stared at Cora as she sat in front of the fire, her back to them both.

"*Dad* is out. Working," Amelia said without looking away from Cora and the fireplace. Daniel tightened his grip on the door handle.

"Of course he fucking is," Daniel growled. Amelia glanced at him, her brows creased, but said nothing and went back to watching Cora.

"What's wrong with Cora?" He crossed the room to kneel next to Cora as her shoulders shook up and down, shuddering as she cried. Amelia stayed where she was, watching. "Cora?" He wiped at her face, her tears pouring down her cheeks freely.

"This isn't working anymore!" she cried. Daniel frowned. She was holding the Ouija board up for him to see. The letters were all faded now, the board covered in lines going from one end of the alphabet to the other like tracks left in the dirt on the road.

"What do you mean?" Daniel took the board and turned it over. The back was bare apart from the game company's logo on the bottom.

"She hasn't talked back to me in ages! She won't play with me because I won't do what she wants!" Confused and mildly concerned, Daniel regarded Cora before turning to Amelia for answers, but only terror was etched onto her face.

"Who, Cora?"

"Mam!" Daniel sat back and landed softly on the floor next to Cora with a sigh. He set the board back down onto the rug in front of the fire.

"What does she want you to do?" Daniel asked as tears streamed down her face.

"She wants me to stay with her. But says I can only do that if none of you are here." Amelia's voice was like a whisper, shaky and quiet.

"That's not Mam you're speaking to."

Daniel turned to her, "Amelia-"

"What! It's not!" Amelia leaned forward, knocking the puzzle book onto the floor.

"It is too!" Cora almost screamed it at her, her little face scrunching up and turning pink.

"No, it's not!"

"Then who is it?" Cora had turned around fully now, facing Amelia.

"I don't know, but Mam is dead, and she is not going to come back to talk to you through that thing." Amelia glared at Cora.

"If it's not Mam then who gave me this doll?" Cora retorted and reached over to the end of the couch where her doll was sat, facing the fire, out of sight. She pulled it out and shoved it into the air, proudly. Dangling around its neck was something shiny. The light from the fire bounced off the necklace and caught all of their eyes. When Amelia spotted it, her face drained of colour. Her hand reached for her neck. The little gold 'S' glittered back at her, almost teasing her.

"*Where* did you get my necklace from?" Cora twisted the doll around and touched the chain as if noticing it for the first time. Her face illuminated with glee, and she hugged the doll close to her chest.

"I knew she wasn't angry!" At the same time that Amelia moved, Daniel sprung to his feet, but Amelia was faster than him and grabbed the doll from Cora's arms, yanking the necklace free from the toy. She stepped back, away from Daniel and Cora who had started screaming at her. "It's MINE!"

With shaking hands, Amelia fastened the chain around her own throat, her eyes welling up with tears. Daniel's jaw tightened.

"No, it's mine! Mam gave it to me ages ago!"

"Well, now she gave it to me!"

"No, she didn't, she's dead, Cora, she couldn't have given it to you."

"But she did! She put it on the doll she gave to me-"

"Shut up, Cora!"

"Woah, Amelia, don't be such a bitch to her-" Amelia rounded on Daniel then. Her eyes were brighter than they had been for weeks, fiery, even. She stormed across to them, pushing past Cora, kicking the doll away, and picked up the Ouija board from the floor. At first, she stared down at it for a few seconds, then, without a word of warning, she shoved it into the bright flames of the fireplace, her shaking hands pushing it deep into the fire as if she didn't feel the heat of the blaze kiss her skin.

"NO!" Cora was screaming, diving towards the grate, her hand outstretched as if she was going to try and get it back out. Daniel moved quickly, scooping Cora up and holding her wriggling body against him as she thrashed and screamed. He faced Amelia who panted heavily, crying now.

"How am I being a bitch? Because I want my necklace back? Because I want you to stop eating my food? Because I am the only one who realises what is really going on here?" She was distraught.

"And what's going on here? Huh? What? So someone had some of your cereal and Cora found your necklace- what's the big deal? Cop on, Amelia." Daniel was still wrangling Cora, but he set her down so she could stand now and held her shoulders. Amelia scoffed.

"Me? You think I need to cop on? You go around slamming doors, swearing and shouting as soon as Dad asks you to pick up some socks, and you think I'm the hysterical one? You aren't the only one who lost a parent, Daniel, you do realise that, right?"

"Well, at least I don't hear a bump in the night and need a fucking exorcism. Look at you, you're a mess, and because of what? You were told a scary story?" Daniel was fighting to control his temper, to keep his voice level. He now clung to Cora's shoulders to steady himself as much as her.

"What's going on in here, then?"

Neither Daniel nor Amelia looked at Mark in the doorway. It was only Cora who did, and when seeing him, she pushed even harder against Daniel to be freed and ran to him, wrapping her arms around his waist and streaming a bubbling mess of words out.

Amelia rubbed at her eyes with her sleeve and cleared her throat, facing Mark. Daniel faced the fire, watching the game board's demise to nothing more than firewood.

"Amelia threw... my game... away... and took... my...necklace." Her words were a mess of stutters between choking sobs

"It's *my* necklace. She had it on her stupid doll." Amelia was back to almost shouting. Daniel stood, holding onto the mantlepiece, waiting, composing himself before he tackled his father.

"You burned the Ouija board? Why, sweetheart?" Mark knelt next to Cora and kissed her gently on the cheek. "Don't worry, we'll get you another one."

"Dad, you can't! That's what's caused all of this! She's been talking to... *something*... and it is haunting us now-"

"Amelia, what are you talking about?"

"Everything! How am I the only one noticing it all? The footsteps, the banging in the walls...?" Mark met her account with silence. Daniel turned to see Mark getting back to his feet, taking a deep breath. His eyes flashed towards Daniel, finding a way to blame this on him, he supposed, like everything. But Daniel wouldn't take it this time. Or ever again.

"Honey, I don't doubt you are hearing these things in the house, but you have to remember how old this house is. Things make noise in old houses, you know this." His tone was condescending, his expression pitiful. Daniel could see Amelia's shoulders round, she wrapped her arms across her chest, chewing her lips as tears silently travelled down her pale cheeks. The fire in Amelia died, the fight in her receding. "It's probably my fault, for giving you my draft."

"No, it's not that, Dad. I *know* that there's something here. I... I... I just do. Stephen told me what happened here and... I think it's happening to us, too." Her voice cracked on the words. Mark seemed to take the words and chew them over. From here Daniel could see how his mind was already working them into his story, working the hysteria into a new scene in his head, and felt a heat rise up his neck, his hands starting to tense.

"Okay, well, we only have to be here for another couple of weeks and then we will be going home. Just two - maybe three - weeks and then you'll be in your own bed." Amelia looked desperate, her anxiety almost palpable as her fingers tore at the strands on her jumper, her eyes starting to water again.

"But, Dad, we'll miss the start of school…?" Amelia was wiping at her eyes. Mark shrugged.

"It'll be okay, you'll catch up." A sob broke from Amelia.

"What about the anniversary?" Amelia was trying to speak through her tears. Daniel's eyes fell to the floor. No one spoke, no one answered her.

When someone did speak, it was Mark in his most patronising tone, "I really shouldn't have let you read the book, Amelia, I'm sorry. Maybe it's too scary for you."

"Yeah, maybe it's your story," Daniel muttered. "What is this one about? Is it about the family that was murdered in this house or about the kid that went missing in the area? Or is it some mixture of the two?" Mark was staring at him now, straightening his shoulders, his head tilting to the side, his lips relaxed, but his jaw was tightening. "I'm just wondering why strangers are telling me to keep an eye on my sisters here. Why would they be saying that?" Mark waited a moment before responding.

"Is there something you want to get off your chest, Daniel?" Mark had one of his hands resting on Cora's head, the other on her shoulder.

"There's a few things, yeah."

"Go ahead," Mark prompted him with nonchalance.

"Firstly, why don't you tell us what happened in this house? Why people keep telling us about slaughtered families and satanic bullshit?"

"You of all people should know how rumours work, Daniel, how people spin yarns- what did people say about you? What did they write about you after your mother died?"

Daniel's breath came out hot and fast through his nose. His nails dug into his palms.

"So, tell us the truth."

Mark paused, looking at his three children, his eyes lingering on Cora as she leaned her head back to look up at him.

"I don't think it's a suitable story for your sister to hear."

"Why not? If it's only rumours then they aren't true, are they? You wouldn't bring your kids somewhere dangerous, would you? You wouldn't bring them anywhere where... say... kids are going missing, would you?"

"Daniel-"

"No, tell us why you brought us here? To a house that is driving Amelia insane, in a town where kids are getting picked up off corners and never seen again. Tell us." Daniel's voice was rising, he fought hard to keep himself from shouting.

"Daniel, kids go missing every day; I'm sorry that it was a friend of yours, but that has nothing to do with why we are here."

Daniel's whole body was tense. "Okay, then why are we?"

"You want to know what happened in this house?"

"Yes!" Mark looked at Cora's tilted face and gave her a reassuring smile, followed by a wink. He took a breath, glanced at Amelia, and finally met Daniel's eyes.

"From the reports, an American family moved in about 45 years ago. One night, someone crept into the house while they slept and killed the two of them. What else do you want me to say?" Mark shrugged.

"How did they get killed?" Amelia was gripping the couch with white knuckles. Mark shrugged.

"Does that matter?"

"You wouldn't be writing a book about it if you didn't think it mattered," Daniel stated simply. Mark sucked air through his teeth.

"The residents owned a hardware store. The husband had just finished doing renovations here. The person who killed them used a chisel to decapitate the man and used a drill to - for lack of a better term - lobotomise the woman before he," Mark set his hands over Cora's ears for the next part, "sexually mutilated their bodies. He was never found." Amelia leaned back against the couch, chewing her lips.

"So, they could still be here? Somewhere, in this town?" Amelia's voice was strained. Mark shook his head.

"It's highly unlikely, pet."

"And their baby? What happened to her?" Daniel watched as surprise flickered across Mark's eyes until he quickly composed himself.

"Indescribable things, probably. But the child was never found," Mark said.

"Just like the kids in the last few years? They've never been found either, have they? And you still believed it was a good idea to bring us and Cora here?" Mark's brow furrowed, his façade of calmness peeling away now.

"Cora has never been in danger here, Daniel. You're trying to be combative now."

"How would you know? You're *never* here!" Daniel's rage was coming out and he could no longer contain it.

"When was the last time you were even here for dinner? Or to put Cora to bed? When was the last time you went shopping for us?" Daniel was shouting, his body getting hot. "When was the last time you did anything for anyone but yourself?" Mark was coming towards him, moving past Cora and Amelia, and standing on the other side of the coffee table.

"When do I do things for you? How, Daniel, do you think you get fed? How do you think you can pay for your school and running equipment? I work, Daniel. I do things to pay the bills." Mark was yelling as well. "Life isn't neatly tied up in a bow, not everything is as easy as we'd like!"

"Yeah, you write your shitty horror novels that has one kid believing that she's being haunted, while the other thinks she's talking to ghosts! You're so busy writing and running away that you haven't noticed how your family has turned into a horror of its own. Maybe when something bad happens to us you can write a bestseller!" Daniel's whole body was trembling, his vision painted red. He couldn't see the others in the room, only his father.

"I lost my wife, Daniel, don't you think I get to grieve, too? Or is it just you that gets to do that?"

"You lost your wife, while the three of us lost both of our parents that night." Mark took a step backwards, his shoulders relaxing as a kind of calm came over him.

"Do you really believe that Daniel?"

Daniel nodded with his jaw clamped tight.

"That's not fair."

"Why not? It's true. You're a piece of shit drunk who cares more about his terrible novels than his kids. At least when Mam was here we had one parent."

Mark parted his lips, choosing his words with the precision of a writer readying the quote for the front of his novel, and stared straight at Daniel when he spoke.

"And whose fault is that?" The words had enough force to crush a tower. "Your mother wouldn't have been out that night if she wasn't looking for you. You were so drunk that you were passed out on some random couch covered in your own vomit while your mother was crushed to death in her seat, her head caved in as she choked on her own blood, as her organs spilled into her lap, held together by her *fucking seatbelt*! Because of you, your mother died alone and afraid." Mark's pent up resentment had exploded. His face was a bright red, his eyes wide and pinned on Daniel, his hand clenched in front of him, with a single finger pointing towards Daniel.

There was a loud buzzing inside Daniel's head. He couldn't tell if Amelia shouted his name before or after he lunged forward, tackling his father to the ground. He couldn't control himself. They knocked the old coffee table over in the hustle, Daniel feeling something hard hit his leg as they toppled to the ground, his father flat on his back. They struggled, Daniel trying to get his leg over his father to straddle him. His hand hit something solid and there was a loud crunch, a dull pain in his knuckles. Strong arms deflected his fists as he attempted to hit him.

Just when he thought he might get his leg over, Mark grabbed his arms and swung his leg to lock in with his, twisting himself around so that he was now over Daniel. He shoved against Daniel's chest with great force and slammed him to the ground before he staggered to his feet. He shoved against Daniel's chest again and his head hit the carpeted floor in a dull thud. Mark backed away from his son, lifting his fingers to his bloody mouth and holding his palm out to Daniel as if trying to ward off a vicious dog.

Daniel rolled to his feet, panting, not quite sure what had just happened. His eyes flickered to Amelia, who stood watching in horror, her hands holding Cora as she hugged Amelia's waist, her face buried in Amelia's jumper. She was screaming. Daniel and Mark locked eyes, both panting, both unable to speak. After a moment, Mark lowered his palm and turned his back on Daniel, stopping only to reach into his pocket and extend cash to Amelia. He did not say anything before he left through the front door. Daniel stared at the floor until the sound of the tyres squealing disappeared down the drive.

His face was burning to the point that he felt it would be hot to the touch. The crackle of the fire was the only sound. His breathing was deep and long, his heart racing in his chest.

Soon, his knuckles would start hurting. Soon, the weight of what he just did would settle in. Until then, he had to get out of here.

He didn't look up from the floor when he went towards the door, ignoring his sister's calling. He was almost running by the time he got outside, jumping down the porch steps and racing towards the trail to numb himself.

Chapter 23

"What do your children think of your work?" The reporter will ask, pointing to the photograph on his desk of his family.

"Amelia loves horror, always has. She reads every one of my books. Cora, she's too young to understand, she just knows that her dad writes stories. But mostly they just see it as my job." He will hold on to that picture frame, his finger grazing over each of their faces with tenderness, the reporter will note how much he loves his family.

"And you have a son, too, don't you?"

"Daniel, well, Daniel is a teenage boy, so there's that." The reporter will smile, mimicking his own.

Once his son had been everything that Mark had wished he was himself, he had lived vicariously through him; now, he encompassed everything he resented. His entitlement, his anger, his foolishness, his blatant disregard for everything but himself. His wife's death. That was all he saw whenever he looked at Daniel. And what topped it off, what tormented him as though he were trapped in the ninth circle of hell, was the uncanny likeness the boy held for his mother.

It was a cruel joke how everything he loathes about himself was packaged up to look like what he had most dearly loved in life.

Did Mark love his son?

Did Frankenstein love his monster?

He was his firstborn. His first failure. He had thrown everything he had into the boy, teaching him everything he hoped would get him through life with success. Then that night happened and no matter how much he told people otherwise, how much he swore to himself that he would try, he couldn't not blame Daniel.

Cora sat on her honkers in front of the fireplace, watching the last of her game board melting to ashes in the hot flames. She felt a sort of pressure in her belly, one that made her uncomfortable to think about. It got worse whenever she pictured her dad and Daniel wrestling on the floor. They looked like they were really angry, and that had made Cora scared. Now her dad had gone off in his car and Daniel was running up and down the hill outside.

Cora had once tried going up that hill, but like the shop back home, she knew she wasn't allowed to go any further than that alone - that and she didn't really like the woods, even though Susan liked to explore it and Daniel often went off in it, Cora wasn't quite brave enough for that just yet. She would be soon, but for now, she was happy to stay in the garden. Besides, the garden was plenty big.

Cora hoped that her dad would remember to get her new game while he was out.

She was still angry at Amelia and every time she thought about that, she would frown. She was angry at her for being mean to her and especially for throwing her board into the fire. She wanted Amelia to apologise, but all she was doing was staring out the window, watching Daniel run.

To Cora, it seemed like everyone was fighting. She knew they wouldn't be fighting forever because a family has to like each other, but she wished that they would hurry up and stop it already.

"Are you okay?" Amelia was kneeling next to her. Cora shuffled on the carpet, turning her back to Amelia. "Cora…?"

"Go away."

"How can I make this up to you?" This, Cora knew, was an offer that came around only so often. She had gotten a new Polly Pocket off of Daniel the last time she had heard it. But she sighed, thinking that not even a new bear could make up for what Amelia had done.

"I wish everyone would stop yelling," Cora told her. "Mam hates it when Daniel or you shout." Amelia crawled around her so that she faced her now. Her brows were coming together over her eyes.

"Do you see Mam a lot, like in your dreams or when you're playing with your dolls?" Amelia asked. Cora found the question funny. She couldn't stop herself laughing. What did Amelia mean by that? She wished Mam was there to hear her say it.

"No! I see Mam all the time, like in real life." Cora was smiling, more than Amelia was, but she couldn't understand why; didn't Amelia want to see her too?

———

Daniel watched Amelia move around the porch, stepping over the broken slats beneath his room, the ones he was yet to move, and come down the back steps. She was walking towards him by the time he had turned around and was heading back up the hill. He wondered what would happen if he were to keep running when he got to the top of the hill; if he was to disappear into the forest and go until he could go no more. How long could he keep running for?

His leg was hurt, sore to put pressure on, and was becoming more noticeable now that his adrenaline was starting to slow, his blood cooling, his temper taming. Amelia was still walking towards him when he got to the bottom of the hill. He turned around and started back up it, forcing himself to move through the pain he was feeling in his leg and hand.

"Daniel!" Amelia called out to him from the bottom of the hill. He didn't answer her; instead, he continued running through the trees, skidding to a stop and turning around again. By the time it took to get back to the crest of the hill, Amelia was halfway up the slope, clinging to the long grass to steady herself in the ascent.

"What are you doing?" He set his hands on his hips. When a shooting pain started in his right hand, he set them by his sides, opening and closing his palms into fists. He winced with each movement.

"You ran off-"

"If you're here to give me some bullshit lecture you may save it. I genuinely couldn't be arsed hearing it." Amelia was panting when she got to the top of the hill. She hugged her arms to her chest and visibly shivered.

"I'm not. I wanted to see if you were okay," she said. Her eyes dropped to his hand, and she grimaced. "Can I see it?" Daniel lifted his hand, his jaw hardening. Amelia frowned when she saw the swollen knuckles. "I think you need to go to the hospital."

"I'm fine." Daniel pulled his hand away before she could take it and set it behind his back.

"Where's Cora?" Daniel looked down at the house. The gathering clouds overhead made it look like a house from a horror movie Daniel had once seen. Uninviting and ominous, it looked straight from a Hitchcock film.

"She's upstairs, playing." Daniel couldn't see Cora in her room.

"Is she angry with me?"

Amelia shrugged. "That wasn't fair what he said to you in there, Daniel. It really wasn't."

Heat ran down Daniel's neck.

"No? It's true though, isn't it- it's what you all think. What everyone thinks, what they said in the papers." He took a breath, his chest shifting uncomfortably in the movement as a ball formed in his throat. Even at the funeral, he could see people's scathing stares, their blaming eyes. From the moment it happened, people said it was his fault. It had been a session at a friend's gaff. He was told not to go, had been grounded, but he went anyway and drank too much. He had passed out on the couch and woke up the next evening to the news of his Mam's crash. No one had come to get him. His dad had left him there, to find out alone, surrounded by classmates.

He had gone out for a few drinks, so what? He hadn't meant for that to happen. Would never have hoped for that to happen. That didn't matter to anyone else, though.

Amelia was shaking her head.

"It's not. You didn't kill Mam. The drunk driver did."

With a shaky breath, Daniel lifted his hand to examine his fist. His fingers shook as he closed over his hand, his knuckle already double its normal size. He couldn't be sure, but it was probably broken. With any luck, Mark didn't fair out any better.

"Mark doesn't seem to think so." His jaw was set stiff. He could feel a bubble in his throat.

"No, he... Dad is different since it happened."

"All Mark cares about is himself."

"I miss her. A lot." Amelia muttered.

"Me too." Somehow, without agreeing to, they sauntered through the trees, walking along the worn trail. Amelia's gaze moved slowly through the forest, seeing it up close for the first time. There was a moment of silence then as Amelia regarded him. It was a quiet moment when they both seemed to realise the same thing: they had spent so much time fighting each other that they forgot they were on the same team.

"Well at least you don't have to get your dad to buy you tampons," Amelia joked, her cheeks blushing pink.

"Dad? When has he ever gotten them? Maybe he pays for them, but it's your brother who has to go get them!" he teased, knocking against her with his shoulder, playfully.

"Probably even more embarrassing, then." Amelia shook her head.

"Nah, what are big brothers for, eh?" Amelia half smiled and brushed her hair back from her face. "What's wrong?"

"I just… I feel like with Mam not here, I kind of feel like I'm doing this whole thing alone, you know? Like… it's hard being the only girl," she paused before adding, "that has gotten to puberty, I mean." Daniel's stomach clenched unexpectedly. He had never considered this before.

"Yuck," Daniel teased her, smiling. "No, I'm joking."

"And the whole *boy* thing." Amelia was fidgeting with the sleeves of her jumper. Daniel took a deep breath.

"Listen, I know it's not ideal, but if you need to talk about that shit, you can talk to me." Amelia's brow rose with scepticism.

"You?"

Daniel raised his hands in surrender, smiling. "I said it's not ideal, for either of us." Realising they had come too far and that the house was no longer in view, Daniel turned back. "I mean that though, if you need someone to talk to you can talk to me."

"Thanks." Amelia bounced off Daniel this time, before pulling all of her hair over her shoulder. They stopped on the crest of the hill, not quite ready to face the inside of the house. Daniel knelt to tie his shoelace, the echo of a dark bruise already appearing on his thigh from where he had hit the table.

"How did you find out about the missing kid?" Daniel glanced at his sister; she was chewing her fingernails.

"Ellen told me about it." He got to his feet and shook out his legs, his muscles tired from the exertion. He bent to stretch them out. "Weren't you reading his new book? Didn't you know what it was about?" Amelia shook her head vehemently.

"No. I only read the beginning, until… everything started in the house." Her eyes danced around the trees, focusing anywhere but him.

"And you really think the house is, you know, haunted?" he said it, trying to keep his voice free from judgement, free from the sarcasm that he usually expressed. Amelia was hesitant, as though she was gauging whether she wanted to articulate herself. Eventually, she decided she did.

"I know it is. The house has always felt off, even from the day we moved in, but it really began when Cora found that Ouija board. I think I'm being targeted, too."

"What do you mean?" Daniel was standing in front of Amelia now, on the edge of the hill. If she were to push him, he would fall backwards down it and probably break his neck.

"I can't be the only one that's heard the banging in the walls at night, or the footsteps in the hall even though there's nobody there," her voice was strangled, her eyes wide as she said it. Her body was tense, her breathing rapid. Daniel listened to her and if he was honest, he had heard the noises at night, had heard the knocking on his wall. But that, to him, meant they needed a plumber more than a priest. The footsteps… he hadn't heard any… or had he? No, he thought, remembering the day he and Ellen had heard Cora on the landing – the day she had thrown the Virgin Mary figurine at Ellen's head – when Ellen had said it didn't sound like his sister. This was madness. Of course it had been Cora. There're no such thing as giggling ghosts, and humouring Amelia – fuelling this mindset – wouldn't help her get over it.

"Amelia, don't you think there's a rational explanation for these things?" She was shaking her head aggressively.

"There *is* an explanation. I *know* there's something in the house with us. The missing food, Ellen's bra disappearing… the sounds at night. It's been getting worse, getting stronger and I think something bad is going to happen to one of us if we don't leave-" a look of pure terror spread across her face and she stopped speaking, her voice caught in her throat. Daniel frowned, waiting for her to go on but his sister was transfixed on a thought. Her mouth moved, but no sound came out.

"Amelia…? Amelia!" Daniel set his hands on her arms and went to shake her. Her hands grabbed onto his shirt, gripping it so tightly that he thought she might rip the fabric. Her eyes moved to his face then, and her voice, so small that he focused on reading her lips as a single, terrified tear rolled from her bloodshot eye, down her cheek, and fell from her chin to land, lost, in the dirt and soil under their feet.

"I... can... see... it... now..." her voice was trembling, strained and squeaky. Daniel was confused, shaking her.

"Amelia, what are you talking about?" Her gaze seemed to move through him then, her face so pale that he feared she might collapse.

"Behind... you..." Daniel, still holding on to her, turned his head slowly, not sure what he was expecting to find. What he did see, however, was something that chilled him to his core and was something he had not seen in his worst nightmare.

From the crest of the hill, Daniel could see directly into the bedrooms at the back of the house, and from here, he watched as Cora played in her room with her doll. Across from her, moving in twisted, contorted, unnatural ways, was another figure on all fours. The figure was not the transparent apparition that terrorised Amelia's mind, but a whole, tangible person, crouching in a familiar navy bra and thin, women's underwear, barely concealing the man's bulging groin. Long, tangled, knotted grey hair swung side to side as the head of the man shifted back and forth while he crawled around the room, nearing Cora with every movement, as his little sister laughed.

Daniel's heart was leaping in his chest when, suddenly, the intruder stopped and stared straight out the window to where Daniel and Amelia stood. There was a split second, that dragged out for a long time, when Daniel and the emaciated man stared into the eyes of one another.

Then Daniel was moving.

He ran, as fast as he could, skidding down the steep slope of the hill towards the house. Behind him, Amelia was screaming in terror. He ignored her calls and raced to the porch. He wrenched the back door open and came hurtling through the kitchen, jumping over the black cat, swaying his tail on the other side of the door. He reached the stairs, and his stomach sank when he heard Cora's scream. There was a raucous upstairs. Daniel launched himself up the winding stairwell as fast as he could and ran to his sister's bedroom.

When the door flung open, Daniel dove to the ground. The man's body had mostly disappeared through a space under Cora's bed, his hands the only visible part as he clung to Cora's ankles, dragging her with him. Daniel stretched out, feeling the tips of Cora's outstretched fingers slip from his clutch and fall through the space under her bed.

Daniel was panting heavily now, his mind a whirlwind as he tried to comprehend it. He jumped to his feet and in one swift move, upended the entire bedframe, sending it soaring to the other end of the room. A small square in the floorboards alluded to a hatch. There was no handle. Daniel pressed his fingers in the crevice of the frame, tugging with all his might, but the small hatch only rattled.

Before his mind could understand what his body was doing, he was running back towards the stairs, his mind a flurry of thoughts, and he was down the steps and running beneath the corkscrew stairs.

The library had been untouched since he had last been in the room. He went directly to where the shelves opened out and exposed the alcove. Gripping the two edges of the wall, Daniel slammed his foot against the wood panelling. In his rage, the wood gave way easily. When there was a big enough gap, he used his hands, blind to the pain in his fist, and tore at the splintered wood. He was yelling as he did so, screaming Cora's name. His body was pure adrenaline, his mind nothing but rage.

A lock on the inside of the wall came exposed, and Daniel reached in, behind the wall, to undo it. Space opened from the hidden door and Daniel shoved himself into the gap, trying to fit, not knowing what he was doing, where he was going to go. Wires impeded him, made it difficult to get through the gap. When he kicked at them, knocking them dangerously out of place so that they were exposed, he tried to shimmy himself into the gap in the wall, however, after only a second, he realised that he could not fit. He was too big to fit. He could not get in.

As panic set in, as fear reared its ugly head, Daniel heard screaming from outside.

"Daniel!" It was Amelia. *"Daniel! Out here!"* Daniel sprung towards the broken window in the library. Through the grimy glass, he could see Amelia at the bottom of the hill now, her face a mask of hellish horror. Then, from beneath the porch, a figure appeared. The near-naked man had crawled under the house, tugging Cora along with him, and had appeared outside. Cora was fighting him now, seeing Amelia, but the man lifted the child and flung her over his thin shoulders, staggering forward. Amelia went to go towards him. Seeing this, the man stopped before her and unleashed a sound that was borne from the pit of his stomach. It was a growl unnatural to man. Amelia fell back against the bank as recognition dawned on her face, as though she had heard this noise before. She called for Daniel again.

Daniel tried the window, not wanting to lose sight of Cora or the man, but there was no give to it and so he ran out, came through the foyer and out the front door. His foot caught on one of the steps on the porch, his foot crashing through the plank. It sent him flying forward and left a bloody trail in his wake as the skin on his shin was torn open. He stumbled free and started running to the back of the house. Amelia was coming towards him, crying out.

"Daniel! They went that way, to the forest!" She was hysterical. Daniel couldn't stop.

"Go! Call the Guards!" He ran past her, going towards the dense trees. He couldn't see them yet.

Only when Daniel passed the tree line, his body fuelled by pure adrenaline, did he spot them. Bouncing along in a zigzag motion was the man carrying his sister. They weren't far, they wouldn't get far. Daniel started into a run like he had never run before, everything else around him a blur but the outline of the decrepit man holding Cora.

Without slowing down, Daniel ploughed full force into the man's back. The three of them tumbled forwards, Cora rolling away from the two men. The man growled like an animal and now that Daniel was up close to him, he could see just how old and gaunt he was. His flesh was sunken to the bone, his cheeks pressed against his skull. His eyes were black and bloodshot, his teeth protruding from his receding gums. He snapped and snarled at Daniel, like a vicious dog trying to wriggle away from him, like a rabid animal, but Daniel was much bigger than him and pinned him easily. The man scraped at Daniel's face with talon-like nails, his hands like curled claws. His whole body looked sick, contorted.

He fought Daniel, twisting, and turning, always reaching towards Cora. It was then when Daniel realised the man was still trying to get to his sister, that understanding dawned on Daniel and he let go of everything he had been feeling for the last twelve months. Every angry thought, every muttered rumour, every disappointed stare from his father escaped through him as he knelt over this man.

The fury that exploded from Daniel was catastrophic. He punched the man, watching as his face broke under his fists, as his teeth loosened, as his jaw broke. Blood spluttered from his mouth as he choked on his own teeth, as his eye socket broke inwards. Even when he could barely tell where his features separated, Daniel continued to pound his fists into the man's face. There was no sound but for the rhythmic thumping of his clenched fists against his skull; flesh and bone grinding together to a crescendo in the peaceful forest.

The man's temple imploded on one side. And Daniel continued.

Hot tears streamed down Daniel's face, mixing with the man's blood.

He continued. Putting every ounce of anger into this man.

At some point Amelia found them.

Daniel could not stop.

"Daniel..." Amelia screamed out at him. "Daniel..." she was right behind him. "Daniel!" She was hysterical. She pulled on his shoulder, to no avail, and fell back onto the dirt and fallen leaves. She crawled to where Cora lay.

For every bump in the night, for every missing breadcrumb, for every minute of stolen sanity, Daniel pounded his fists against the man's face until there was a mess of blood beneath him.

"She's not waking up! Cora! Cora! She's not waking up, Daniel!"

Out of breath, out of energy, with broken knuckles and sprayed with somebody else's blood, Daniel fell off the man and landed on his side, in the soil and foliage of the forest, his breathing heavy. A single orange leaf was moving against his lips with every inhalation, and away again with each exhalation.

"She's bleeding, Daniel! Her head! I think she hit the rock!" Daniel could barely hear Amelia speak, there was a ringing in his ears, a thumping in his chest.

"I think she's-" Amelia stopped herself from saying it at first, then, she spoke. "Cora's dead." The words were like a foreign language, he couldn't understand her. Hot blood pumped through him.

He was numb. At last. He was numb.

He looked to where Amelia was laying over Cora, her lifeless body limp, her little face grey and colourless. Her mouth lay slack, her lips parted slightly as Amelia tried to pick her up. Her hair at the back of her head was slick with blood, her arms splayed out on the forest floor, looking as if she might be sleeping.

One of her shoes had fallen off, revealing the polka-dotted socks she wore. Her eyes were closed, never to open again.

Amelia had been right.

They had been haunted. But not by a ghost.
Daniel wished it had been a ghost.

Chapter 24

"Do you think it's hard to write a horror that's never been done before?" the reporter would ask him, her high-heeled shoe balancing delicately on the end of her foot.

"No, I think it's impossible. There isn't a story out there that is completely original, in my opinion. Instead, I think readers choose books with expectations for the genre." He would lean forwards, smelling her perfume, a waft of sweet rosewater would envelop his senses.

"And what do you think they are?" Her nails would be a vibrant red, long, and narrow at the top, shaped like coffins.

"I think that in fantasy, readers expect an adventure, in historical fiction they expect a historical retelling. In horror, I think people expect something horrible."

ACKNOWLEDGEMENTS

As a writer I know I owe an awful lot to patience; the patience of you, hungry reader, to sit through the thousands of words that I have written, to the patience of my family and friends, who have helped, encouraged, and supported me whilst I am selfish enough to work on something that can be seen as nothing more than a passion project to a lot of people, and then to my own patience for which without it, I would have stopped this hobby of mine a long time ago. As the saying goes, *'patience is a virtue'*. Not only is it a virtue, but it is a skill as well. As with all skills, it can take time to hone them. This irony is not lost on me.

A special thanks to the man who this book is dedicated to, Mikey, whose competitiveness would shadow Daniel's. Thank you to my sisters for always being a set of listening ears, helping hands, and having encouraging words. They are appreciated. A nod of thanks to my friends who without there would not have been the break-up scene between Ellen and Daniel in the story - apparently it was necessary. My parents deserve a thank you, too, as do Thinus and James. An honourable mention to Natalie, for loving crap horrors as much as I do – I hope this isn't one of them. A massive credit to Rachel, for the poem at the beginning of the novel. It is creepy and perfect.

Lastly, thank you, patient reader. I hope this story sent a shiver or two down your spine.

AUTHOR'S NOTE

Horrible was written at a strange point in time, when the world came to a stand-still and none of us really knew what to do with ourselves. I was presented with an opportunity to take my love of horror and mix it with my passion for writing. What came from this concoction was a story that surprised me. I had planned it to be a novella length nail-biter, what it unfolded as was a creative outlet for my frustrations – my sister even noting that it seemed like I was getting out a lot of pent-up energy with it (can you tell she is studying to become a therapist?) - with that novella wordcount left in a cloud of dust in my rear-view mirror!

If you took the time to get this far into reading it, I think I owe you an explanation of sorts: who has been haunting the Owens family? Well, that is a question with several answers, with most of them leading to further questions. The one I like to think of as the best one is 'themselves'.

Make of that what you will.

Sarah McCormack is an Irish author living in Dublin, Ireland. Contact the author on Instagram @sarah.mccormack1 to see what she is reading and working on next.

Printed in Great Britain
by Amazon